# Praise for Catherine Bybee

## Wife by Wednesday

"A fun and sizzling romance, great characters that trade verbal spars like fist punches, and the dream of your own royal wedding!"
—Sizzling Hot Book Reviews, 5 Stars

"A good holiday, fireside or bedtime story."
—Manic Reviews, 4 1/2 Stars

"A great story that I hope is the start of a new series."
—The Ror    ʾdio, 4 1/2 Hearts

## Married b

"If I hadn't already added M            .ny list of favorite authors, after reading this            . compelled to. This is a book *nobody* should mi              . it contains is awesome."
Booked Up Reviews, 5 Stars

"Ms. Bybee writes authentic situations and expresses the good and the bad in such an equal way . . . Keep the reader on the edge of her seat . . ."
—Reading Between the Wines, 5 Stars

"*Married by Monday* was a refreshing read and one I couldn't possibly put down . . ."

—The Romance Studio, 4 1/2 Hearts

## Fiancé by Friday

"Bybee knows exactly how to keep readers happy . . . A thrilling pursuit and enough passion to stuff in your back pocket to last for the next few lifetimes . . . The hero and heroine come to life with each flip of the page and will linger long after readers cross the finish line."

—*RT Book Reviews*, 4 1/2 Stars, Top Pick, Hot

"A tale full of danger and sexual tension . . . the intriguing characters add emotional depth, ensuring readers will race to the perfectly fitting finish."

—*Publishers Weekly*

"Suspense, survival, and chemistry mix in this scintillating read."

—*Booklist*

"Hot romance, a mystery assassin, British royalty, and an alpha Marine . . . this story has it all!"

—Harlequin Junkie

## Single by Saturday

"Captures readers' hearts and keeps them glued to the pages until the fascinating finish . . . romance lovers will feel the sparks fly . . . almost instantaneously."

—*RT Book Reviews*, 4 1/2 Stars, Top Pick

"[A] wonderfully exciting plot, lots of desire, and some sassy attitude thrown in for good measure!"

—Harlequin Junkie

## Taken by Tuesday

"[Bybee] knows exactly how to get bookworms sucked into the perfect storyline; then she casts her spell upon them so they don't escape until they reach the 'Holy Cow!' ending."

—*RT Book Reviews*, 4 1/2 Stars, Top Pick

## Seduced by Sunday

"You simply can't miss [this novel]. It contains everything a romance reader loves—clever dialogue, three-dimensional characters, and just the right amount of steam to go with that heartwarming love story."

—Brenda Novak, *New York Times* bestselling author

"Bybee hits the mark . . . providing readers with a smart, sophisticated romance between a spirited heroine and a prim hero . . . Passionate and intelligent characters [are] at the heart of this entertaining read."

—*Publishers Weekly*

## Treasured by Thursday

"The Weekday Brides never disappoint and this final installment is by far Bybee's best work to date."

—*RT Book Reviews*, 4 1/2 Stars, Top Pick

"An exquisitely written and complex story brimming with pride, passion, and pulse-pounding danger . . . Readers will gladly make time to savor this winning finale to a wonderful series."

"Bybee concludes her popular Weekday Brides series in a gratifying way with a passionate, troubled couple who may find a happy future if they can just survive and then learn to trust each other. A compelling and entertaining mix of sexy, complicated romance and menacing suspense."

## Not Quite Dating

"It's refreshing to read about a man who isn't afraid to fall in love . . . [Jack and Jessie] fit together as a couple and as a family."

"*Not Quite Dating* offers a sweet and satisfying Cinderella fantasy that will keep you smiling long after you've finished reading . . ."

"The perfect rags to riches romance . . . The dialogue is inventive and witty, the characters are well drawn out. The storyline is superb and really shines . . . I highly recommend this stand out romance! Catherine Bybee is an automatic buy for me."

## Not Quite Enough

"Bybee's gift for creating unforgettable romances cannot be ignored. The third book in the Not Quite series will sweep readers away to a paradise, and they will be intrigued by the thrilling story that accompanies their literary vacation."

## Not Quite Forever

"Full of classic Bybee humor, steamy romance, and enough plot twists and turns to keep readers entertained all the way to the very last page."
—Tracy Brogan, bestselling author of the Bell Harbor series

"Magnetic . . . The love scenes are sizzling and the multi-dimensional characters make this a page-turner. Readers will look for earlier installments and eagerly anticipate new ones."
—*Publishers Weekly*

## Doing It Over

"The romance between fiercely independent Melanie and charming Wyatt heats up even as outsiders threaten to derail their newfound happiness. This novel will hook readers with its warm, inviting characters and the promise for similar future installments."
—*Publishers Weekly*

"This brand-new trilogy, Most Likely To, based on yearbook superlatives, kicks off with a novel that will encourage you to root for the incredibly likable Melanie. Her friends are hilarious and readers will swoon over Wyatt, who is charming and strong. Even Melanie's daughter, Hope, is a hoot! This romance is jam-packed with animated characters, and Bybee displays her creative writing talent wonderfully."
—*RT Book Reviews*, 4 Stars

"With a dialogue full of energy and depth, and a twisting storyline that captured my attention, I would say that *Doing It Over* was a great way to start off a new series. (And look at that gorgeous book cover!) I can't wait to visit River Bend again and see who else gets to find their HEA."
—Harlequin Junkie, 4 1/2 Stars

# Making It Right

# Also by Catherine Bybee

## Contemporary Romance

### Weekday Brides Series

*Wife by Wednesday*

*Married by Monday*

*Fiancé by Friday*

*Single by Saturday*

*Taken by Tuesday*

*Seduced by Sunday*

*Treasured by Thursday*

### Not Quite Series

*Not Quite Dating*

*Not Quite Mine*

*Not Quite Enough*

*Not Quite Forever*

*Not Quite Perfect*

### Most Likely To Series

*Doing It Over*

*Staying For Good*

## Paranormal Romance

### MacCoinnich Time Travels

*Binding Vows*

*Silent Vows*

*Redeeming Vows*

*Highland Shifter*

*Highland Protector*

### The Ritter Werewolves Series

*Before the Moon Rises*

*Embracing the Wolf*

### Novellas

*Soul Mate*

*Possessive*

### Erotica

*Kilt Worthy*

*Kilt-A-Licious*

# Making It Right

## *A* Most Likely To *Novel*

## CATHERINE BYBEE

*NEW YORK TIMES* & *USA TODAY* BESTSELLING AUTHOR

Published by Montlake Romance, Seattle

www.apub.com

Amazon, the Amazon logo, and Montlake Romance are trademarks of Amazon.com, Inc., or its affiliates.

ISBN-13: 9781503943599
ISBN-10: 1503943593

Cover design by Shasti O'Leary Soudant

Printed in the United States of America

*This one is for Andrea . . .*
*I miss you every day.*

# Prologue

The sun shot daggers into Jo's eyes as she opened the door of Zoe's home. It was already noon, but she and her best friends couldn't be bothered to wake up early on the day after their high school graduation. The bottle of tequila they'd managed to put a pretty good dent in twelve hours prior resided in her duffel bag for later use.

"It burns," Jo said with a laugh as she covered her eyes.

"You dork." Mel, the third part of their trio, brushed past her and opened the door of her car before tossing her yearbook in the backseat.

Zoe hovered in the doorway of the double-wide.

The three of them had stayed up most the night talking about their futures.

Well, Zoe and Mel had been the ones predicting the next year of their lives while Jo listened and drank Jose Cuervo until her head swam.

Mel had another seven weeks of life in River Bend before she was off to California to fulfill the River Bend High's class prediction about her future. Being voted most likely to succeed was about the highest praise a gaggle of eighteen-year-olds could manage.

Jo tossed her bag into the back along with Mel's yearbook and turned to Zoe.

"When are you going to talk to Luke?"

"I don't know."

Zoe had told the two of them that she needed to break up with her boyfriend of two years in order to get away from River Bend. From the looks of the broken-down dump of the Brown family home . . . and the graduates' predictions that Zoe was most likely to never leave River Bend . . . it was no wonder Zoe wanted to flee.

Making matters worse, Zoe's father was the well-known felon in their small town. He was serving a sentence of fifteen-plus years for armed robbery, but that didn't stop the kids of River Bend from giving Zoe crap anytime they could. As if it was Zoe's fault her dad was a complete lowlife.

"Please don't say anything to him," Zoe pleaded.

Jo and Mel exchanged glances. "We wouldn't dream of it."

"I'm going to miss this place," Mel said with a sigh.

Jo's eyes shifted to Zoe.

"That will make one of us," Zoe said.

Zoe wouldn't miss the family home where when her father wasn't in jail, he did a fair amount of drinking and beating up his family. Mel would miss it because she'd only known the Brown home as a place to crash in the last couple of years. And Jo wouldn't miss it at all because she had no plans to leave.

A higher education would consist of something at the community college level at best, along with a lot more partying while she was still young enough to enjoy it. She considered a move to Waterville, a town only an hour away with a lot more going for it, but she doubted her father would foot the bill.

She had the summer to figure it out. Who knew, maybe she and Zoe could find a place together?

"I'll be back at eight to pick you up for tonight's bonfire," Mel told Zoe.

"You're coming, right, Jo?" Zoe asked.

Jo slid around the passenger door. "Someone has to bring the booze."

Zoe closed the front door behind her a little more. "Shh!"

"See ya later." Jo didn't bother with a seat belt, even after Mel pulled out of the driveway.

The short drive into town and down the street where Jo lived was met with silence. "You sure you don't want a ride to Grayson's farm tonight?"

"I'm going to con my dad into giving me back the keys to the Jeep. I did manage a B average this year."

"I don't think it was your grades that worried him."

No, Jo's dad was River Bend's sheriff. Jo hated the label of cop's daughter from day one. Everyone expected her to be Little Miss Perfect, be a stupid pillar of the community. All she wanted was to be herself, a teenager out to have fun and live life every day. Unfortunately that collided with being the cop's kid. Most of the teens in town drank, many of them smoked a little pot, and occasionally someone would bring something stronger into town. Her dad called her on every indiscretion. Made her run cross-country in the summer and had her running sprints every spring for the track team.

But no more. High school was officially over. She planned on tossing her running shoes in the bonfire later that night.

Mel pulled into the driveway of the home Jo had grown up in. Her dad's squad car wasn't blocking the garage door. She sighed with relief. Twenty questions about what she and the girls had done the night before wasn't something she wanted to face. Not with the slight hangover she'd been nursing since she woke up.

"See you tonight," Jo said as she stepped out of the car, dragging her duffel bag with her.

She peered into the car after closing the door.

Mel gripped the steering wheel as she looked down the street toward where she lived. "My parents suck."

Jo tried to make her friend feel better. "All parents suck. It's in their job description."

"Yeah, but they couldn't even wait until I was off to college before telling me about the divorce. Now that's all I'm going to think about all summer."

"We're going to party all summer, Mel Bel. You won't have time to spend on your parents' screwed-up world."

Mel pointed a finger in Jo's direction. "I'm depending on you to distract me."

"I got ya covered."

Mel gave her a half-assed smile and pulled out of the drive.

Jo stepped into the empty house, dropped her bag on the kitchen table, and headed toward the bathroom. She pulled her dead cell phone from her back pocket and plugged it in to charge. After digging into the bottom of her personal drawer, the one filled with tampons and pads, she found the birth control pills her father didn't know she took and popped the tiny orange contraceptive into her mouth.

Much as she wanted to crawl back into bed, she opted for a shower in case her father came home early. The man had the uncanny ability to smell alcohol on her skin after a night of drinking.

Fifteen minutes later, with her hair wrapped in a towel and her bathrobe tied around her waist, she left her bathroom for the short walk down the hall to her bedroom.

The outline of her father standing in the hall, holding a half-empty bottle of tequila, caused her to stumble to a stop.

"Care to explain this?" His even, controlled voice always unnerved her.

Jo's breath caught in her chest.

Her dad wasn't a small man. Six two with a good 220 pounds of muscled bulk made him look like he needed to be a linebacker playing for the Ducks. Only instead of shoulder pads and a helmet, he wore a gun, a badge, and a hat on his head.

She wanted to lie, somehow convince her dad the bottle wasn't hers. But he had been the one to drop her off at Zoe's the night before, and Jo didn't want to rat her friends out.

Instead of playing stupid, she stuck her chin a little higher in the air. "It was my graduation night."

"You're eighteen."

"I didn't drive."

"You don't have a car."

"None of us drove."

He stood silent for the space of a breath; his eyes bore down on hers. "None of you . . . you mean Zoe and Mel?"

It was Jo's turn to play quiet.

"Where did you get the liquor?" His voice was calm, almost too much so.

"I'm not ratting out my friends."

"Zoe?"

"No."

"Mel?"

"No, Dad, stop. It's not the end of the world. It's just a little alcohol." She moved past him and grabbed the duffel bag he'd rifled through to find her stash.

"That Julian guy in Waterville?"

The guy she needed the birth control pills for supplied her with more than booze.

"Let it go, Dad. I'm an adult now."

She tried to move around him but he blocked her way.

"Did you steal it?"

Jo looked at the floor before remembering to make eye contact.

5

Her hesitation was all her dad needed to sniff out the truth.

"Damn it, JoAnne."

"I didn't steal it," she lied.

"Bullshit." His voice edged higher.

"You never believe me."

"You're always lying to me. Now tell me where you got this." He waved Jose in the air.

"No."

His jaw twitched. "I can't have my daughter running around town stealing liquor from our neighbors."

"I didn't—"

"Do I need to put you in handcuffs before you're going to learn to keep your nose clean?"

She shot both hands toward him, her wrists close together. "Go ahead, Dad. Arrest me for having a bottle of alcohol, something just about every kid in this town my age has access to."

Joseph slammed the bottle on the table. "That isn't the point. You're *my* daughter. I can't have you breaking the law."

"Because you're a cop."

"I'm *the* cop!"

Something she'd always hated. "And because you play sheriff, I have to wear a fucking halo and pretend I'm prim and innocent."

"No one is expecting you to be a Disney character."

"Good. I'm glad we understand each other."

She tried to move around him again.

He didn't budge.

"No more of this, JoAnne."

The noose of his presence, his uniform, started to cut off the air in the room.

"I hate that you're the sheriff."

Her words did nothing to him. She'd said them before.

"I'm going to find out who this belongs to, and you're going to face them, apologize, and hope they don't want to press charges."

"No one presses charges against you, Dad."

"This isn't about me. One of these days I'm not going to be able to stop you from sitting in that jail cell."

She glared at him. "So you believe what all those assholes at the school said about me, too?" Voted most likely to end up in jail had been her sentence from the graduating class at River Bend. And obviously her father had read that in her yearbook.

"I believe that if you don't start having a little humility, a little respect, you're going to hate life."

"I already hate my life."

Her father visibly winced. "I'm not a perfect father, I know I've made mistakes, but you don't have it that bad."

Her teenage hormones wanted to scream. "I'm a cop's kid. I've always had to be something I'm not. Right now half the graduating class is waking up with a hangover, and I bet their parents are yelling at them."

"We've been through this—"

"We have, and you know what? I don't give a shit what you think."

"That's enough!" He yelled loud enough to rattle the china in her late mother's cabinet. "You will respect me in my home."

"What are you going to do, kick me out?"

"If I have to."

He wouldn't.

Only his eyes said he meant business.

"Is that what I have to do, JoAnne? Does something tragic have to happen in order for you to get your crap together?"

She'd lost her mother to a car accident when she was just a kid, which helped prompt her rebellion.

"High school is over," he said as if she didn't know. "You're eighteen now. You get caught stealing, even liquor, and I have no choice but to put you behind bars. That doesn't go off your record."

"You're worried about how it will make *you* look."

"I'm worried about my kid screwing up her life for something as stupid as this." He pointed to the bottle. "I think you should join the military."

She shook her head, the towel holding her hair started to come undone. "I'm not joining the military!"

He lifted his hands in the air. "Well, you're not doing this all summer. You're getting a job if you're living here."

"I help out at Sam's."

"A real job. To keep you out of trouble."

"Where do you suggest I get one in this one-crap town?"

Her dad stared her down. "I don't know if you can get a job in this *one-crap* town since you can't be trusted."

The image of the words in her yearbook scrolled in her mind: JoAnne Ward, most likely to end up in jail.

Instead of saying anything else, she grabbed her bag from the table and shoved past her dad into her bedroom. She slammed the door and took less than two minutes pulling on a pair of jeans and a sweatshirt. With wet hair, she charged into her bathroom, grabbed the cell phone and the charging cable, and went ahead and shoved her birth control pills into her bag. A few changes of clothes made it into her duffel before she stormed out of her childhood bedroom.

Her father sat at the kitchen table, the half-empty bottle of tequila was winning a staring match.

When he heard her, he glanced up.

"Where do you think you're going?"

"To find a job," she told him, having no intention of actually looking.

He sighed. "Sit down, JoAnne. Let's try and talk about this."

"Why? So you can tell me what a crappy kid I am? How I disgrace you and your position in this town? I don't think so." She ran out of the house and half jogged the five miles of back roads and shortcuts to Miss Gina's Bed-and-Breakfast.

Once on the steps of the inn, she dropped her bag and caught her breath.

She hated her dad, hated this town.

It choked her every damn day.

The screen door to the inn opened, and Miss Gina, with her gray-speckled long hair, sixties throwback skirt, and flowing blouse plopped down beside Jo on the steps. "Well, look what the wind blew in."

"I hate him, Miss Gina."

Miss Gina wrapped an arm over Jo's shoulders. "You don't hate him."

"He doesn't understand."

It took a lot to make Jo want to cry, but she was fighting back tears.

"C'mon inside and you can tell me all about what Sheriff Ward doesn't understand."

# Chapter One

*Twelve years later*

Red and blue lights from Jo's squad car lit up the night sky, and the rarely used siren bounced off the pine trees in eerie opposition to the quiet country road. Josie had called Jo personally to ask her to stop by and handle a couple of locals that were raising the anxiety levels at R&B's. The only real bar in River Bend sat nestled off the main road leading out of town. It took Jo less than five minutes to climb into a ready uniform, strap on her duty belt, and back out of her driveway.

Gravel churned under her tires as she pulled to an abrupt stop in the parking lot of Josie's bar. A half a dozen motorcycles along with a dozen familiar pickups and off-road vehicles told her the place was close to capacity. Not surprising for a Friday night. She straightened her sheriff's hat on her head and doubled her stride up the steps to the single-level tavern.

Inside, music pumped from the jukebox, and the smell of stale beer from one too many party fouls wafted from the floor.

She stopped just inside and scanned the room.

Josie stood behind the bar, her eyes narrowing on Jo before she nodded toward the back of the room in a silent signal of where the trouble brewed.

Jo wove her way through the bar, nodding in acknowledgment as many of the patrons said hello, using her first name instead of her title.

Steve Richey and Billy Hoekman crowded a table opposite the Ryan brothers. The four men had been friends at one time, but that was before Dustin Ryan ditched Billy's baby sister shortly after they were engaged. Never mind that the rumors around town were pointing to Billy's sister having a second boyfriend in Waterville, the blame of the breakup went on Dustin. In their midtwenties, the four men should know better than to take their problems to the bar. Unfortunately, alcohol only brought out their differences in bright, shiny sparkles.

A few yards away, separated by half a dozen people, Jo heard the jabs over the music and scraping of chairs on the old laminate floor, which was covered in a layer of sawdust to help soak up the nightly spills.

"Let it go, Billy." Cody was the younger Ryan by only a year. The two brothers didn't give Jo any trouble, and as she saw it, were probably the ones keeping the fists from flying.

Billy, on the other hand, had brushed elbows with her more than a few times. He wasn't a happy drunk, but he knew better than to push her.

"A man stands by his promises. Then again, maybe you're not a man. Maybe you like men . . . that pretty face of yours probably attracts all kinds of boys when you're in Eugene."

Dustin, who had been sitting with his fingers clutching a longneck beer, pushed his chair away from the table with the last insult and turned his six-foot frame toward his would-have-been brother-in-law.

Everyone had a breaking point, and it looked like Dustin had met his.

"Boys?" Jo stepped close enough to the party of four to be seen and heard, but far enough away to avoid a fist if one were thrown.

Cody noticed Jo first and visibly took a step back.

Dustin never stopped looking at Billy as he nearly bumped chests with the man.

Steve flanked Billy's side; his gaze skated over Jo with a look of contempt.

"I've heard just about enough of your mouth, Billy *Ray*."

A few nearby patrons moved away from the five of them, and the noise in the bar started to dwindle. Everyone knew that Billy Ray didn't like his middle name being used. It sounded hick, according to the man, and he refused to be labeled as such even if the title fit.

Billy bumped up against Dustin, the move just shy of a shove.

"You really wanna do this?" Billy asked.

"Hello? Am I invisible?" Jo stepped closer.

She knew both men saw her, but only Dustin hesitated.

"C'mon, Dustin." Cody took hold of his brother's arm and pulled him back.

Jo looked to Steve to do the same for his team.

He didn't.

"I really don't think your mother wants to bail you out of my jail, Billy. My guess is her hip still aches since her fall last winter." Jo wasn't above using family guilt to have her needs met. Besides, processing a bar fight and having to sleep in her chair all night because she had someone in the one holding cell in River Bend's sheriff's station didn't sound like a good time for any of them.

Buddy, the short-order cook from the back of the bar, stepped to the other side of the party, his size and presence there in support of Jo, should she need it. "Josie doesn't want any trouble."

Jo watched the flick of the fingers, the twitching of the eyes . . . the breaths of both men facing each other off.

Cody tugged his brother a second time and broke the tension. "He's not worth it."

Dustin pulled out of his brother's grip but did the right thing and backed away.

Jo released the breath she held when Billy lowered his eyes for one brief second.

His body language changed in a heartbeat and he charged Dustin's turned back.

*Well, hell!*

Jo jumped in, one hand reaching for Billy's wrist at the same time her forearm pushed into the space just above his elbow. With a pivot and a full-body push, Billy Ray Hoekman was flat on his face with Jo reaching for her handcuffs.

He reared beneath her, would have had a shot at bucking her off if her knee wasn't grinding into the man's kidney. She took a breath only once he was cuffed.

Cody held Dustin back, and Buddy stood between her and Steve.

"Damn it, Billy . . . you just couldn't leave it alone, could you?"

"She's my sister, Jo."

"That's Sheriff to you, Mr. Hoekman. And Opal is capable of dealing with her own relationships. You don't need to beat up her boyfriends in front of a cop."

Billy cussed in a not so quiet way, the sawdust pushing away from his open mouth as he lay on the floor. Every patron in the bar had their eyes focused on them. The only sound came from the jukebox, which blared out a Led Zeppelin song from the seventies.

"Okay, folks. Show's over." Josie made her way to Jo's side, shaking her head. She knelt down so Billy could hear. "I don't wanna see you in here for six months, Billy . . . you got that?"

"C'mon, Josie . . ." Even from the floor, Billy was trying to work his way back in.

"Six months!"

Jo brought Billy to his feet, sawdust stuck to the side of his face. He stumbled, evidently from one too many drinks. She glanced over to Steve, his eyes glossy. "I think you might need to walk home, Steve."

He shuffled his feet, turned away from Buddy, and walked out the back door.

"Dustin, Cody . . . you should probably make your way home, too." Jo didn't expect an argument.

The patrons of R&B's parted a path and held the door open for her as she passed through. Buddy walked behind her as far as the bottom steps. "You got this?" he asked.

Jo had to smile. "I'm good."

Hours later, Billy snored in the holding cell, and Jo clutched an ice bag to her left forearm. The takedown was going to leave a bruise. She lay down on the worn brown leather sofa in her dad's old office and put her head on a tiny pillow.

"You know, Dad," she said to the ceiling, as if her father was hovering over her in some angelic, biblical way, "I always thought you were full of it when you said you slept on this couch. I always thought you had a girlfriend you were keeping from me when you didn't come home at night."

The room grew silent when she stopped talking to the air.

Her father didn't answer.

But she smiled into the thought that maybe he heard her as she closed her eyes and let the clock lure her to sleep.

~

"Knock, knock!" Zoe's voice shot Jo out of her sleep and straight up off the sofa.

"Holy . . ."

Daylight.

Office.

Bar fight.

*Billy Ray.*

She grabbed the back of her neck, certain she managed whiplash with the simple task of jumping from a dead sleep.

"Did I wake you?" Zoe was all smiles and rainbows.

"What time is it?" Jo closed her eyes against the light.

"Six thirty."

Zoe held a basket that smelled of yeast and sugar. "Got a call from Josie late last night letting me know you were probably camped out here keeping watch over Billy Ray. I thought you might need something to eat."

Jo's hand moved from her neck to her back as she stood. "I'm getting too old for this."

Zoe laughed as she turned away and into the center of the station. "You're not even thirty."

"Another month."

Jo followed her out, forcing the kinks out of her joints with every step. She probably should get a new sofa for her office, even if the budget couldn't afford her one. Summer always posed the opportunity for her to spend a night in her own jail. On the right side of the bars, at least.

Jo glanced around the reception desk and scratched her head. "Is Glynis here?"

Zoe removed what looked like something sinfully sweet, along with a small crock that smelled of eggs and cheese. "Nope. She doesn't come in until eight, right?"

"How did you get in here?"

"C'mon, Jo . . . really? We're the ones that hid the spare key the summer of our junior year."

She dumped yesterday's day old coffee into the sink and rinsed it out. "I'd forgotten all about that."

"I can't believe you talked me into breaking into your dad's office back then."

"We didn't break in . . . we had a key."

Zoe licked her finger as she leaned against the table. "Oh, yeah . . . and what would you say to anyone who gave you that line now?"

Jo paused. "No wonder my dad was turning gray before he hit fifty." She'd been thirty shades of shitty when she was a kid, something she could never atone for since her father was gone. She scooped out the coffee grounds and made a thick blend that would help her wake the dead, namely her.

She glanced at the offerings Zoe brought. "I should probably check on Billy."

"Oh, he's fine. Sleeping like a baby."

The door leading to the one holding cell was cracked open enough to hear him call out for help but closed enough to not hear his snores, which had threatened to keep her up most of the night.

Jo settled into a chair, pulled the warm pastry from the basket. "You're like Mary Poppins with a bag full of goodies."

"It's a basket," Zoe said with a smile.

"Even better." She tore off a chunk and popped it into her mouth. Jo closed her eyes and hummed. "Have I told you how much I love you being back in town?"

"If I didn't know you, I'd swear you're using me for my culinary skills."

Jo pulled off another piece, talked around the food in her mouth. "Oh, I am. No doubt about that."

They both laughed.

The coffeepot buzzed, signaling it was time for a hefty dose of caffeine.

Jo offset the bitter brew with a truckload of sugar. "Have you heard from Zane?" she asked as she took her first sip.

"He called night before last. Said he might be moved from Virginia to North Carolina."

Zoe's brother, Zane, had joined the marines shortly after Ziggy, their father, had been shot and killed the previous year. Sheryl, Zoe's mom, sat in a woman's penitentiary for voluntary manslaughter for shooting her husband. Even though the woman was protecting her children, she still ended up with a three-year sentence with a mandated one year to be served. Jo didn't think the courts would keep her all three years. Ziggy's long history of violence and abuse weighed heavily on the case. The chances of her getting out and being anything but a mouse in need of a hole to sleep in were slim to none. She'd been beaten down her whole life; she would suffer even more behind bars.

"More training?" Jo asked, redirecting her thoughts to Zane.

"He said something about tactical. He sounded excited." Zoe smiled like a proud sister should.

"I'm so happy he joined."

"Me, too."

Rattling of metal on metal brought their attention to the door to the holding cell. "Jo . . . I mean, Sheriff . . . you out there?"

Jo took another swig of her coffee before setting the cup aside. "Looks like I'm on."

Zoe tapped her toe against the air as Jo made her way to the back.

Billy Ray's bed head hair, rumpled shirt, and bloodshot eyes suggested his night was just as bad as Jo's. "Look who sobered up."

He looked past her to the open door. "I take it my mom didn't want to come down and pick me up?"

She leaned against the door frame. "She didn't answer the phone. I'm not even sure I had the right number." There was no way she was getting his mother out of bed to take care of his drunk ass.

Billy narrowed his eyes. "You have everyone's numbers."

"Everyone who ends up on that side of the bars," she corrected.

"But I've . . ."

Yeah, he'd been there before. "Dustin isn't pressing charges," she told him.

Billy sighed in relief.

"But disobeying a direct order from a peace officer . . ."

Billy looked up and met her gaze.

"I'm sorry, Jo. Steve and I had been drinking. Opal's my sister . . . I couldn't just sit there."

She took a step forward. "You didn't just sit there, you ended up sleeping here. Is Opal's broken engagement worth a police record, Billy? Do you think your mom needs to deal with this kinda thing?" Billy had always been a mama's boy, hence the reason he was still living with the woman at twenty-five.

"I'm sorry."

Funny, the man actually looked sorry.

She grabbed the key to the cell and moved to open the door. "In case you missed it, you're not invited to R&B's for six months."

He muttered something under his breath.

"And if I see you anywhere near Dustin causing trouble, I'm going to cuff you first and ask questions later . . . got it?"

Billy nodded like a bobblehead doll.

She inserted the key in the lock and paused. "You have running shoes, right?"

"I have sneakers, if that's what you mean."

"Good." She clicked open the door. "Bring them with you tomorrow when you meet me at River Bend High at six in the morning."

He ran a hand through his hair. "Six in the . . . what do you want?"

She opened the door wide. "Six a.m., River Bend High."

She didn't expect an argument, and Billy was sober enough to understand that.

"Thanks, Sheriff."

Yeah, he'd thank her now . . . but tomorrow, after three miles on the track . . . not so much.

She followed him out the door and found Zoe snickering as he walked by. "Mornin', Billy."

He mumbled a good morning and hustled out the door.

Once it closed, Zoe started laughing. "I swear you've turned into your father."

"I run faster than he did."

Zoe slid off her perch. "I better get back to Miss Gina's. Breakfast won't cook itself."

"Thanks for this."

"Not a problem. Always great to see you playing cop."

They hugged before Zoe walked out the door.

*Playing cop* . . . yeah, that's how it often felt.

Jo put together her essentials: gun, duty belt . . . keys to the squad car, before gathering the spoils left by Zoe. Once outside the station, she locked the door and looked around the silent streets of River Bend. Saturday morning held little interest for early risers unless there was some kind of town event or holiday to celebrate.

Not that weekend.

Her eyes landed on the cornerstone bronze plaque of the station, the one that told anyone who could read the date the building was constructed. Taking a step closer, Jo noticed where Zoe had pushed aside the vining jasmine to find the key they'd tucked into the underside of the building's facade. Pleasant memories of her youth kept her staring at the building for quite a while before she stepped away.

Out of habit, she drove the few blocks of town, around the block, and back down the main street before making her way home.

She left the squad car in her drive and unlocked the front door of the single story bungalow. There was a time in the not so distant past she didn't bother locking the door to her house. Her father never had, and they never needed to. Only the previous fall, around the time of Ziggy Brown's death, the weight of a thousand eyes bore down on Jo like a thick fog choking the town from the ocean.

Jo had started locking doors, looking behind her back, and changing her routine. Looking behind her back and changing her routine lasted about a month longer than the eyes watching her. Or perhaps she grew used to being under someone's radar. Either way, she was getting sloppy again. At least according to Agent Burton, the Fed who had become a friend over the past couple of years.

Jo started undressing before she turned down the hall and into the master bedroom. It had taken two years for her to move her father's stuff out and take over the space to make it her own. For almost eight years she'd been sleeping in his room and performing his job.

For nearly ten years she'd been living his life.

The bed called out to her, suggesting she catch another couple of hours of sleep.

Instead she turned to the shower and turned the volume of the rock band of the hour on high.

# Chapter Two

Jo, Mel, and Zoe sat in the parlor of Miss Gina's Bed-and-Breakfast for their weekly girls' night. Most of the time they had to use Jo's house for their gatherings due to the B and B having a full house. But Tuesday nights and even the occasional Wednesday this early in the spring meant the inn had one, maybe two rooms occupied.

Miss Gina entered the room carrying a red pitcher of her famous lemonade. Her worn Birkenstock sandals made squeaky noises against the floor as she walked, her ever-present tie-dyed skirt swishing at her ankles.

Mel stood. "I'll get the glasses."

A tray of guilty pleasures sat on the table: chocolate, cheese, and fruit that Zoe had thrown together. Anyone else would have put a bowl of Hershey's kisses and small chunks of cheddar, but not Zoe. Jo could identify two of the four cheeses, and the chocolates looked like the gourmet category that one picked up at the mall in Eugene. Even the fruit had been prepared with some kind of cutesy knife that offered deckle edges to the melons.

"You'll be happy to know my cookbook is now in production." Zoe picked up a small chocolate and nibbled.

"What does that mean?"

Miss Gina spoke first. "It means Felix and his crew are coming into town by the end of the month to start filming."

"Did I know about this?" Jo tried to place the information inside her head and came up blank. "I remember talking about the possibility—"

"Probability." Mel set the glasses on the table and started to pour. "Felix set everything up, right, Zoe?"

Zoe was dressed down to jeans and an oversize shirt, her long black hair pulled back in a simple ponytail. "Felix put together a small team—"

"How small?" Jo was more interested in the safety of large truckloads of film equipment sitting around for long periods of time.

"I'm not sure."

"Guess."

Zoe glanced at the ceiling. "No less than ten people, probably more like a dozen."

"And trucks? How many trucks?" The size of the town and simple politics meant there weren't permits needed for filming, but if someone wanted to cause problems, there was county-wide red tape that could be pulled.

"Just one, probably," Zoe answered.

"Why do you ask?" Mel sat back, her bare feet tucked under her bottom as she made herself comfortable.

"So I can head off any issues before they become a problem."

"You think there's a problem?" Miss Gina asked.

Jo shook her head. "No. Most of the people in town love it when Zoe's people are around. It makes everyone feel like they are the famous ones."

"I'm not famous." Zoe rolled her eyes.

Jo shook her head. "Who here has *not* been on TV multiple times with celebrities all over the world?"

Miss Gina, Mel, and Jo raised their hands.

"Who here *doesn't* have a zillion frequent flyer miles on their airline of choice for filming said TV spots?"

Three hands went up.

"Who here doesn't have fan mail, has to dodge autograph requests, or has an agent—"

"Okay, okay . . . so I'm a *little* famous."

Jo laughed. "Anyway, if I know what's coming, I can give a heads-up to those who might need to know, and maybe the few busybodies in the area, to avoid any trouble."

"If there is any trouble, we will sic Felix on them. He's great at making everyone get along."

Jo took a sip of her drink and decided to not finish the glass. She wasn't on duty, but the thought of not being able to jump on an issue if needed didn't sit well with her.

"Hope can't wait to see the crew."

Hope, Mel's nine-year-old daughter, was blossoming into quite the prima donna of Miss Gina's Bed-and-Breakfast. With her innocent smiles and fluttering of her eyelashes, the crew handed her the keys to their hearts the minute they arrived.

"She wants to make some money off that swear jar you have in the kitchen." Miss Gina groaned. Her pocket had grown empty in the two years Hope had lived in River Bend, and her language had cleaned up considerably.

"Smart girl," Jo said.

Mel took another swig of her drink. "The high school has managed to lure me into the alumni committee," she told them.

"For the reunions?" Zoe asked.

"Yep."

"How hard can that be? How many kids were in our graduating class, fifty?"

"Ish," Jo said.

"Yeah, but this year's ten-year reunion is going to be triple the size."

Zoe found another chocolate, kept nibbling. "Baby boomers of River Bend?"

They laughed.

"No, Waterville High had a fire during the holidays that year," Mel told them.

Jo narrowed her eyes.

"I forgot about that," Miss Gina said.

"I don't remember anything about it," Jo mumbled.

Miss Gina patted Jo's knee. "You had a hard year."

She sure had. Before her father's death, she was working odd jobs in Waterville and renting out a bedroom from a divorcée who needed the extra money. When Jo would come home, she'd often stay with Miss Gina. She and her father had just started talking without massive fights right before his death. Jo attributed the peace to the distance.

"I can't believe it's been ten years." Mel's voice softened.

"Feels like forever."

Miss Gina made a humming noise as a slow smile inched across her lips. "Your dad liked his beer, but he had a soft spot in his heart for my lemonade."

"My dad never kept beer in the house."

"That's because you'd drink it!" Miss Gina never minced her words.

"And when did he have a chance to drink your lemonade?" Jo asked.

"Joseph made the trip out here a few times that last year you girls were in high school."

"He did?" Jo didn't remember hearing about him going to Miss Gina's except for the occasional drive through and checking on people when the weather was bad and the power was out. Which, where they lived, happened quite a bit.

"To check on you, mostly."

"How come you didn't tell me?"

Miss Gina tipped her glass back. "I told him I wouldn't. Besides, if I told you back then that your dad and I talked, you wouldn't have come to me when things were hard for you."

"I came to you for just about everything."

"We all did," Zoe added.

Mel removed her honey blonde hair from her ponytail and ran her fingers through the ends. "I remember the day we had that counselor come to the school to talk about teenage pregnancy. We all came here to get the facts from you."

Miss Gina nodded with a grin.

"You told us abstinence was what the preachers tell their daughters to practice about six months before their illegitimate babies were born." Zoe's words brought back the memory.

"Then we had a road trip into Waterville and came home with condoms and the number to the family planning clinic for pills when we needed them."

"I used that number," Jo told them.

"I didn't have to. Miss Gina handed me three months' supply when she heard that Luke had asked me out."

"You didn't have sex with Luke for, like, six months," Mel protested.

"Seven, but I started the pills sooner."

Jo laughed. "That's because you thought you'd get pregnant by just thinking about sex."

Zoe rolled her eyes. "I did not."

"Did, too," Mel said.

"You were paranoid, Zoe." Miss Gina waved her glass in the air.

For a minute it looked like Zoe was going to protest; instead she nodded.

"So what did my dad and you talk about? Not birth control pills, I hope."

Miss Gina shook her head. "He never flat-out asked about that part of your life, but I did remind him that you were smart and didn't want to be a teenage mother."

"He probably knew I was having sex."

"Oh, he knew . . . he just couldn't figure out with who. Bugged the crap out of him that you didn't date any local boys."

"Which is exactly why I didn't date anyone in town."

"You didn't date anyone here because they all knew your dad," Mel corrected her.

"It's a good thing as it stands. It's hard enough policing River Bend, imagine if it were filled with exes."

"I would laugh my ass off all the time." Zoe chuckled.

Miss Gina tucked a long strand of silver-speckled hair behind her ear. "Your dad wanted to know you were safe and getting by. He offered to give me money once in a while to help you out so long as I didn't tell you about it."

This was news to Jo. "And did he . . . give you money?"

"Yep, and I took it, too. You kids emptied my pantry every time you showed up."

Jo had no idea. "Why didn't you tell me about this before now?"

"You weren't ready to hear this right after your dad died. Would have made you fall even deeper in your grief. But your dad loved you. He didn't always know how to handle you, and that summer after high school he had to put his boot down or risk losing you to the wrong crowd. Especially after Zoe left and Mel was in California."

"I *was* with the wrong crowd," Jo said, remembering the party lasting for months.

"Yes, but you called me to pick you up when things were a little hairy, and you never ended up in jail."

"Dad locked me in his more than once."

"Not the same." Miss Gina looked beyond them in her memories as she spoke. "He did that to scare you."

"All it did was piss me off."

"It scared you or you would have ended up in someone else's holding cell."

Neither of her BFFs offered a protest.

Mel refilled her glass and topped off Zoe's. "So Jo's dad came here often?"

"The year Jo was living in Waterville. He'd come by after you'd visit." Miss Gina nodded toward Jo. "He wanted the real story . . . did I approve of your friends? Had I met them? Were you getting enough to eat? He was a worrywart, your dad."

"He never showed that to me." Jo wasn't sure if she should be relieved to know how much her father thought of her back then or distressed to know he didn't tell her directly.

"He had to keep it from you, JoAnne. You needed to be on your own two feet in order to realize how much you had with him. The harder you had to work, the less time you had to party."

"It's no different than you telling Billy Ray to run with you at the school," Zoe said. "That's hard to do sober, forget about it if you're hungover or drunk."

"He still checked on you. Kept in contact with the sheriff in Waterville, enjoyed a glass on the back porch with me." Miss Gina waved her half-empty glass. "He knew you were turning your life around."

*Yeah, but he didn't live to see it.*

Jo winced.

The weight of all the eyes in the room silenced the thoughts in Jo's head.

Mel offered her a soft smile and Zoe changed the subject. "Luke and I have decided on the first weekend in September for the wedding."

The conversation turned to dresses and color choices, tents and food. Luke and Zoe were officially engaged the previous Christmas.

Jo weighed in on the conversation where she could, but her thoughts kept rolling back to her father. How was it possible she knew nothing about his trips to visit Miss Gina? His knowledge of Miss Gina's vodka-infused lemonade?

What else didn't she know?

The graduating class the year her father was murdered put triple the amount of people in the town during the days around his death. Something she'd never considered while she attempted to find his killer.

All these years she'd studied the town, the people . . . the gossip. The reports on her father's death that pointed to "accidental."

"Hey, Jo . . . you still with us?"

"I am . . . but I just thought of something." She stood. "I gotta go check . . ." She left the lie on her tongue.

"Jo?" Mel's unasked question was left unanswered.

Jo grabbed her keys off the table, smiled, and promised to see them all the next day.

~

"I'm worried about her." Mel watched the taillights of Jo's Jeep leave the driveway.

"She isn't happy." Zoe's words put an exclamation point on Mel's thoughts. "She isn't even faking it anymore."

"She didn't even drink tonight." Not that Jo needed liquor to make her happy, but she'd always have at least one cocktail with them on girls' night.

"All that talk about her dad got her thinking again," Miss Gina said. "She pulls into a ball when she reflects back. I don't think she's ever forgiven herself for being a rebellious teenager."

"She wasn't that bad."

"She really wasn't," Mel agreed with Zoe. "But her dad didn't see it that way."

"I'm not so sure about that."

Both Mel and Zoe looked at Miss Gina.

"Joseph knew more about what you kids were doing than he let on. He didn't always show his cards."

"Are you kidding?" Zoe protested. "He helicoptered Jo and the two of us all the time."

Miss Gina shook her head. "He watched over you because he knew of the trouble in your house. He watched over Mel because she was the straight-A student that pulled Jo back every once in a while."

"I didn't pull her back," Mel denied.

"You did. You just didn't realize it," Miss Gina said. "You both anchored her when it was possible she'd spin out of control. Joseph watched all of you and made sure her circle of friends in town were the good kids."

"He didn't control that."

"He fostered it." Miss Gina sighed. "You both were kids, you didn't see him as a man or realize why he did the things he did. Raising a daughter by himself, being the sheriff . . . it wasn't easy for him. The stick up his ass didn't help, but I did my best to wiggle that free."

"Did you?" Zoe asked.

Miss Gina picked up her glass and winked. "I managed."

# Chapter Three

"Agent Burton?" With the phone to her ear, Jo sat behind her desk, staring at the walls of her father's office. Her office.

"Sheriff, how are you? I've been thinking about you."

"Good things, I hope?"

Shauna chuckled. "Anything new on the eyes in the dark?"

From anyone else, Jo would think Shauna was being sarcastic. But cops, law enforcement, even the FBI knew better than to ignore their instincts. "It's been quiet. Too much so."

"I never trust silence either. Is there something I can do for you?"

Jo tapped a pen against her notepad, the only sign of nerves she let herself have. "I want to know if I can take you up on that training course we talked about last year."

"Honing your skills, Jo?"

"It's not like I have a lot of use for them in River Bend."

They both laughed. "I think the next course is late April. Outside DC."

A little over a month away.

"That will work."

"It's a weeklong deal, you able to get away from there that long?"

No, but she'd make it happen. "Yeah. I have vacation time coming."

"I'll get back to you later this week with the details."

Jo hung up the phone with a smile.

"Proactive, not reactive," she muttered. For the first time in a long time, she looked forward to the next month.

~

There was a push, a pull, and a whole lot of red tape to make her trip to DC work. The training would last Monday through Friday, but Zoe and Mel convinced her to take the weekend before . . . for herself.

Once the plane leveled off at 32,000 feet, Jo ordered a drink and let herself relax.

She was just a woman on a plane . . . and until the training started on Monday, she'd just be a woman. Not a cop, not responsible for anyone but herself, not Sheriff Ward's daughter from River Bend.

Just a woman.

The first bar she went into was all suits and ties. Lawyers, lobbyists . . . office jockeys who held no appeal. She didn't even bother with a drink. Dressed in tight jeans and a tank that Zoe insisted she wear to prove to anyone who looked that she was a woman, Jo felt entirely underdressed.

The second bar was a little farther from the city center and slightly better. The ties were off, but it was obvious the men ditched them in their sedans before attempting a night out.

She picked up her cell and texted Shauna.

Burton, you there?

Hey, Sheriff. What can I do for you?

I'm in DC. Flew in early. Are you here yet?

I fly in tomorrow. What's up?

Looking for laid back bar. No suits and ties. Any suggestions?

The dot dot dot that followed told Jo that Shauna was either read-ing between the lines or checking a nightclub app.

Uber to Marly's. Dive bar-ish, so no suits. Sane enough to avoid cuffing anyone while you're there.

"Perfect," Jo muttered to herself.

Thanks!

While Jo looked up Marly's on her phone, a final text from Shauna proved the woman read through the lines. Be safe. Use condoms.

At Marly's, Jo hit pay dirt.

Loud and smoky despite the laws suggesting people not smoke indoors, and littered with hard bodies and hard liquor, Jo felt at home.

A few heads swiveled her way as she moved toward the bar. That's when she saw him.

He had his back to her, a tight T-shirt stretched across a thick layer of muscles built by hours at the gym, and maybe a few steroids. She really hoped steroids were not this guy's thing. Ink peeked out on both his arms just above the sleeve line. A shadow of growth gave evidence that his baldness was by choice. He had a nice ass. Now if only his face matched.

She waited until her gaze inched up his spine like an insect in the forest on a hot summer night.

He turned, and her heart stopped.

Good Lord, God broke the mold with this one. His goatee was trimmed, immaculately so. His lips were full, his jaw tight . . . and his eyes. Dark, almost haunting. Dangerous. He did a once-over, and when his eyes met hers, he lifted one side of his lips in a half smile. One that asked . . . who the hell are you?

She let her eyes linger, her mouth drop open the slightest amount.

She'd bet her badge he had priors. Warning bells screamed in her head as he took the first step her way.

The bartender took that moment to ask her what she wanted.

"Jameson on the rocks," she said before turning her back to the stranger walking her way. "And a Stella."

The bartender turned to collect her order.

He was behind her, she felt it before she turned.

Jo waited until the bartender handed her the drink before lifting her chin. "Hello," she said, knowing he listened.

"A woman who knows how to drink. That's rare."

His voice was chocolate, not rough as she expected. The contrast excited her more.

"I graduated from wine coolers last week." She turned and took in the full effect of the man. He was even bigger close up, his look of warning in sharp focus. Jo ignored the inner voice, the one that told her to walk away . . . the angel that sat on her shoulder, telling her it was a trap, needed to shut the hell up.

"Lucky me," he said, his grin lethal.

She responded, all of her. She'd flunked chemistry in high school but knew it was hitting her upside the head now. *Flirt*, she told herself.

"And what are you drinking?"

The bartender set her beer down, along with a bill.

"Wine coolers."

Jo leaned against the bar, noticed when his eyes found her breasts. She took a deep breath and finished the whiskey in one pull.

"Prove it."

He signaled the barkeep.

Jo waited to see what he would do.

"Wine cooler." The fact he said it with a straight face made the bartender turn as if he was asked for that every day.

The man nearly tripped as he turned back around. "Excuse me?"

Viking Man grinned, changed his order. "I'll have what she's having."

The bartender, a skinny man with hair too long and a narrow face that matched, nodded. "That's better."

"I've never seen you here before," Tall, Dark, and Dangerous said.

"Never been here before."

"Do you plan on being here again?"

She met his eyes, eyes that she could fall into and lose herself if he was the right kind of guy. "No."

"So you're in DC for one night?"

"That's about it."

The bartender set his drinks down. Jo took a drink from her beer. The whiskey was already warming her head.

"What's your name?" he asked.

Yeah, that wasn't gonna happen. "Does it matter?"

His grin grew. "No, I guess it doesn't. Saying *hey you* doesn't work, however."

"How about Anne?"

"You don't look like an Anne."

That was the point. "What should I call you?"

He hesitated a beat. "Rocco."

Not his name . . . again, she'd bet her badge. "Rocco fits," she told him.

"So I've been told."

Her eyes moved to his chest, her hands itched to touch, to test his thickness.

Rocco tossed back his drink, chased it with his beer.

Her eyes lingered on his Adam's apple, and as the beverage moved down, she dropped her gaze.

He stood perfectly still until her eyes took their time moving back to his.

He was smiling. Full-watt danger in a grin. "Like what you see?"

She looked again, really hoped he didn't bulk up on stimulants. "I haven't seen anything . . . yet." The invitation was there, left open for him to take.

After reaching into his back pocket, Rocco slapped a couple of bills on the bar and grasped her hand. His lips reached the lobe of her ear. "Back out now if you're going to."

Instead of retreat, she reached out, grabbed a firm hold on his bicep.

He growled as he pulled her from the bar.

~

Rocco, for all intents and purposes, handed Jo his helmet before straddling his Harley. DC in spring was cold . . . at least at eleven o'clock at night. The diversion of discomfort would snap all concerns from Jo as he tore through the streets of DC on a mission. When he took the second, third, and fourth curve with sharp edges, Jo grasped his waist and held on. Only then did he ease into the drive. He was firm, everywhere. The thing she missed most about her life. The thing she told herself wasn't important.

The long-term resident hotel they pulled into wasn't a shock, but if Jo were honest, a disappointment, as Rocco turned into the lot and cut the engine.

He led her into his room, which was surprisingly clean. A single king-size bed, a dresser with an old TV, a small refrigerator, microwave, and two lamps rounded out the visual interest inside the small room. She had less than thirty seconds to study the interior before Rocco tossed the keys to his bike on the dresser and invaded her personal space.

"Can I get you a drink?"

She shook her head and licked her lips.

Rocco's gaze swept her face. "I'll just be a minute," he said before disappearing behind the bathroom door. She heard the water turn on and switched her attention to the side table in the room. What would be in there? Did he have stacks of the same clothes he wore now? The desire to know more about him clashed with the desire to know nothing at all.

Jo sat on the edge of the bed to keep her hands from opening drawers and learning his secrets. There was a weapon in the room somewhere, she could smell it.

When Rocco emerged from the bathroom, his eyes fell on her and that half grin emerged once again.

"You look comfortable," he said, his eyes lingering on her breasts.

She leaned her elbows back on the bed; let her girls reach a little higher. "I could be better." It felt good to tease and say the things she wanted to without censure.

Rocco's smile said he approved.

"A little thing like you should be scared."

He approached slowly, like a predator. Only his grin gave him away.

"I can handle myself."

He narrowed his eyebrows. "Can you?"

She had a few tricks up her sleeve to get away from a situation if she needed to. Hoped to learn a dozen more before the week of training was complete. The only thing she didn't have with her was her weapon, but she didn't think she needed it.

Instead of answering him, she looked at the ink on his arms. "Does that go all the way up, or have you just started?" In her experience, people that liked ink, loved ink. If they could afford it, they had more than one tattoo with the plan for more.

Rocco took her invitation to remove his shirt slowly.

Breath caught in Jo's chest. He was gorgeous. Tight. His right arm had a band that looked like a rope, the left arm had a band that looked like barbed wire. His chest was bare, but she'd bet money his back was not.

She lifted a finger in the air and made a rolling motion.

He took the hint and turned around.

Jo's eyes settled on his ass first.

Her mouth watered.

"You like?"

Damn, his ink . . . she was supposed to be looking at his tattoo.

"Oh . . ." It was an eagle, a massive statement that spread over his entire back, with wings that touched the edges of his shoulders. Jo leaned forward on the bed and reached toward him, her fingers touching the edges of the bird. "That's . . . wow." She stood and felt the muscles under the ink until her focus was on the man.

His chest expanded when she traced the outline of his shoulders with both hands before letting them fall to his narrow waist. At the waistline of his jeans, she squeezed. "I definitely like."

Rocco moved quickly for a man his size. He turned and grasped her waist in his big hands and pulled her hips to his.

His lips torched hers with the first touch. He tasted like fire and a little bit of sin. When she opened to him, his indecent, open-mouth kisses became the fastest addiction Jo had ever experienced. She held on to his neck, lifted on her toes to kiss him back.

For a libido that sat dormant for years at a time, it sure knew how to fire to life when needed. Everything strained toward this Viking of a man.

His hands splayed down her waist, her back, and held on to her hips.

The erection she felt but couldn't see didn't appear to be one shrunk by steroids. She smiled into his kiss and started clawing at her shirt to take it off.

Rocco helped her.

He grinned as he stared, and Jo was thankful Zoe had talked her into a new bra that enhanced the parts of her that were all woman.

Viking Man trailed his lips down her jaw to the top of one breast.

She closed her eyes when she felt the bite of his teeth through the thin material. "Yes," she mumbled more to herself than to him. He nestled between her breasts before matching a nip to the other side.

When his hands reached the globes of her ass, she lost the ability to hold still. Jo jumped up, wrapped both legs around his hips to maximize contact, and forced his lips back to hers. She wasn't sure, but she thought he laughed as he backed her up against the bed and settled his weight once she was lying down.

Everything was a blur from there. Clothes flew, hands took their fill . . . and no, Viking Man didn't use steroids.

There was a condom, a curse, and the satisfaction of him filling her completely. He stopped the second he was inside her.

"Don't stop."

"Catching my breath, sweetness."

Sweetness. No one called her sweet.

Jo clenched every inner muscle she had and lifted her hips as much as she could with a 230-plus-pound hulk on top of her. "Breathe later," she demanded.

His laugh was deep as he started to move. The heat of his body, the friction of his touch . . . the warmth of his kiss brought her to the first crest and had her humming after the fall.

He slowed his movements but wasn't close to being done. "Feel better?" he asked.

When she dared to open her eyes, he was smiling down at her. Satisfied in his possession.

Jo crossed her ankles behind his back. "I'm getting there."

His laugh was contagious before he reached to kiss her again.

~

Jo slid the key into her hotel room door just before four in the morning. Viking Man hadn't stirred when she rose from his bed, quietly found her clothes, and put them back on before she disappeared from his room. The Uber driver met her at the corner, and she was back at her hotel in ten minutes.

It was better this way, she told herself, a late night dash instead of any awkward morning-after conversation. Much as she'd have liked to see what the man could do in the daylight hours, she was afraid to sit around to find out.

She showered before climbing into the hotel bed and smiled as she drifted off to sleep. The man was surprisingly gentle for one so big. She'd ache in the morning but would welcome the discomfort with memories of the night. The one sad truth was the inability to find that kind of a man who fit in her life.

The town sheriff didn't date a man like *Rocco*.

She put them in cuffs and behind bars. Then again, maybe he wasn't all that.

Who was she kidding? His Harley was more important than a home. The transient motel. There wasn't one knickknack or sign of personality in his room, which meant he didn't have any. Men without ties were either married and using the motel as a crash pad . . . the thought had Jo staring at the ceiling. Or the lack of ties meant he was on the move. Probably running from someone. A man the size of Mr. Viking wasn't going to run from trouble; he'd probably avoid the law, however.

Weighing which she liked better, a felon on the run or a married man cheating . . . man, that was a rock and a hard friggin' place. Neither suited her.

Jo punched her pillow, turned it over, and tried to push thoughts of Rocco out of her head.

Only the last thought as she drifted off to sleep was him whispering *sweetness* in her ear.

# Chapter Four

Jo took a train down to Quantico, Virginia, from DC. She wondered, briefly, if she could get back into DC overnight and try and find *Rocco* again before she disappeared from the East Coast for good. The plan was to finish her training Friday afternoon, nurse her wounded everything she was sure was going to hurt, and fly out of DC Saturday afternoon.

Viking Man kept her up the first night by action, the second night by memories.

Why did she do this to herself? Why put herself out there, make her want something she couldn't have, only to walk away somewhat satisfied but seriously desperate for more? She should probably just invest in a crate full of cats and be done with it.

Burton told her to dress in Friday casual, no dresses—not that Jo owned any—and bring a change of clothes to work out in. And her badge.

Her shoulder length honey brown hair was pulled back in a ponytail, and a tiny dusting of blush enhanced her cheeks. Her lips sported a hint of rose, but that was it when it came to makeup. A lack of cover-up kept her from hiding the fading purple mark on the base of her neck . . .

the only leftovers from Viking Man's touch. Wearing simple blue dress pants, black shoes with the smallest heel she could get away with, and a silk blouse she borrowed from Zoe, Jo walked into the training center and approached the front desk.

The man behind the desk wore a suit and tie. His stern expression matched just about every movie she'd ever seen when it came to agents and the FBI.

Jo attempted a smile.

He wasn't amused.

"Agent Burton is expecting me," she told him. "Sheriff Ward."

The man scanned her up and down. "Badge and ID, Sheriff."

She reached into her back pocket, found her slim wallet, and presented him her credentials.

He looked at the ID and her badge twice, and her three times before lifting the phone at the desk and punching in a few numbers. "Sheriff Ward is here," was all he said.

Fed Man handed her back her documents and then lifted a camera attached to a computer. He didn't ask her to smile, he simply snapped a picture and turned back to his computer. "Take this," he said, sliding her a visitor badge. "Wear it at all times until this one is available."

Jo pinched the badge on the silk shirt and hoped it didn't make a permanent mark. She didn't want to return Zoe's shirt with dents in it.

She waited a breath, expecting the man to give her further instructions.

He didn't.

Thankfully, Agent Burton saved her any confusion as to where to go by walking down a corridor that led to a bank of elevators.

Ease washed over Jo when Shauna approached in attire very close to Jo's. The woman seemed to understand the business side of life and mix it with just enough femininity to not look like she was pretending to be a man. In the grand scheme of things, women in law enforcement were accepted. There were still small pockets of doubters out there. Men who believed women couldn't do the job. Jo had been dealing with that since she joined the academy. Burton told her that wasn't quite the case with the bureau. Women reached into all positions and were needed in places that men simply couldn't go. And vice versa. The respect was on all ends here. Something Jo looked forward to experiencing, even for just a week.

"Agent Burton," Jo said with a smile.

"Sheriff . . . good to see you again." They greeted with a hug.

Shauna addressed the man behind the desk. "Thanks, Francis."

He snarled.

"I take it you were kind to our guest."

Francis offered a noncommittal nod. "He hates everyone," Burton whispered as she walked away.

Jo kept to her side and took in everything around her.

Burton spoke as she stepped into the elevator. "I have a meeting first thing this morning but will join you later on this afternoon for the hand-to-hand stuff. "My partner, Agent Clausen, will show you around until I can meet up with you."

"I hope I'm not a burden to her."

"Him," Shauna corrected. "You won't be. He's big and scary but a teddy bear once you get to know him." They stepped off the elevator with her still talking. "Most of the men around here are happy to have women around. There're a few old-timers who think we shouldn't be here, but most of them aren't at these training exercises any longer."

Jo chuckled. "Probably because they can't keep up."

"Exactly!"

They rounded the corner to find several agents talking and drinking coffee in what looked like a lounge.

"Here's Agent Tall, Dark, and Scary now."

Jo's skin started to tingle.

"Gill?" Shauna called out. "Sheriff Ward is here."

Shauna's voice reached the back of the man. As he turned, Jo felt the world tilt.

*Holy shit!*

"Agent Gill Clausen, Sheriff JoAnne Ward."

"Jo," she managed to choke out.

Rocco, who exchanged a T-shirt for a suit and tie, managed to look her up and down in the space of a breath. His half smile emerged. "Sheriff Ward." He extended a hand. "I've heard a lot about you."

Jo forced her cold palm forward. "A pleasure."

His hand squeezed hers . . . twice. "Have we met?"

The question was meant to unsettle her.

It did.

"I don't believe so."

His left eyebrow lifted. "I'm sure we have."

She squeezed his hand, dug what nails she had into his palm before letting go.

"No one would forget meeting you, Gill." Saved by Shauna.

Shauna introduced her to the other agents in the room. None of the names registered.

*Get it together, Jo.*

"I've gotta go," Shauna said after checking the time on her watch. "Be nice, Clausen. Remember, you're scary to those of us who know you."

Jo met Agent Gill Clausen's eyes. "She looks like she can handle me."

Shauna narrowed her eyes. "I'll be back by noon."

Jo waved her off and pulled in a deep breath.

Well, this was going to be a load of shits and giggles. Here Jo prided herself on being able to read people. Never once in the time she spent playing tonsil hockey over the weekend did she peg Rocco—Viking Man—Gill, as a Fed.

The water cooler room filled with other agents and kept Jo and Gill from saying anything they were thinking. What was he thinking? He kept eyeing her like an enigma. Which was probably how she appeared, looking at him.

"Burton was assigned to your town for that missing girl a couple years ago, right?"

Jo directed her attention to the man talking. She'd already forgotten his name. "That's right."

"How's the kid?"

"Hope is great, thanks for asking."

The five men in the room watched her.

"It's always nice when it works out," another agent said.

"Yes, it is."

Gill put his coffee down and caught her attention again. "Well, *Sheriff*, we only have you for a week. Let me get you where you need to go."

Jo forced her eyes to look directly at him. She would not cower . . . not be embarrassed. She hitched her backpack higher on her shoulder. "Lead the way, Agent Clausen."

They walked in silence down the same hall she'd just used with Shauna.

He ate up the path with quick strides, making Jo take another step to his in order to keep up.

They stepped into the elevator together, the reprieve from a private conversation came in the way of a woman joining them before the doors shut.

Her fist clenched her backpack and Gill chuckled softly.

She refused to look.

The elevator emptied them back into the lobby, where he directed her toward a long, busy corridor.

She doubled her step and matched him shoulder to shoulder. "Where are we going?"

"Training complex."

He pushed through an exit door, the sun blinding her.

Gill fished sunglasses out of an inside pocket of his jacket, set them over his eyes, and didn't miss a beat.

He stepped to a dark blue sedan, one that screamed FBI, and opened the passenger door.

Looked like their silence was over.

Gill managed to put his frame behind the wheel and turn over the engine before he uttered a word. "You left without saying good-bye."

No use pretending. "I didn't think I'd see you again."

He backed out of the parking spot. The training center sat on a military base of over five hundred acres. Driving to each location made more sense than walking. "Burton tells me you're here to better your tactical skills, investigative skills . . . survival skills."

Jo found her sunglasses in her backpack, felt relief when she knew Gill couldn't see her eyes. "That's right."

His head turned toward her briefly. "Lesson number one. Don't pick up strangers in bars."

Oh, the nerve. Anger in the form of heat shot up her spine. "Like you did?"

"I'm a man."

She couldn't help it. Jo laughed.

"You think I'm kidding."

"I think you're a hypocrite."

He made sure to look at her again, kept looking until she met his stare. "I could have snuffed you out, cut you into tiny pieces, and hidden your body in a place so remote they wouldn't discover it until it was an anthropological find."

"You've given this some thought."

His jaw tightened, his eyes darted back to the road in front of him before he turned in the direction of what Jo assumed was the training center. "You do that often?" Something in his voice changed.

Sarcasm was needed. "Every Saturday night. Living in a small town affords me all kinds of opportunities to pick up strangers. The seedy motel is a little hard, however. Is that a government approved hotel, or just your personal choice?"

He pulled the car to an abrupt stop, threw it in park. "I know what to expect in places like that."

"Armed criminals in the next room?"

"Sometimes."

"You left your weapon in the bathroom once we got there, didn't you?"

Gill whipped off his sunglasses and stared. "The fact you didn't know I was carrying one should tell you something."

Actually, she assumed he did . . . but didn't think he wanted to use it on her. He had other needs.

So did she.

"I'm not an invalid, *Rocco*."

His eyes narrowed with the use of the name that wasn't his.

"And I'm not an idiot. If you wanted to hurt me, I would have sensed it before we left the bar."

"You don't know that."

It was her time to look over the brim of her glasses. "Did you hurt me?"

"That's not the point."

She pushed her glasses higher, reached for the door of the car. "Yes it is."

# Chapter Five

There wasn't much that ruffled Gill. He knew at the time something about *Anne* wasn't up-front. But a small town sheriff? No, he didn't see that coming. When he'd woke just before dawn and she wasn't there, he was surprisingly disappointed. She'd been demanding . . . a little needy, even. Then there was the fire that she lit with a touch. JoAnne Ward . . . Little Miss River Bend Nowhere, Oregon, gave as much as she took and asked for more. They'd gone at it for hours. Not something he often did. It was like she was saving it up, soaking it all in to last.

Yeah . . . that crack about hooking up in a small town was laughable. He'd have to ask Burton about what she knew when it came to Sheriff Ward's love life.

He watched her ass as she moved through the doors of the training center. There were plenty of law enforcement officers there for the very same training as Jo. They mingled on the sideline while several receptionists took in the newcomers.

Gill approached the desk by Jo's side.

"Agent Clausen? What are you doing here?"

Gill shook hands with an old friend. "Agent Ault, this is JoAnne Ward. Sheriff of River Bend, Oregon. She's on the roster this week."

Agent Ault looked over his printed sheet, found her name, and checked it off.

"Welcome to Quantico, Sheriff."

"Thank you," Jo said.

Ault twisted a waiver in front of her. "You need to sign this."

She skimmed the document . . . the one saying if she was hurt or killed she had no right to sue the federal government. The part about her being dead and not being able to sue never managed to be questioned.

"Have you been with us before?" Ault asked.

"No. First time."

Gill made sure Ault knew to take care of her. "She's a close friend of Agent Burton," he told him.

"Ah, right. Shauna said she was coming in later to help with the hand-to-hand. Had a friend coming."

"This is her."

"Great. Locker rooms are in there." He pointed down the hall. We'll be starting in fifteen." He looked at her feet. "I hope you brought running shoes."

Jo smiled, something Gill had yet to see since she arrived.

He liked it.

"Burton suggested it."

"You're all set, then."

Jo stepped away and turned toward him. "Well, Agent Clausen, thanks for getting me here."

"I can't let my partner down."

Jo put her hand out as if she was shaking it good-bye. "It was a pleasure."

He took her one hand in both of his briefly before she pulled away. "No, it was mine."

A tiny bit of heat rose in her face before she walked down the hall to the locker rooms.

As she did, he envisioned the tattoo she had on the small of her back. The simple, geometric design women want when they're young as a form of rebellion but have no true idea what they want in life.

Didn't matter if it was rebellion or not . . . Gill thought it was sexy. He'd wanted to eat breakfast off it the morning after.

Only she'd left.

"You and Burton are on tap for instruction this week, right?"

"We volunteered to help."

"See you out there."

~

Dressed in dark blue from head to toe, with *FBI Training* written on her T-shirt, her hat, and even the belt they'd given her . . . Jo walked out with several other female law enforcement officers with the same purpose.

They met their male classmates in a large room that housed close to two hundred of them.

Gill hovered in her head. The idiocy of him suggesting she couldn't take care of herself burned.

He didn't know what he was talking about. And after this week, she'd be even better equipped to ward off any unwanted man.

She'd wanted Viking Man.

Arrogant Fed that he was.

She forced his image from her brain and switched her attention to those around her.

Reminiscent of her days in the academy, Jo stood shoulder to shoulder with the other officers while the instructors filed out in front of them.

As they lined up, the room grew silent.

When Jo saw him, she cussed under her breath. She didn't see where Gill's eyes fell from behind his sunglasses, but she felt the weight of them nonetheless.

"Ladies and gentlemen, I'm Agent Ault. Welcome to Quantico. Where we help take your skills you've obtained in your local law enforcement agency and help you find your weakness and attack it. We will hone and teach you what you may not know . . . use what you've forgotten, and remind you every day that you're one bullet away from being a statistic. We're here to help you stay alive, help you keep your civilians breathing, and above all else, know what you are capable of doing and what you are not. We are not on a military base by accident. This week will feel like boot camp. It will challenge you, leave you bruised and exhausted. Welcome the pain. It will make you stronger."

The woman standing to Jo's right shifted and muttered something she couldn't hear.

Jo looked back up and felt Gill staring.

Agent Ault explained how the days would progress before dismissing them to their preassigned groups.

Jo didn't bother looking for a group number, she walked right up to Gill, knowing his half smile that bordered on a smirk was meant for her. "What a surprise," she said without humor.

He tilted his glasses enough to make sure she saw his dark orbs. "Time to see what you're made of, Sheriff."

Jo knew, without a doubt, this was going to hurt.

~

They started at the range. A place Jo felt comfortable. Her father had raised her with guns in the house, and there wasn't a memory there that didn't involve her safely using every gun available to him.

Small towns didn't have a ton available, however. And with the price of finely tuned weaponry, Jo didn't have the budget to add to her personal arsenal.

Gill introduced his group to the range officer, who went over the plan for the morning.

"We want to know your baseline . . . want you to know it. I'm sure you're accurate with your service weapon. What about your perpetrator's weapon? When you manage to disarm your suspect and have need to use their guns?"

Gill took up where the range officer left off. "We want you to team up with another person who uses a weapon different from your own. Who uses a forty?" he asked.

Several hands went up.

"The nine millimeter?"

Jo raised her hand.

He went down the short list of backup weapons after that, before pairing the groups.

Jo found herself with Lenny, a deputy from somewhere in Ohio, and Sal, a vice cop from Chicago. Both men had half a foot or more on Jo and several more years on the force than she. When she introduced herself as the sheriff of River Bend, the men exchanged unconvinced glances.

"It's a small town," she explained.

"How good a shot are you, Sheriff?" Sal asked. Sal had a long, lean face that belonged on top of a thin body . . . instead it bobbled on a thick neck that made the man look completely out of proportion.

"I hold my own," she said as she loaded the clips for her weapon of choice.

"I'm a betting man . . . how about you, Lenny?" Sal asked.

Lenny, a little younger than Sal, glanced at Jo. "Small town girls grow up with guns," he told Mr. Vice. "I'll stay out of that bet."

Sal smirked as he loaded the forty-caliber Glock. "What about you, Sheriff? Put some money behind your skills?"

Jo saw Gill approach.

She stopped being a sheriff for two seconds and gave Sal the sweetest smile she could muster. "I don't know, Sal. You probably get all kinds of practice in a big city like Chicago."

Sal tilted his head. "Where's your confidence, Sheriff?"

She knew Gill heard the bet. "Twenty dollars says I'm a better shot with my nine than you are with your forty."

Sal approved with a nod.

"And . . . just for shits and giggles, twenty more says I'm better with your forty than you are."

He blinked. "Fifty."

Jo forged insecurity with a dip of her chin. "Small towns don't pay well." Before he could back out, she agreed. "But I'll take that bet."

Shots started to ring out around them.

Jo covered her ears with the protection provided and pushed her sunglasses higher on her face.

Out of the corner of her eye, Gill watched.

Her target was twenty-five yards out. The first round suggested the sights on Sal's gun were a little high. She adjusted her aim and concentrated. The rapid succession of bullets flew through the air until her clip was empty. She dropped the clip and set the empty gun down and stepped back.

Lenny sat with his arms crossed, a smile on his face.

Gill smirked.

Sal wasn't happy.

"Your turn, Chicago," Jo said.

Gill walked by, patted Sal on the back. "Never bet your lunch money against a woman at the range. She'll take it every time."

Seventy dollars richer, Jo happily moved on to weapons she didn't have as much experience with.

The .45 shot a lot like her 9mm with a little more kick. Her backup .38 was easy, but when put in a smaller weapon, she found the target moving around. Or perhaps she wasn't hitting it.

Sal wasn't a sore loser, and gave her pointers on the smaller weapon.

Gill would walk by on occasion and offer one of them a pointer they hadn't thought of that helped them improve their game.

When they moved to the outdoor long range, Jo asked Sal if he wanted to win his money back.

He hesitated, and Lenny reminded him that there was more open space in rural Oregon than there was in the city of Chicago.

Sal passed.

This was where the best military snipers in the service came to train. There was something inspiring about the grounds. The group training wasn't there to hit their targets at five hundred yards with scopes and spotters . . . but with what they'd actually use in real-life scenarios they'd face.

Agent Ault and the range officers spoke of offense and defense when being called for backup.

When he asked how many of them hunted for sport, less than half of them raised their hands. Though Jo didn't do it any longer, she had when her dad was alive. The small hunting cabin her father had used for years sat high in the forest above River Bend collecting spiders and dust. She'd been a couple of times since his death, just to make sure the place wasn't overtaken by raccoons, but couldn't bring herself to stay. It was the one place she left exactly as it had been since the day her father passed. Removing any of his things felt like a sacrilege. So she left all as it was and thought one day she might bring herself to use the space.

Or maybe she should just open it up to Luke and Wyatt, not that either of them hunted for venison. The place was off the grid, completely unavailable outside a two-way radio that her dad had kept with him in case of extreme emergencies. When he'd been sheriff, he never really took any time off away from River Bend. Even the cabin wasn't outside of the zip code.

When she was older and didn't go up to the cabin with him, he'd come back from a weekend refreshed and ready for a new month, a new season.

She smiled fondly into the memory and remembered that he was the reason she was there.

"Sheriff?"

Jo jumped. How someone the size of Gill could sneak up on her was a mystery.

"Agent Clausen."

He looked out over the range and back to her. "You looked lost in your thoughts. Uncomfortable with rifles?"

"I hold my own."

He smiled.

"I don't have a lot experience with ARs. We trained with them, but it isn't what I carry in the squad car. I'd use a range rifle when we'd hunt," she confessed.

"We'd?"

She looked past the man, tried not to imagine the ink she knew was under his FBI T-shirt. "My father and I."

Gill turned a chair around and straddled it. "Burton told me about your father. I'm sorry."

He sounded as if he was.

"It was a long time ago."

She watched Sal struggle with a lever-action 558, paid attention when Lenny instructed the man.

"I was surprised to hear your father died of an accidental shooting."

Lenny looked behind his shoulder and waved her over.

"Yeah," she said, standing up. "I was, too." Without more, she placed her ear protection on and moved in, leaving Gill behind.

Later, when they'd moved to the ARs, Gill took a space beside her and took over the instruction.

The man was distracting. When he called her on a lack of concentration, she focused and went through the paces of becoming more familiar with a weapon she hardly ever shot. Problem was, this gun was available to most anyone out there who had the money. Unfortunately, law enforcement in rural Oregon didn't think she needed one enough to put it in her budget. Once she started shooting it, however, she made a note to lobby the deciding parties to change their stance. Even without the use of the scope, the gun was a dream.

Gill stood behind her when she shot, a pair of binoculars in his hands. The targets were as close as one hundred yards out and as far out as three. Hitting the mark wasn't easy, and it took more concentration than would work in any real-life uses.

Once she'd squeezed the trigger, she'd wait to hear him call out if she hit, if the shot was high, or if it was too low.

"High and to the right," he told her.

She adjusted.

"Too low."

Another breath, her eye peering down the barrel at the sights, she missed her target again.

"Lean into that gun, Sheriff," Gill called behind her.

She squeezed.

"Closer." Gill stood behind her, his chest pressed into her back, his face close to hers. "Get closer to the weapon."

He moved away far enough to not be hit by the casing as it exited the chamber.

She didn't need him to tell her she hit her target. So did the next six shots.

When she pulled the clip and sat back, Gill was smiling. "A couple hundred more hits and I might consider you efficient."

She'd argue with him if he wasn't telling the truth.

He waved one of her trio over. "You're up, Lenny."

By lunch, she was already tired . . . and they hadn't even started the hand-to-hand yet.

# Chapter Six

Shauna met Jo during lunch. "How was the first half of your day?" she asked, sitting with her sandwich and soda.

"Intense." Jo moved her tray over to give her room.

"Gill said you're a pretty good shot."

Jo couldn't stop her eyes from searching the man out in the crowd. He sat with a few instructors.

"Did he?"

"Hey, that's high praise, coming from him."

"He's an intense guy." Gill took that moment to feel the weight of her stare. He met her eyes and didn't flinch.

Shauna glanced over her shoulder and back. "Well, look at that."

From across the room, Gill appeared to laugh before moving his attention to the people he was with.

"Look at what?" Jo picked up her sandwich and attempted to focus.

"He's single," Shauna said, a smirk covering her face.

"Who's single?"

"Gill . . ."

Jo felt her face flush. "Did I ask?"

"Your eyes did."

So did the rest of her, but Jo kept that to herself. "Not interested," she said.

"Liar! But I'll let it go. We haven't had a chance to really talk since last fall. How is everything in River Bend?"

Jo was happy to change the subject. "Quiet."

"That's a good thing."

"Considering all the excitement in the past couple years, yeah. It's also a little unnerving."

Shauna shifted in her seat. "I don't like sitting idle either. A place like River Bend would grow cobwebs on my feet in no time."

"Yeah, that's why I'm here. My badge feels like a target or a noose." The words escaped her mouth before she could retract them.

"Target I get . . . but noose?"

Jo wasn't one to really talk about her emotional stress on the job, but if there was anyone who might understand, it was someone who carried a badge of her own. "Some kids inherit their family business . . . auto shops, plumbers . . . even a restaurant. I somehow managed to inherit a badge. Not the path I thought I'd find myself."

"You don't like it."

Jo gave up on her lunch, pushed it aside. "I'd like it more if it wasn't such a marriage to an entire town. I'm more of a play the field woman, commitment phobic. Watching out over the same street, the same neighbors week after week, year after year, makes me feel old."

Shauna shrugged. "Then why do it?"

Jo thought of the flag that hung over her fireplace. The one that had been draped over her father's casket at his funeral. "I need to finish what I started."

"What am I missing, Jo?"

"This summer will be the ten-year anniversary of my father's death."

"And?"

CATHERINE BYBEE

Instead of coming out and telling Agent Burton every thought, every fear . . . Jo asked, "How many men or women in uniform 'accidentally' shoot themselves with their own weapons?"

Shauna laughed as if it was a joke, but then her face lost her smile. "Wait, didn't the investigating officers determine your father accidentally shot himself?"

"That's what the report said." Jo left her thoughts open.

"You don't believe it."

"My father was a smart cop . . . an avid hunter, and a man who respected his weapons more than any marksman here. I believe my father *accidentally* killed himself about as much as I believe you can out arm wrestle your partner." Jo's eyes moved to where Gill had been a few moments before.

He wasn't there now.

"So you became a cop to get answers."

Jo set both arms on the table and leaned forward. "I became a cop because it was what my father would have wanted. I followed his steps in River Bend to find the truth."

"And what have you found after all these years?"

She released a painful sigh. "That my father led a very boring and unfulfilling life. The only dirt on the man was what I created when I was a teenager."

"Sounds depressing," Shauna said.

"Sounds like bull. My father was a good-looking guy. More than one single woman in town tried to get his attention that I remember, but he didn't bite. Not that I found out about."

"Maybe he went out of town for that part of his life."

Yeah, she'd thought about that more than once. Even Waterville didn't bring up any hits when she'd asked around.

"Where do you go when you want to let loose?"

Once again Jo found her gaze rolling over the room in search of Viking Man. "Anywhere but River Bend."

"Seems to me you need to start looking in Anywhere, USA, instead of River Bend."

Jo glanced at her watch when the other students started to get up and clear their lunch trays.

"Well, this is about as far from River Bend as I can get without leaving the country."

They both stood and moved their half-eaten lunches to the garbage.

"I'd be happy to look over the reports on your father's death. Not sure if I can help, but I'm willing."

Jo smiled. "I'd like that."

~

Barefoot, on mats, in sweatpants was only attractive if you were kicking ass . . . which Jo was not.

She'd always considered herself competent in hand-to-hand combat . . . or at the very least, able to take a perpetrator down despite her size and weight. But for every move in her cop's toolbox, Shauna had one of equal or greater value that neutralized Jo's efforts. While Shauna worked with Jo and a handful of other female classmates, Gill knocked around several of the men in an effort to show them their weaknesses and where they could grow.

Then they switched.

"And this is where I get my ass handed to me," Jo said under her breath.

It wasn't that Gill smirked when he approached . . . wait, yeah, that was exactly the expression on his face. An *I'm going to show you who the strong one is, babe* look.

Jo was teamed up with a half dozen women; none reached the height of Gill, and only one competed with his girth. And Bess didn't look like she spent all her time at the gym. *Big boned* was the polite term that would be tossed around River Bend.

From the east side of the room someone rolled in a cart full of replica weapons and started dropping sets off with each instructor.

Gill addressed their group as the weapons were passed out. "Chances are you'll have a weapon on you, and your opponent will know it. So for the purpose of these exercises, we're going to increase your chances of overtaking your opponent's weapons or ensuring yours stay with you."

Gill glanced up, met Jo's eyes. "Jo*Anne*?" He motioned her forward.

"Jo is fine."

"Great . . . take a weapon, *Jo*."

She grasped a purple mock handgun similar to hers and turned toward Gill.

"Some of these tactics you've seen before, some you've practiced, but my guess is you haven't spent a lot of time on mats perfecting your skills like you did when you were training to carry a badge." Gill kept talking. "It's one of the things that separate this department from yours."

Jo stood beside Gill, waiting for him to finish.

"Jo, you work in a small town, right?"

"That's right."

"When was the last time someone went for your gun?"

She thought about the scuffle in Josie's bar and shook it off. "I can't say anyone has." Saying that out loud made her realize how inept she was.

"All right then . . . let's begin."

Three times Gill had her point the gun at him at point-blank range, three times he disarmed her before she could blink and had the gun on her. Each time he took her weapon away, he did it differently, from several angles and positions. The fourth time, he had her gun, and her pinned to the ground.

"In tiny, little pieces, *Anne*!" he said so only she could hear.

He stood, held out a hand for her to take.

"Now let's slow all that down and practice," Gill addressed the class.

Jo limped off the base hours later with the need for an ice pack and a shot of anything, as long as it was strong.

~

Gill sat beside Shauna at a bar not far off base.

"So, Sheriff Ward?" Gill opened the conversation over a beer.

Shauna glanced at her watch, huffed out a laugh. "Less than two minutes, Clausen. Not bad."

He twisted his frame on the supersmall bar stool and glared. "What?"

"She's single."

"Who?"

"Jo. Sheriff Ward. Keep up!" Shauna tilted her glass back with a grin. "Go on . . . you want to know something about Jo?"

Right. He wanted to know something about the mirage that shimmered out of his weekend and walked into his week. "What's her story?"

Shauna studied the inside of her glass. "I already told you. River Bend's sheriff, had a steady head when I was there investigating the disappearance of the girl. We chat once in a while." A look of concern crossed his partner's face before she took another drink.

"And?"

She shook her head. "I think she's bored in that small town. Probably ready to find something new to keep her in law enforcement."

He and Shauna hadn't been partners for very long. In fact, he'd moved to Eugene to help the West Coast arm of missing persons a few months after the Hope Bartlett case. He knew where River Bend was on a map, but he'd never been there.

"She grew up there, right?"

"Yeah, her dad was the sheriff before her."

"Was?"

Shauna lifted both hands and made quotation marks in the air. "'Accidentally' shot himself ten years ago. Jo joined the academy and the town voted her in as soon as they were able."

"She's a little young to be the sheriff."

"Not for River Bend. They adore her."

He could see why. Honey brown hair, snarky grin, with enough spice under her skin to make him think about her long after she'd left his bed. He knew when he pulled her into his room it would be a onetime thing. But when she'd been gone in the morning, he'd craved.

Gill never craved.

Lost in his thoughts, he felt his partner's stare and met it.

"I have her cell number."

So did he; he pilfered it off her paperwork.

"She's single," Shauna said again.

"I don't remember asking."

Shauna laughed and turned back around in her chair. "She's a smart cop. Level headed . . . too good for where she lives, if you ask me."

"You think this week is an exercise to see if she's ready for something else?"

"I think there are a couple of things eating at Jo, one of which is her desire to move on to something bigger than Nowhere, Oregon."

Gill waited for Shauna to elaborate.

Only his partner took another pull on her beer and didn't.

"What would the other thing—"

She interrupted him. "If I thought you were interested in Jo for professional reasons, I'd tell ya, but since I think this is a boy girl thing . . . I'm going to play the gender loyalty card and suggest you call and ask her yourself."

Shauna gave a sideways glance and a smirk.

"When's that divorce of yours final?" he asked, knowing full well she was in the middle of trying to keep her retirement she'd managed to build in the time she'd been an agent. Her soon-to-be ex worked in security but wasn't a Fed. His benefit plan for old age was nothing compared to hers.

"Not soon enough."

It was Gill's turn to smirk. "I'll remember to play the 'gender loyalty' card when it is."

"Touché."

## Chapter Seven

The beat-up sedans were tinted and framed with extra bumpers to keep those inside the cars as safe as they could be while on the 1.1-mile track housed by the TEVOC training center. Jo's excitement over the Tactical and Emergency Vehicle Operation Center driving course fueled the smile on her face as she sat in the passenger space of the car. Lenny buckled in as the driver, and she was supposed to keep him informed of what was happening around him when things got dicey.

And things were about to get dicey!

"Don't kill me," she told Lenny as she fastened her seat belt.

"Ha!"

The radio in the car paired them with an instructor, while the other cars on the track also housed students with a set instructor talking to them.

"Have you done this before?" she asked.

"Not here. Have you?"

"Academy. Pit maneuvers, high-speed basics. Nothing I've had to use that often."

Lenny turned over the engine. "You're in luck, I've had my share of chases and haven't killed my partners yet."

"Let's keep it that way, Deputy."

"Car five . . . are you ready?"

They were car five out of six on the track.

"Standing by," Jo said into the radio.

"Okay, kids . . . ease onto the track and take the third position. Don't let anyone pass you."

Jo glanced at Lenny . . . "Something tells me there will be more than one person vying for third."

Sure enough, car six was side by side within seconds of making the first turn. When the pace car sped up, so did everyone else.

Car six pulled back.

"Where'd he go?"

Jo swiveled around to notice the other cars on the track spread out. Car six sped up.

"Coming around your blind side."

Lenny positioned the car to keep six behind him and not on the side.

They slowed on the turn, and six spent a few seconds in the dirt before moving behind them again.

"Looks like they're positioning for a pit maneuver." All the other cars had eased back, and the two in front kept the pace.

Sure enough, car six kissed the corner of a back bumper as Lenny sped up. They swiveled a few times, but Lenny managed to keep the car on the track.

"Car five . . . work your way into the lead."

Jo kept her eyes darting from car to car. "Guess we passed."

Lenny hit the gas and wove in and out until he set the pace.

Several laps later, four of the cars peeled away from the track, leaving them and car two.

They were instructed to hold their speed and stay alive. That was all the warning they received before out of the passenger window of car two, the long barrel of a paint gun slid toward them.

"Brake!" Jo yelled.

Lenny listened, and the red paint ball whizzed past the front of the car.

"There are civilians in the street, car five," the instructor over the radio said.

"Pit him," Jo suggested.

Lenny sped up, dodged another paint ball as he attempted to get into position.

Each time they came close, the armed car outmaneuvered them.

Paint balls started hitting the car.

Jo swiveled around. "Shit, another car behind us."

"Well son of a—" Lenny hit the brakes and swung the car around, skidding tires as he went.

Jo held on to the door and the dash to keep from being flung around. By the time she knew what Lenny had done, he'd managed a 180-degree turn and positioned himself behind both cars.

"Well played car five . . . now what?" the instructor taunted.

Jo picked up the radio. "Is backup available?"

Jo glanced at Lenny. "Worth a try."

Lenny swerved away from flying paint.

For a brief minute, Jo thought the third car pulling up behind them was backup.

That was until a splash of green paint hit the side of her window.

They managed another lap before they were forced off the road and ended up boxed in.

When the instructors called time, both Lenny and Jo sighed in relief.

Lenny lifted a fist in the air. "Nice dying with ya, Jo."

She managed a fist bump before they stepped out of the car.

Jo wasn't at all surprised to see that the shooter from the first car was a familiar face.

Gill walked up, set his paint gun on the front of their car. "Sheriff . . . Deputy . . . not bad."

"Not all that good either, we'd be dead if this were real life," Lenny conceded.

"We normally tap newbies out with two cars."

Jo swatted Lenny upside his left arm. "Way to drive, Ohio."

The course filled up with new drivers while Gill and another instructor went over the things they did right, the things they could improve. By the afternoon Jo was in the driver's seat, a little better prepared for what to expect.

Only when it was her turn, only two cars were needed to stop her and put her in the kill zone.

While the frustration was there, so was the sheer adrenaline rush from the exercise.

The clocked rolled around to the end of their day. Jo stood beside Lenny, Bess, and a few of the other trainees before they changed out of the FBI standards and into their civilian clothes.

Out of the corner of her eye, Jo saw Shauna walking toward her.

"Hey, stranger," Jo said. "I haven't seen you all day."

"I've been helping with hand-to-hand. How did it go out here?"

Jo leaned against a beat-up car, arms crossed over her chest. "Makes me wanna build a track like this close to home to practice."

"That good, huh?"

"You'd have to come up with old cars," Lenny said.

Jo thought of the many cars that broke down and had to be towed out of River Bend or risk cluttering up the back lots of forgotten farms. "Finding the cars won't be hard . . . making sure they run would be the challenge."

"Or we can meet here every other year or so."

Jo liked Bess's suggestion.

"I don't think my department would go for that. Hard enough to get the okay to be here this time." Sal dusted his hand on his pants. "Well, kids, I've had it."

A chorus of *see ya tomorrow*s went up as Sal made his way into the locker room.

"Wanna grab a bite to eat?" Shauna asked Jo. She looked to the others in the group. "There's a local dive, great burgers, some decent beer on tap."

Lenny's eyes lit up. "You had me at burgers. Beer sealed the deal."

A couple of others decided to join, while two peeled off to rest for the next day.

The way Jo saw it, she could rest when she flew back home.

Shauna drove Jo to what she labeled a dive.

Bar stools and oak filled an entire wall in what appeared to be a bar dating back over a hundred years. Two side walls were floor-to-ceiling brick, with the only windows framing the front of the building. Class in this place was defined by age. From the smells coming from the kitchen, the burgers would be memorable.

Like many bars, this one sported a couple of dartboards and a pool table that had a dozen or so players milling around it.

Lenny pushed through, did a quick head count. "I'll get us a table for eight."

"Make it nine," Shauna said over the noise of the crowd.

Lenny scurried off in search of open space.

Wearing jeans and a slightly less revealing shirt than she had on when she'd met Gill in DC, Jo felt a little more at home. She left her hair loose, something she found herself doing less and less in River Bend. Only when she was with her friends did she try to relax. For some reason, her hair in a tie changed her attitude from play to business.

"Place is busy for a Tuesday night." Jo studied the crowd.

"This place is always crazy."

"Lots of military boys?"

"Yeah." Shauna's gaze swept down the torso of a man a good ten years younger than she was. "Fresh."

Jo laughed. "You haven't told me much about your divorce. How is it going?"

"Not fast enough." She leaned in. "We can talk about that when we're alone."

Jo took the hint and dropped the subject.

Lenny waved them across the room and their group followed.

Music flowed from a stereo in the walls, but a small stage was available for live entertainment in the back of the room. The waitress took their drink order and left after dropping off menus.

"How often do you get out here, Agent Burton?" Lenny had a knack for keeping the conversation going and including everyone within earshot.

"I'm in DC a few times a year, try to get here at least once."

"Don't you have to retest annually?" the woman next to Lenny asked. Jo tried to place her name. Nina . . . or was it Mina? Jo had forgotten but knew she was from Kansas City. Why that fact stuck out, Jo couldn't say.

"Quarterly quals are four times a year . . . fitness, annually. Clausen and I hold a firearms cert, so that's something we need to prove every year."

"Sounds like a lot of testing," Bess added.

Jo leaned in. "Yeah, well . . . when you call in the Feds, it's nice to know they aren't sending some overweight, underskilled fat cat counting his time toward retirement."

Shauna nodded. "What she said."

"We have a few of them in my department."

"There's a few of those in every department," Lenny said.

"I haven't seen one overweight, underskilled anyone here," Jo said.

"They are . . . they're just hidden."

"Who's hidden?" Jo swiveled around to see Gill standing over her chair, asking. He'd changed into a T-shirt that stretched over his chest like a glove. It wasn't all that different from the shirt he'd worn the night they'd met.

Jo's mouth watered.

"Not you, that's for sure," Bess said from the other side of the table. She pulled out a chair to her right and patted it. "Saved you a seat, Agent."

Gill glanced at Jo, smirked, and moved to the other side of the table.

Good, he wasn't close enough to smell. And he was far enough away to look at without being obvious.

"I was explaining how often we have to prove ourselves to our boss."

Gill shrugged like it wasn't a big deal. It helped that he looked like he lived in the gym.

"Jo?" Lenny moved the conversation around the table. "How many deputies do you have working with you?"

"It's a small town." Here with so many law enforcement officers, surrounded by the FBI and marines on leave from the base, Jo couldn't help but feel like a little fish in a great big pond.

"How small?" Bess asked.

"I have one full-time deputy, and two part-timers I pull in from Waterville that help with relief when my second or I are occupied."

"So there are only two of you?" Mina/Nina asked.

"It's a really small town," Shauna explained.

"I'm not sure if that's good or bad," Lenny said.

"I'd go apeshit crazy."

"Oh, I don't know . . ." Gill said. "There's been enough trouble in River Bend to keep you busy."

Jo switched her gaze from Shauna to Gill. The two had obviously talked.

"Trouble in River Bend usually means trouble with people I know, which makes crime personal."

Lenny tossed a hand in the air. "I'm out. I don't want to be slapping cuffs on my friends."

"Forget that, what about family?" Mina/Nina asked.

"Maybe your family," Bess teased.

The discussion moved to dysfunctional brothers and deadbeat cousins. Jo was happy to switch the spotlight away from herself. Who knew policing such a small town held embarrassment? She hadn't felt that coming. Since she had taken the position of sheriff, she'd worn her badge with pride and taken everything she did seriously.

Jo always considered herself a strong person, one that didn't bend to peer pressure or cower in any way. Yet for the next hour, while their group enjoyed a couple of drinks and ate some of the best burgers she'd ever tasted, Jo said as little as she could to keep the conversation off her.

~

Gill watched her disconnect. Almost like a computer being powered off, the fire in Jo's eyes twinkled down to a dim spark until she appeared to be nothing other than a shell. He waited until they'd gotten through their meal and she was ordering another drink before he engaged her.

"Hey, Jo."

She met his eyes from across the table.

"Yeah?"

"You're a competitive sport." He nodded at the vacant dartboard on the other side of the room. "Wanna lay a bet on who can toss a better dart?"

Jo swiveled in her seat before narrowing her eyes. "What kind of bet?"

He liked her tiny smile. "Round of drinks, twenty bucks? Whatever you want."

Shauna nudged Jo's arm while keeping on with the conversation with Lenny.

"Round of drinks and twenty bucks." She stood. "You're on."

"Give her your money now, Clausen. I saw her on the range," Lenny said.

The chair scraped against the floor as he left the table and followed Jo to the dartboard. He couldn't stop his eyes from lingering on her ass any more than he could stop breathing. It helped that he knew what it looked like without the tight jeans she now wore.

Jo Ward was many things, but a sluggish, small town cop working toward retirement, she was not.

She finished her drink and set it on the tabletop closest to where they were going to play.

"I'll have a Stella," she told him before moving to the board to retrieve the darts.

"Afraid you'll lose and downgrading your drink now?" he taunted.

"Slowing down the liquor so I can beat you." She nodded to the tiny cocktail waitress with blue hair as she walked by. "You order whatever you want. You'll be buying."

Some of her earlier spark came back.

"Two Stellas," he told the girl.

She wrote it down and walked to another table.

Jo erased the scores from the previous players from the chalkboard before adding their names. Only instead of Jo and Gill, she wrote an *A* and an *R*.

He chuckled under his breath.

"Are we playing 501?" she asked.

"Sure."

"Double score to win, or just get to zero?"

"Double score."

There was a little swing in her hips as she walked back. "You're entirely too confident," he told her.

She gathered up one set of darts and pivoted toward the board. "You live in Eugene, right?"

"Yep."

She didn't look at him. "Big city."

"It's not New York."

She poised a dart on the tips of her fingers and motioned toward the board a couple of times. "River Bend has one bar and zero nightlife outside of that bar." She let the dart fly, hitting the twenty-five-point green bull's-eye. When she turned back toward him, a satisfied grin lifted both sides of her cheeks.

Gill liked her like this, at ease and sassy.

The waitress dropped off their beers and Gill opened a tab.

He took one of his darts and moved close enough to Jo to breathe in her scent. "Where I live now holds little weight on my dart playing ability."

"Oh?"

It was his turn to twist the dart in his fingers before pulling back and letting it fly. It slid right along hers, but directly in the center, where a proper dart needed to be this early in the game.

He reached around, made sure his arm met with her shoulder as he grabbed his beer. "I grew up outside of Spokane, where my dad still owns a small town bar. My mom helps out with the bookkeeping."

Jo looked at the board and then him. "I'm guessing you helped your dad. Bouncer?"

Gill answered her with a nod and a grin as he sucked on his beer.

She reached for hers and smiled through her eyes as she drank.

With a sigh, she set the beer back down, reaching across him to do so, and filled her lungs with a fortifying breath. "And here I thought this was going to be easy."

She did a little rolling of her head on her neck thing, along with the shaking of her right arm, before tossing her next dart. Instead of aiming

73

for the center, where his dart might very well deflect hers, she set her dart in the triple score of the twenty-point zone.

"Oh, game on!"

Pride washed over her face when she turned around.

His hand stopped shy of slapping her butt when she reached for her beer a second time. He glanced over his shoulder at the party going on with their group. Yeah, ass slapping was going to have to wait for another time.

Less than ten minutes later, Jo was handing him twenty bucks and ordering another round. "I want another shot."

He glanced at their drinks. "You're not driving, are you?"

"I know about Uber," she told him.

"Does River Bend have Uber?"

Her eyes were a little glossy, something he didn't think happened all that often.

"River Bend has me."

He erased their scores and started over.

"You taxi people around?"

"There have been a few times I've been called, mainly by Josie."

He sat down, waited for their drinks before starting the next game. "Who is Josie?"

"She owns R&B's, the bar I told you about."

"Josie calls the sheriff to drive drunks home?" Gill wasn't sure his father had ever done that. Then again, the small town he grew up in had an actual police department with more than two men stationed there. And his father wasn't the only one with a bar.

"Most of them can walk, but yeah . . . sometimes."

"That's a hell of a service you have there, Sheriff."

"It's a pain in the ass," she admitted.

The waitress dropped off their round, slapped a bowl of nuts on the table. The increase of salt would increase the drinks. A trick Gill had learned from his father.

"Then why do you do it?" Gill asked her.

"It beats the heartache of having to haul them in for drunk driving, or worse. Besides, it isn't like everyone calls. Policing the town where you grew up has its upside, and its downside. Downside is, those who know me, call."

"And the upside?"

Jo blinked at him a few times, narrowed her eyes. "Free meals."

Gill chuckled. He wasn't about to tell her that once in a while his meals were comped, too. And most of the law enforcement in the room had plenty of free meals from local businesses without driving anyone's intoxicated uncle home from a bar.

She stood, grabbed her darts, and nodded toward the board in question. Technically he should take the first turn for the next game, but he agreed, and Jo turned toward the board as she spoke. "The worst part isn't driving drunks."

"Oh?"

The dart flew, not that he didn't bother looking where it landed.

"The hardest part about policing River Bend is trying to erase my youthful transgressions." She sat back down and twisted her beer in her hand.

"You were a wild child?" he asked.

"Quintessential cop's daughter. Defiant, skipped school, got caught drinking early on."

The way she looked beyond him said she was remembering one of those teenage days. "Sounds like a lot of people I knew growing up."

She sipped her beer, pointed at him when she was finished. "But your dad ran a bar. My dad ran a town."

"I guess it was expected that I drank, and mandated that you stay sober."

"I hated it." The words sounded like a confession.

He leaned forward on his elbows, the dart game forgotten. "Then how did you end up taking over your father's world?"

If Gill wasn't watching her so closely, he would have missed the wave of brief pain that washed over her. "He died before I could redeem myself. Before I grew up enough to know I'd acted like an idiot. Going to the academy, talking the right people into putting me on the ballot to become sheriff even though I was *too young* and *too green* . . . it's what my dad would have wanted me to do."

Probably. But was it what she wanted to do?

He was about to ask when someone tapped his shoulder.

He twisted to see Shauna smiling. "You kids having fun?"

"Relieving Jo's wallet of her spending money," he said.

"I'm going to take a few of these monkeys back to their hotel."

Gill saw Jo glance at her watch, start to stand. "I should probably get going, too."

He tried to think of an excuse for her to stay. "You wouldn't earn your money back anyway."

She sat back down and Gill grinned.

He found himself doing that a lot around this woman.

"I don't have room in my car anyway," Shauna informed them. "You can give Jo a ride, right, Clausen?"

The memory of her straddling the back of the bike, the heat of her pressed against his back, moved all the blood in his head south. "Yeah, I have it covered."

"Good, I'll see you both tomorrow."

Gill noticed the women exchange glances. Jo's held wonder, while Shauna's was filled with mischief.

# Chapter Eight

It took Jo a couple of miles to settle on the back of his bike and for her arms to slide around his waist to hold on.

Gill would have liked to take a long way to get to her hotel, but there weren't many alternative routes that didn't shorten the ride.

It was past midnight, the lot was quiet and lit only by the street-lights that spotted the front of the hotel.

He cut the engine the second he turned into a small space.

Jo hesitated before swinging her leg around the back of the bike. She removed the helmet and shook out her hair.

The pink in her cheeks from the cold night air gave her a childish glow: *cute*. A word Gill was pretty sure she wouldn't appreciate, so he kept it to himself.

"Thanks for the ride, Clausen." She handed him his helmet.

He placed it on one of the handlebars.

"Anytime."

She shuffled her feet once. "And thanks for taking my forty bucks."

Yeah, that wasn't exactly gentlemanly of him, but hey, a bet was a bet. "I did buy your drinks."

He liked her smile.

"Yes, you did." She glanced up at the hotel behind them.

He swung a leg around and stayed sitting on the bike, looking up at Jo as silence was broken by the song of crickets.

"I should go."

But she didn't.

"Probably."

A playful, short laugh accompanied a roll of her eyes.

"Okay, I'm going . . . I'll see you tomorrow."

He let her turn, but didn't let her take a step.

"Jo?"

She glanced up from the ground she was staring at.

Gill placed a hand on her waist and pulled her between his legs.

"What are you—"

He reached for her head with his free hand and pulled her down for a kiss.

Jo moaned and opened her lips to let him explore.

When he felt her fingers dig into his shoulder and move closer, he thought, *there you are*.

He forced himself to stay on his bike, didn't stop kissing her until she pulled away. The smoky desire that glazed her eyes made him want her even more. But no. He decided before that evening began that he wasn't going to jump back into any one-night anything with this woman. And after listening to her spill many of her secrets, her hates, and her desires regarding her life, he realized two things. JoAnne Ward didn't think she was worthy of anything more than a one-night stand, and second, Sheriff Ward had yet to really live.

"Do you want—"

He cut off her invitation to her room with a finger to her lips.

"I want to," he confessed. "But I'm not going to."

Her eyes narrowed.

Gill spread his fingers on her lower back slowly. "You deserve more than a couple hours of my time."

"We spent the whole night together."

"You need more."

It was a tricky thing, turning a woman down who wanted you in her bed.

"You know what I need now, do you?"

"I'm a really good listener, Jo. Besides, you have a big day tomorrow."

"So you're letting me sleep alone to save my strength."

He shook his head. "No. To save mine."

Some of the disappointment disappeared from her eyes.

"I'm only here for a few more nights."

"I know."

Her chest lifted and fell slowly before she stepped out of his embrace.

Gill grabbed the helmet he'd let her wear and pushed it over his head. "Good night, JoAnne."

"It's Jo."

He winked and turned over the bike.

~

"Isn't it like midnight there?"

"He kissed me and then left, Zoe. What man does that?" Jo spoke into her cell phone as she moved around the hotel room, toeing off her shoes.

"Well, hello, Jo . . . how was your day?" Zoe laughed.

Jo paused. "Hi, Zoe. Yes, it's after midnight. Now answer my question."

"About kissing and leaving?"

"I offered myself. And it isn't like he hasn't been there, so why would he say no?"

"I love you, Jo . . . but you're going to have to back up a little. We haven't talked since you got to DC, so start at the beginning."

Jo sighed and moved into the bathroom. "I met this guy in DC. My kind of guy."

"Let me guess: big, bulky, tats, and available."

The mirror showed evidence of Gill's kiss. Her lips were swollen, her cheeks flushed.

"Right. All that. Supersexy. It was . . ." She paused. "Epic."

"I'm still listening."

Jo shook off the memory of his naked ass. "We hooked up. I left before he woke. I'm not coming to the East Coast again anytime soon. No need to stay around for pillow talk in the morning, right?"

"Right." Zoe's voice softened.

"Then I arrive in Virginia, and guess who happens to be Agent Burton's partner?"

"No!"

"Yes."

"How does that happen?"

"I don't know. In the movies, mostly. Come to find out my Rocco is actually Agent Clausen."

"Rocco?" Zoe asked, laughing.

"Fake name. I used one, too."

"So what's the problem?"

Jo ran the water in the sink, dipped a washcloth in when it was hot. "For the last two days we've said next to nothing to each other. We whispered about what had happened, but neither of us brought it up again."

"Until tonight?"

"We didn't talk about it. We stayed late at the bar, everyone else had left. He gave me a ride back to my hotel . . ." She wiped her face, moved the phone to the other ear to get the opposite side. "I wasn't going to offer anything, then he kissed me."

Zoe ahhed into the phone.

"Stop it. It wasn't like that."

"Oh, what was it like?"

Jo stopped washing her face, thought of how soft his touch was tonight instead of the urgency they'd both put into everything while in DC.

"Different," she confessed.

"Good different?"

"Yeah," Jo said with a sigh.

The image of him driving away pulled her back. "Then he left. Said he needed his energy for tomorrow."

"Oh, Jo . . . that's fabulous."

"How is that *fabulous*? I don't have many nights away from River Bend." She tossed the used washcloth on the counter and picked up her toothbrush, loaded it with toothpaste.

"Didn't you say he was Shauna's partner?"

With the toothbrush in her mouth, Jo talked around it. "Yeah."

"Isn't Shauna in Eugene?"

Jo stopped midbrush. "Yeah."

"Maybe Agent Rocco isn't too concerned about your timeline on the East Coast."

Jo started brushing again . . . slowly. "His name is Gill."

"Whatever."

Jo brushed more vigorously, spit out the mess. A quick rinse and she stepped out of the bathroom. "Doesn't explain why he said no to tonight."

"Sure it does."

"How?"

"Because he wants to slow things down. His clock isn't ticking like yours is."

"But when I get home, it's River Bend twenty-four/seven again."

"I don't think your agent understands that. Or if he does, he realizes you can have a life outside of being our sheriff."

Jo sat on the edge of the bed. "Ha!"

"I like this guy already," Zoe said.

Jo frowned. "He's annoying."

"Which is exactly why I like him."

"You're not helping, Zoe."

Her friend laughed and laughed.

~

Jo's eyes opened before the sun made its appearance. After turning over a few times, pounding her pillow into the mattress a dozen times, she sighed and gave up.

Restless for more reasons than she could name, Jo did what she always did. She put her running shoes on and left the hotel on foot.

Her legs warmed into her stride on the second mile and her head finally started to focus. She tried to think about the training courses she'd taken so far, the things she had learned and wanted to take with her when she left Virginia.

Gill's image swam in her head.

She pushed him away. He'd kept her up most of the night by not staying; she didn't want him plaguing her morning run. Some of the day's lesson plan was about investigations, one of the things she wanted to soak in most. Jo thought of what she already knew. Most of what she'd been taught was on how to draw confessions out of a suspect. Interviewing skills with known criminals and not so known criminals . . . stuff that she didn't have a lot of experience with since River Bend was a rather crime-free zone. It was the art of observing, and seeing what others didn't, that she needed to use. That's what she told herself as she rounded on mile three.

*Most murders are performed by someone the victim knows.*

She thought of her father and his case. There was no one, not one red flag. Even the town misfits and drunks stayed sober for his funeral.

*There are no coincidences.*

Whenever something felt too easy, or just "fell into place," it was time to cry foul.

Like the *accidental* part of her father's death.

Too easy. Jo didn't buy it.

Jo turned the corner back to her hotel with her muscles and mind loose and ready for the day.

She jogged up the two flights of stairs and pulled her plastic key from her exercise bra as she walked down the hall.

When she looked up, she hesitated. And then she smiled. "What are you doing here?"

Gill lifted his hands, one held a bag, the other something that smelled suspiciously like coffee. "I've yet to meet a cop who didn't like coffee and donuts."

Her stomach grumbled, and her heart thumped an extra beat . . . almost like it was telling her to notice something.

She swiped the key and opened the door. Then she hesitated in the doorway.

"Since you took my money last night, I guess it's the least you could do."

He smiled and followed her inside.

*What is he doing here? Turned me down last night just to jump in this morning?*

She sipped the coffee before looking inside the bag.

Heaven . . . donuts were sugary gifts from above. She bit into a chocolate glazed and leaned against the dresser.

"Running and donuts?" Gill asked.

"I run to clear my head," she told him, taking another bite.

He smelled fresh, unlike her, and his clothes were professional but not stuffy. All the material on his body hid the ink underneath. It felt like a secret, one she knew but others didn't. The thought made her smile.

He took the bag from her and grabbed one of the remaining pastries inside. "That," he waved a maple bar in her direction, "is a wicked smile."

Jo stopped chewing, moved close enough to smell his aftershave. She leaned forward, took a bite out of the donut he was about to put in his mouth, and turned to walk into the bathroom.

She stopped at the door.

*There are no coincidences.*

Zoe's question bounced in her head.

"What were you doing at Marly's the night we met?"

"Drinking, hanging out?"

Her eyes narrowed. "You go there a lot?"

"When I'm in DC, why?"

"What about Shauna, she go there with you?"

He shook his head. "Too seedy for her. I've dragged her there a few times, but it's not her style."

"Hmmm." Jo popped the rest of her donut in her mouth and turned her back on Gill.

She wasn't going to tell him to leave, wasn't going to ask him to stay.

Jo turned on the water in the shower, peeled off her clothes, and stepped inside.

The small space instantly started to steam.

Gill's massive frame shadowed the doorway through the mirror.

Jo forced herself not to look as she squeezed shampoo into her palm before scrubbing her hair.

"You're killing me, JoAnne."

She smiled the way a woman did when she knew she'd grabbed a man's attention. Besides, he couldn't see her smile, he could only guess.

"You're the one who showed up uninvited. I have somewhere to be in half an hour."

"You didn't like my donuts?"

"Oh, I like your donuts all right," she said to herself. She moved on to scrub the sweat from her body, wondered if there was any silhouette through the hotel shower curtain. "They were okay," she said a little louder.

She heard him laugh, saw a shadow pass by.

She finished her shower and pulled a towel into the steam to quick dry her hair and covered herself before stepping out.

Noise from the bedroom sounded a whole lot like someone tripping over a bed.

Jo forced herself not to look. "You okay in there?"

"Yep, um-hmm. I'm good. I'll a . . . I'll see if I can step up my pastry game next time."

She left her towel in place and took that moment to step to the open doorway.

Gill was in the process of pulling the hem of his right pant leg over his sock.

"You plan on bringing me breakfast every day I'm here?"

The heat of his eyes, as they took in her frame, shot right to her belly.

"I can be persuaded."

"I tried that last night."

His smile fell.

"Besides, my best friend is a celebrity chef. You can't beat what she delivers."

"This friend of yours a woman?" he asked.

"Yeah."

"Then I can beat her." Gill made his exit, called over his shoulder. "See you there."

~

They were on a tactical training course, something she would see one more time before leaving the facility on Friday. The students were working their way through several different real-life scenarios, from hostage situations to mass casualty gun violence.

Jo watched from the sides as several students were placed into what she called an arena, where the instructors were beside them, guiding every move.

Even watching managed to pump adrenaline like she'd remembered in her initial officer training.

"Sheriff Ward?" One of the instructors tapped her shoulder.

"Yes?"

"You have a phone call."

She stood, reached for her back pocket, and realized she'd left her phone in her locker.

Jo followed the instructor out of the arena perimeter and into a building. There, she picked up the phone and pushed the line where her call was waiting.

"This is Sheriff Ward."

"Jo, oh, thank God I got ahold of you. You weren't answering your cell."

The excitable voice of Glynis had images of her sitting behind the reception desk at the station with piles of papers stacked all around her.

"I don't have my phone with me in the field, Glynis. What's going on?"

"Deputy Emery is going to make a mess out of this dog situation. The man doesn't like animals. Remember how he all but bullied the Swanson boy who lived next door to get his dog to stop barking when the other dogs in the neighborhood let loose after midnight?"

"Glynis."

The woman kept talking as fast as humanly possible. "I swear when that little beagle went missing—"

"Glynis!" Jo shouted this time.

"No need to yell, Jo. I hear you."

Jo squeezed her eyes shut. "Start at the beginning. What dog situation are you talking about?"

"You sound annoyed."

"I'm not annoyed." Annoyed wasn't a strong enough word.

"I don't think you're telling the truth. I would have called the Millers, but Zoe and Luke took them to Los Angeles. The auto shop is closed for the first time in years."

"Zoe isn't there? I just talked with her last night." Jo had spilled all her guts and never even asked about her friend.

"They've been in LA for two days. Did you call her cell?"

"Yeah." Jo shook her head. "Why would you call the Millers about the dog situation? And what situation is that?"

"Cherie's rottweiler mix had puppies again."

Cherie Miller, Luke's single aunt, lived about a half a mile outside the main streets of River Bend and had at least eight dogs that Jo remembered counting the last time she'd called on the woman.

Eight adult dogs plus a litter equaled a whole lot of noise for the neighbors, even if the closest one was a quarter of a mile away.

"I had three messages waiting for me when I came in this morning. None of them wanted to call Deputy Emery."

Yeah, Jo wouldn't want to call Karl Emery either. The man really didn't like animals. Jo looked up to see Gill walking toward her.

"Listen, Glynis, I'll call Karl. And I'll call Cherie."

"Good luck, she isn't answering her phone. Probably doesn't want to hear the complaints. It isn't like she can't hear the dogs going on and on."

Gill stood over Jo. "Is everything okay?" he asked in a low voice.

Jo shook her head and rolled her eyes.

"I'll take care of it, Glynis."

"I knew you would. I'm sorry to bug you at your special camp."

"It's not camp."

"Deputy Emery said it was camp."

Jo wanted to growl. "I've got to go."

"Okay, Jo. Sorry I had to bug you. You know—"

"Glynis, I'm hanging up now."

"Oh, okay . . . of course. Have a great day."

Jo disconnected the call and leaned against the wall.

"What was that all about?" Gill asked.

"Glynis runs my office. Dispatch."

"One person?"

Jo wanted to glare. "It's a small town."

Gill smirked. "So what was the emergency?"

She started to say something about the puppies, realized how stupid it would sound, and stopped herself. "Nothing," she said instead.

"Had to be something."

"Nothing important." She pushed away from the wall and started back to the arena.

Gill followed behind. "If you don't want to tell me, fine, but you don't have to lie about—"

Annoyed, Jo stopped and turned. "Dogs, Gill. Barking dogs." The absurdity of it had her laughing with tears threatening. "I'm called out of a tactical lesson where we're learning defense techniques against a dozen possible suspects because one of the neighbors in River Bend thinks she's running a dog breeding program. And my deputy hates dogs. Hates them, so Glynis thought calling me to solve the problem from three thousand miles away was a viable option." Jo acknowledged the tear on her cheek by swiping it away with a fisted palm.

"Hey . . ."

Jo glanced toward the door leading back to the training grounds. "I shouldn't be here. I'm never going to use any of this stuff in River Bend. Resolving neighborhood disputes and escorting the occasional drunk from R&B's is the scope of my practice." Her anger built as she spoke. Anger at herself.

Anger at River Bend.

Anger at the universe.

"If you knew that, why did you sign up for this?"

Even though Gill's question came out soft, her response bordered on violent.

"Because I can't seem to find my father's killer doing what I've been doing for the last eight years of my life. And doing this for the next eight years sounds like my worst kind of hell."

She felt another tear, shoved it away with a fist, and stared at the door.

Instead of joining the team, she turned in the opposite direction and walked away.

# Chapter Nine

Gill kept pace beside her.

The woman walked fast for someone with legs so much shorter than his. She stepped out of the building and into the light. Jo reached for her sunglasses and said without looking, "You don't have to follow me."

Gill covered his eyes from the glare, too. "I don't have to do a lot of things."

He didn't invade the place she was inside her head with questions, even though he had a million running through his.

It was obvious she was walking off steam. And from the way she was muttering under her breath, she was battling several demons all at once.

"Don't you have to be training someone on how to be badass?" Jo threw out over her shoulder.

"Nope. I'm technically done for the day."

"The day just started."

He didn't need to be there at all, he came for the company.

The company that was storming around the building on a mission. He'd been having a hard time getting her out of his head since she walked in the bar in DC. This morning's little show from the doorway to her bathroom just about undid him. She'd offered him everything the night before, and that morning did her best to show him exactly what he'd said no to.

He had to admit, Jo pissed off was turning him on. He'd rather see her pissed than teary eyed. Seeing a strong woman break down was his Achilles' heel.

The East Coast sun was doing a good job of heating him up; the humidity had him pulling the collar of his shirt from his neck in search of air.

Jo rounded the building and walked toward the parking lot.

She stopped in front of what looked like a rental car and patted her back pocket. Her lungs deflated in frustration.

"Damn it." She pounded on the roof of the car and rested her head on her arm.

She was looking a little too weak for his taste.

He placed a hand on her shoulder, was a little surprised she didn't pull away. "Jo."

"You know what the kids that ride skateboards call the kids that don't but who still wear those skinny jeans?"

Her question came out of left field. "I have no idea."

"Poseurs." She lifted her head, nodded toward the building across from the lot where her group was training. "That's what I am in there. I'm wearing skinny jeans and pretending to be something I'm not." Jo turned her back to the car, dislodging his touch.

Gill leaned against the car across from hers and didn't try and touch her again.

"You're not a poseur, Jo."

She didn't look convinced. "Have you ever been to River Bend?"

"No."

"You might think differently if you had."

He folded his arms across his chest. "I have every intention of seeing River Bend. I'll let you know my verdict when I do."

She opened her mouth to say something, but he cut her off. "What's this about your dad?"

The thoughts derailed. "Forget it."

"Mmm, can't do that. Not part of my DNA. He was killed?"

She nodded once. "The report said accidental shooting. My dad was a good cop, an even better hunter. He was never sloppy with his weapons. Any of them."

Accidental shootings happened, but when it came to law enforcement, those accidents almost always happened when said officer was with another person.

"Was anyone with him when it happened?"

"No."

"Where did this *accident* take place?"

"His hunting cabin. It appeared that he was cleaning his guns."

"He shot himself with a hunting rifle?"

Jo wiped the sweat from her forehead with the back of her hand. "His service weapon. Point-blank, to his head."

Gill winced. "Did your dad always carry his pistol with him when he went hunting?"

She shrugged. "I didn't really pay attention. The last time I'd gone hunting with him I was probably fourteen. Then I discovered boys and wanted nothing to do with it."

"You're convinced he didn't shoot himself."

"I know he didn't shoot himself. Guns were never toys in my home. Not even the plastic orange ones you filled with water. Guns were weapons, period! I was taught gun safety before I was potty-trained. He was always careful with his guns and way too smart to leave a bullet in the chamber while cleaning the damn things." She spread her hands to the complex around them. "I thought some of this might help. Focus me again . . . I don't know . . . something."

Just talking about her father had focused her. Gill wondered if she knew how intensely her eyes displayed her emotions. She was convinced, utterly and completely, that she was right.

"I'll help."

Those piercing eyes found his. "You don't have to."

"And I didn't have to follow you out here either."

A corner of her mouth slid up. "I don't know."

"I'm good at what I do, Jo. And from what I've seen, you're good at what you do, too. From what you said earlier, it looks like we're going to lose a good cop if we don't find some answers."

"I never wanted to be a cop."

"I gathered that. Doesn't mean you're not suited for the job."

She hunched her shoulders, didn't comment.

He gestured toward the building. "C'mon. You finish this today, and tonight I'll take you to meet a friend of mine. He might help you focus."

"Your friend's an investigator?"

"Not really. You'll understand when we get there."

She looked over his shoulder, blew out a breath. "I need to call my deputy. Make sure he doesn't do something stupid." Her voice was filled with resolve.

"I'll meet you at your hotel at six?"

Her smile was his answer.

~

Jo was becoming quite comfortable on the back of Gill's Harley. There she could wrap her arms around him and forget nearly everything except the vibrations of the bike and the feel of the man.

She'd nearly lost it after the call from Glynis. All the reasons she wanted to find her father's killer and search for a new life for herself rose up and slapped her in the face with that one call. Dogs. Dogs were the emergency in River Bend, and it took calling her deputy and heading him off before he could make a mess out of things to settle the nerves of her so-called dispatcher. When Jo contacted Cherie, the woman thought it was a social call. It took ten minutes to get through the gossip on her street before Jo managed to get a word in. Cherie agreed to keep the dogs inside at night so the neighbors couldn't complain about their inability to sleep because of the barking. Jo also went on to say that her property wasn't licensed for a kennel, and if the neighbors wanted to make a big deal about the amount of dogs, they could, and Jo would have no choice but to have the dog pound in Waterville step in.

Cherie was agreeable, but Jo knew it was only a matter of days before the complaints would start in again.

By then she'd be home, and hopefully be able to smooth things out.

Until then, she'd enjoy the feel of Gill on the bike and the freedom being away from River Bend was giving her.

Gill followed along the twisted back roads off the interstate until he slowed his pace and turned into a suburban driveway lined with trees. The modest one-story home looked to sit on a half-acre lot. The mature landscape consisted mostly of trees and hedges, with several rhododendrons in various shades of red.

Once Gill cut the engine, Jo climbed off the back, the pattern of removing the helmet and raking her fingers through her hair becoming more than a little comfortable.

Gill smiled at her as she handed him the helmet.

"The ride relaxed you," he said.

"A little," she admitted. Jo snuggled into her windbreaker and knew the ride back would probably be much cooler. "Who lives here?"

"An old friend." He took her hand and led her up the walkway to the front door.

He knocked once before opening the door.

"Better be a good friend," she murmured. Since Gill was letting himself in, Jo had to assume they were expected.

The smell of something savory filled the house and made Jo's stomach rumble.

"Lee?" Gill called once they stepped inside the foyer.

"Back here." The smoker's voice sounded young, if not a little gruff.

Gill led her through the house like he knew the way until they emptied into a family room that connected to a kitchen.

In front of the stove was a tiny Hispanic woman in her late thirties. She placed a kitchen towel on the counter and walked around to greet them.

Jo's eyes traveled to the man behind the gruff voice. He might be close to forty, but not much past. His upper body stretched the confines of his T-shirt, suggesting he spent time working that part of his body out. The rest of him sat in a wheelchair, which Jo forced her eyes away from the moment she realized she was staring.

Gill released her hand to embrace the woman and kissed her cheek before offering introductions. "Consuela, this is my friend, Jo."

Consuela had long, dark hair that fell over her back like a drape. "Any friend of Gill's is a friend of ours."

Jo extended a hand and shook the woman's. "Thank you for having me."

"And this lucky bastard is Lee." Gill did one of those slamming handshakes, followed by a bent-over man hug.

"You're the only one with big enough balls to call me that," Lee said, pushing Gill aside to move his chair closer to Jo. "Let's get a look at her."

Jo offered her hand to shake his and was met with the two-hand shake men did when they wanted to flirt. "Nice to meet you."

Lee held on and looked her up and down. "You're a bit tiny to be taking on this behemoth."

"Excuse me?" Jo managed to get her hand back and look at Gill.

"Ignore him."

"You can't ignore me, I'm the elephant in the room. Hey, baby, how about some beer?"

Consuela stirred whatever was in the pot and turned toward the fridge. "You okay with beer, Jo? I have wine. Not good wine, but it was made with grapes."

"Beer is fine," Jo said.

"How is my bike running?" Lee asked Gill.

Gill sat on one end of the sofa and patted the space beside him while he looked at her.

"Like a dream. One of these days I'm going to convince you to sell her to me."

"Wait," Jo said. "That bike isn't yours?"

Gill shook his head. "Whenever I'm this close to Lee, he makes sure I get her out to stretch her legs."

Lee laughed, and Jo found herself looking at the man's legs. Legs that obviously didn't work for walking on.

"Someone has to," Lee said, chuckling.

"I refuse to drive that thing," Consuela said as she brought their refreshments.

"Did you think I drove it all the way out from Oregon?" Gill asked Jo.

"I didn't even think about it." She was slightly disappointed the hog wasn't his.

Gill twisted the top off one of the beers and handed it to her.

"Gill told me you're training this week," Lee said to Jo.

"I am."

"Thinking of joining the Feds?"

She shook her head. "Nothing like that."

"Jo's the sheriff of River Bend, Oregon."

Lee swept her again with his stare. "Young for a sheriff."

"It's a small town." Jo felt she should just as soon have that tattooed on her forehead for all the times she'd said that during this trip.

"Jo's father was the sheriff before his death."

Lee lost some of the grin he'd been wearing since they arrived. The man was attractive enough, with what looked to be a burn scar on the left side of his face that covered a quarter of his cheek and half of his jaw. "I'm sorry."

"It's been ten years, it's okay."

Lee stared at her now. "So your father passed, and you stepped in."

Gill placed a hand on her knee and kept it there. Unlike when they were surrounded by those at Quantico, he didn't hold back the fact they were more than just acquaintances around his friends.

"You could say that."

"Did you know you were going to be a cop?" Lee asked.

Jo glanced at Gill before answering. "No. It wasn't on my bucket list."

Lee nodded a few times before turning his attention to Gill. "Interesting."

There was some kind of nonverbal communication going on between the men, but Jo wasn't clued in to what it was.

"How do you two know each other?" Jo asked, trying to get the conversation off of her.

"One of those biker fundraisers put on to raise money for kids at Christmas," Lee said.

Gill laughed. "Lee had this badass wheelchair with a Harley plate. I knew we had to meet."

"Gill?" Consuela called from the kitchen, her hand on a tray. "Can you put this on the grill? Five minutes each side, no more."

Gill patted Jo's knee and pushed off the couch. "Anything for you."

Once Gill walked out the back door, Lee continued as if Jo hadn't changed the subject. "Let me guess, your father would have wanted you to take over for him."

"Nothing would have made him happier." Jo pulled on her beer.

"But not you, I'm taking it."

She tried to deny it. "It hasn't been that bad."

"Or that good."

She moved to protest, shrugged her shoulders instead.

"You know what happens when you live your life for other people, Jo?"

Jo couldn't think of an answer, so she remained silent.

"You end up in some godforsaken sand trap, an M-14 strapped to your back, while your buddy steps on a bomb. There aren't enough pieces to pick up of your friend, and you end up spending the next six months on your back in some deathtrap hospital, knowing you'll never walk again. But you were the lucky one. You made it out alive." Lee revealed what sounded like the CliffsNotes version of how he ended up in his chair without venom, just straight facts.

"What branch of the service were you in?"

"Army. Dad joined right after high school. Met my mom somewhere after he'd worked his way up the ranks to private first class. By the time I was in the picture he was a sergeant dragging us from one base to another. Like most army brats, I wanted nothing to do with it."

"You enlisted anyway."

Lee nodded, drank from his beer. "Tried to avoid it. Went to college for two years, hated it. Floated around for another year trying to figure out life. Finally I conceded to the old man. Wanted him to think I was doing something good with my life. Little did he know that all hell was about to break out in the Middle East and my boots were some of the first to hit the ground."

Jo looked at his chair. "This happened over there?"

"Yeah. Six months before my term was up. All because I was trying to make someone else happy."

Jo saw Gill's back through the sliding glass door at the back of the house. She knew then why he had brought her to visit Lee and his wife.

~

"What do you think of Jo?" Gill asked his friend.

Consuela and Jo were sitting by the fire pit in the backyard while Lee smoked his cigarette a distance away.

"Looking for my approval?"

Gill leaned forward on his knees, kept his voice low. "We haven't known each other long."

"Considering you haven't spoke of her, I assumed as much."

Gill glanced her way, enjoyed the way the flames from the fire danced over her face. "She's too good for such a small town."

"She doesn't seem to want anything to do with her job."

Gill wasn't convinced. "I thought so, too, then I saw her in action during this training. She's good at what she does. I just don't think she's doing it in the right place."

Lee pulled in a drag from his smoke. "It's hard to stop chasing ghosts once you start. While she might be good at what she's doing, it doesn't mean she should be doing it."

"I thought you would say as much. Once she puts some closure to her father's death, I think she'll move on."

Lee narrowed his eyes. "What's up with that?"

Gill explained Jo's theory and added that he wasn't convinced the death was accidental either. "I need to see the files, scope out where they found him."

"Open a cold case?"

"The case is completely closed. But for Jo, it's open every day of her life. And it's strangling her."

Lee crushed out his cigarette. "For someone who just met this lady, you seem to know a awful lot about her."

Gill felt Jo's eyes on him. "Not nearly enough."

# Chapter Ten

The syndicator counted down, Jo's heart stayed steady until the red light indicated that the simulation was live. Her weapon out in front, her eyes wide open . . . she waited.

The first person she saw on the left side of the room was a civilian walking from an on-screen grocery store. A noise behind her brought her attention to the image of a car. Behind it, a man held a gun to the head of a hostage. The gunman shouted at the camera, which was meant to simulate a real-life situation, but Jo couldn't talk the man down. This simulation was about gut instinct for when to shoot and when to hold back.

The victim in the image cried and attempted to lean away from the gun pressed to her temple.

The gunman suddenly looked to a place beyond where Jo stood, his attention diverted.

She refused to look behind her.

A split second later the gunman turned that gun toward her and the victim managed to move a half a foot away.

Jo took the shot.

The pretend gunman went down.

Only then did she look behind her.

The fictitious grocery store had several people running from it, all of them screaming.

Jo forced her heartbeat to quiet and she waited.

~

Gill stood beside Shauna as they watched Jo in the simulator.

"She's good," Shauna said, her arms crossed over her chest.

"I wonder if she knows how good she is?"

Jo grazed a bad guy, and took him out on a second shot. "I don't think she's ever tested herself until now. Fear is a great motivator to hone your skills," Shauna muttered.

Gill glanced at his partner. "Fear of what? She makes River Bend sound like a TV sitcom from the fifties."

Shauna never stopped watching Jo in the simulator, her eyes tracking Jo's every move. "When her best friend's daughter was missing, she was hyperaware of everything, her instincts and mind worked like a computer. Like any seasoned agent."

"Don't mess with kids."

"Yeah." Shauna's gaze narrowed. "Then last fall."

"What happened last fall?"

"She was convinced someone was stalking her."

Gill stood completely still, his arms chilled.

"Stalking?"

"Watching her. We all have that sixth sense when someone is looking at us, but it sounded a lot more sinister than that. At least how she described it to me. And since Jo doesn't scare easy, I'm guessing she was right."

Gill moved his eyes to the woman in the room once again. "Nothing came of it?"

"I gave her a few tips about changing her routine, came down shortly after her call. She told me the eyes in the dark stopped after the holidays. Stressful few months for her."

Gill didn't like to think of someone watching her for that long. For any amount of time. "You think that's why she's here?"

Jo fired off several rounds inside the simulator, hitting three out of the five gunmen on the screen. She rolled on the floor to avoid the laser fire that would indicate she'd been shot.

From the ground, she managed to bring down the remaining bad guys.

When she did, the lights in the simulator went on, and Jo laid her head on the ground, her body heaving with deep breaths, her gun lax in her fingertips.

Several agents watching, and many of Jo's classmates, met her success with applause.

Gill felt a strange sense of pride at her accomplishment.

Jo pushed herself off the floor, shook the hand of her instructor. Gill didn't hear the conversation but knew Agent Gutierrez was giving equal amounts of praise and instruction. When she turned away, Gutierrez patted her on the back as she exited the room.

Later, when the final test had been taken and the last weeklong student was done, Gill kicked back with Shauna, Jo, and a much larger group of law enforcement from around the country in the same bar where he'd demonstrated his dart skills.

Unlike when they'd been there earlier in the week, the bar was packed. It helped that it was Friday, and the celebration was also the long good-bye to those who would most likely never see each other again. A band set up on the tiny stage, a small space in front of it would give some room for dancing.

Gill wondered if Jo danced.

A waitress in a tight mini walked by, a tray of shots in her hand. She stopped at the circle of people who joined Jo.

The noise level was too high to hear the exact words, but from the body language, it appeared that one of Jo's classmates challenged her. All Gill saw was Jo waving a hand at the other person before she reached for a shot.

A cheer went up when she poured it back and set the empty on the tray before picking up another.

Laughter erupted by the time the third shots were downed.

Her partner quit, and she grabbed a bottle of water that sat on a table beside her.

Someone moved beside him, distracted him. "Looks like someone has your attention."

Shauna nudged his arm.

He did a double take to find her wearing a halter top, one that showed cleavage. And while he knew she had that, he'd never noticed before. Her hair was down, and if he wasn't mistaken, she wore more makeup than he'd ever seen on her face.

"What the . . ."

She stood back, did a little spin.

Along with the skimpy top were skintight jeans. Apparently Shauna's divorce was helping her remember she was a woman again.

"Someone is on the hunt," he said without censure.

"You can't be the only one hooking up."

"Who says—"

Shauna stopped him with a look that reminded him of his mother, the one where she extracted a confession about the missing cookies with only a stare.

"That's what I thought," she said.

The band started to play a few notes, making conversation even harder in the crowded bar.

Once the music started, several couples moved onto the dance floor.

Gill moved toward Jo without thinking. He paused, looked over his shoulder. "You need backup, just holler." His eyes swept Shauna again before he winked.

"Go." She pushed him away. "You're cramping my style."

Gill knew he was too big a man for people to ignore. Several gave him room as he made his way toward Jo. When the people closest to her parted, her eyes lifted to meet his.

"Agent Clausen."

She was tipsy, he could see that from the rose color in her cheeks to the shine in her eyes.

"Sheriff."

"Little Miss Mayberry knocked it out of the park today, eh, Clausen?"

"She sure did."

If Jo was offended by the title she'd been given, she didn't show it.

Someone to her left started to ask something, but Gill ignored them and reached for Jo's hand. "How about a dance?"

One of the women on her right did a low whistle, and someone pushed her from behind.

Jo smiled. "Since you asked so nicely."

Catcalls followed them as they walked away from the crowd.

The music was fast, but the dance floor was small, so he was able to keep a hand on her while they found the beat of the music.

She moved to the music and placed her hands on a part of her body that made him salivate. This was the Jo he'd met in DC. The one who didn't hold back. He couldn't help but wonder just how loose she would be if given half a chance.

The music changed and they kept dancing. By the third song, he pulled her off the dance floor and over to the bar.

"Not bad moves for a guy as big as you." Jo's half compliment had him grinning.

He leaned close and spoke in her hear. "I think you gave at least three guys out there a hard-on."

She turned around to see who he spoke of.

Gill twisted her back his way and handed her a beer. He put a possessive hand on the small of her back and led her away from those clamoring for drinks.

There wasn't a quiet corner, just one with a little less crazy going on so they could talk.

He lifted his bottle to hers. "To a successful week."

She clicked hers to his and drank.

"Are you glad you stuck around?" he asked.

Jo shifted on her feet. "I am. I learned a lot, even if I won't use any of it."

"We all hope we never have to use it."

"I guess."

"When does your flight leave tomorrow?"

"Eleven. Had to give myself time to drive into DC."

He wasn't leaving until Sunday. Having given himself an extra night to see Lee and Consuela.

"I'll be back in Eugene on Monday."

She sucked on her lower lip before drinking.

It was his turn to shift in order to make more room in his jeans.

He lifted his hand, palm up, her way.

"What?" she asked, looking at it.

"Your cell phone."

When she didn't move to get it, he reached around, let his fingers linger on her ass before he lifted the slim device from her back pocket.

He was surprised to see there wasn't a lock screen. Then again, she did live in Mayberry and carried a gun. He couldn't imagine anyone jacking the information in her phone.

Gill put his number in, along with his name, before returning it to her pocket.

Jo leaned forward, her lips close to his ear. "Was it good for you?"

He laughed, and instead of letting her back away, he held her hip and pulled her against the length of his leg and the heat of the erection she was provoking.

The playful grin on her face slid, and her nose flared.

Awww hell. He'd wanted to wait . . . wait for them both to be away from Virginia, away from the place of temporary and back in their home state. But her blatant stare, the way she pressed into him . . . the smoldering huff of her breath cracked his resolve.

Gill set his beer down, took hers from her hand, and dropped it beside his before using both of his hands on her hips to guide her out a back door of the bar.

Once they broke free of the noise, he pulled her around the side of the building and pressed her against the bricks. His lips were on hers with the same heat and passion they'd shared that first night.

Only this time, it was so much better.

Her hands were on his chest, his hips, his ass. All the while Gill explored every inch of her mouth until they were both breathless and panting.

He broke away. "Not here."

"My hotel," she said.

Gill kissed her, briefly, and pulled her toward his ride.

Unlike the previous times on the bike, this ride proved erotic. Jo didn't rest her hands on his waist to hold on, she let them linger lower, her fingers stroking him through his jeans. He pushed through a few stop signs and broke a few speed laws as he drove the short distance to her hotel. Once there, he followed her until she stopped at a door and fished out a key from the wallet she kept in her back pocket.

Gill let her get through the door, let it shut before he reached for her. "C'mere, sweetness."

Jo moaned in his embrace as she clawed at his clothing.

He pinched her breast through her shirt, felt her knees give just enough to know she liked it. Then he lifted her in his arms and walked the short steps to her bed.

He followed her down, her legs wrapped around him like a snake holding on to a limb of a tree. The way her hips moved to his, even fully clothed, pushed his limits. "You're the most passionate woman I've ever known," he told her as he ravished her neck and the top of her breast.

"I need practice," she said, her hands moving to the fly of his jeans.

He saw stars when her hand reached for his bare flesh. "I'm in trouble."

She laughed, lifted one leg over his, and used a move he'd taught her to have him on his back.

"Big trouble," he repeated.

Jo leaned over him and pulled out of her shirt, unfastened her bra, and tossed it to the floor.

Gill's mouth watered before he let his tongue seek her flesh. Her breasts fit his hands perfectly, and tasted like sugar. Or maybe that was the shots of whatever it was she'd been drinking before leaving the bar. He grinned into the thought and teased her nipple with his teeth. Either way, she tasted divine, and he wanted more.

Her hands were everywhere, and she had too many clothes on.

Gill rolled her around, took the dominant position, and unbuttoned her snug jeans. Jo lifted her hips and helped kick them free.

She slid a free hand into the elastic of her panties and he stared. When she reached farther down, he pulled her down the bed by the backs of her knees and slid his hands up her thighs.

"Too much staring, not enough doing," she complained, her voice husky.

He unwrapped her, tossed her panties across the room, and dropped to his knees. He started at her knee, a nibble, a kiss, and as slowly as he could, worked his way up. He teased with the tickle of his beard, the heat of his breath.

Jo tried to push closer and cussed under her breath.

Still Gill took his time until it was he who couldn't hold out any longer.

Sugar and sex hit his senses, and Jo's moan had to be doing a good job of waking her neighbors. He wanted to know her, learn what she liked, what drove her wild.

Like any map, he studied and learned by the signals she gave, until finally her hips rose from the bed, her short pants and words telling him not to stop when he'd found her spot.

He smiled into her when she cried out the loudest and sensations became too much to bear and she pushed him away.

Gill looked up the length of her body, her head to the side, her hair wild on the bed, the smile on her face as radiant as any satisfied woman he'd ever seen. He leaned over, took a swig of the water she had sitting by her bedside, and found a condom in the back of his wallet.

"Let's do that again," he suggested.

Jo spread her hand over her stomach before helping him with the latex and pushing him onto his back.

His sex strained toward her, and she didn't make him wait.

Jo took control, and he let her. Only when she begged him to finish did he let himself go.

Once they were both breathing normally and Jo rolled off to snuggle into his arms did she say, "We're really good at that."

He kissed the top of her head. "We are."

Half an hour later, when he'd slipped out of Jo's arms after she was fast asleep to use the restroom, stared down at her lax body and realized how much he liked the woman.

He slid under the sheets, pulled them up over her shoulders, and pulled her close.

For a woman who claimed to always sleep alone, she had no problem seeking the heat of his body. Gill made himself comfortable, knowing that if she wanted to wake alone, he would be the one that would have to leave.

And he wasn't going anywhere.

# Chapter Eleven

As liberating as it was to leave River Bend, the feeling faded quickly as the chains started to slowly link back together the closer Jo came to landing.

Rain met her return, which was fitting.

Zoe waved from the doors of baggage claim, not that Jo had anything but her carry-on backpack for luggage.

"Now look who is jet-setting across the country," Zoe teased with a hug.

"I don't have frequent flyer miles like you."

Zoe might be dressed in jeans, a button-up shirt, and a jacket, but she looked like she'd just stepped through the pages of a fashion magazine. The contrast between how she dressed now and when they were kids always stunned Jo when she saw it after a week away.

"Tell me you had fun."

Jo smiled. "I had fun."

Zoe narrowed her eyes. "So Agent Hottie stepped up?"

Jo's smile grew. "Yes, he did." She kept the details to herself.

Her friend blew out a breath and turned toward the doors of the airport and out to the curb, where some travelers were waiting for rides. "Good. Otherwise I was going to have to book you another flight this spring, and I don't think River Bend would survive it."

"Has it been bad?"

"From my perspective. Cherie and Deputy Emery nearly came to blows. One of the neighbors called Luke because the yelling overpowered that of the dogs barking."

Jo ducked into her jacket as they crossed to the covered parking lot. The rain was coming down steadily, which made her wonder what the road conditions were in River Bend. Then again, River Bend was two hours away, and the weather could be clear there. Not that her weather app said it was. "I thought I had that all cleared up. Cherie was supposed to keep the dogs inside at night."

"Which I think she was doing, but according to Emery, a complaint came in during the day, so he had to go over and put his foot down."

Jo checked her messages on her cell phone. Nothing from Glynis. "When did this happen?"

"Yesterday."

"Emery called the pound in Waterville—"

"He what?" Jo interrupted.

"Said he had no choice."

"He had a choice," Jo muttered. She'd have to have a talk with the man. Something she seldom did unless forced to. He was twice her age and had worked under her dad. He didn't adjust to her being boss for some time, and now, so long as she didn't go out of her way to tell him what to do, they worked well together.

"That's what the Millers thought. Either way, they came in and cited her, gave her a big fine, and told her she had two weeks to find homes for four of her dogs."

"Not the puppies?"

"The puppies would need to go, too, but not until the eight-week mark."

Zoe opened the back of her SUV, and Jo tossed her backpack inside before climbing into the passenger seat.

"What a mess," Jo said once she was buckled in.

"Yeah. The woman has too many dogs, we all know that, but how Emery went about it was just wrong."

"He has the law on his side, but I can't disagree. If she hadn't let her dog get knocked up, this wouldn't have happened."

Zoe backed out of the parking spot and worked her way out of the lot.

"Everyone knows Emery hates animals."

"His bias shouldn't come into play," Jo said.

Zoe offered a smile. "I'm glad you're back."

Jo groaned. "Any other messes I'm walking into?"

"There's a big pothole in front of Sam's diner."

"Pothole?"

"Almost like a sinkhole."

*Great!*

"Anything else?"

"Yeah . . . I think Mel is pregnant."

Jo lost air turning her head. "She's what?"

Zoe lifted her palm in the air. "She hasn't said anything to me, not sure why . . . but she was in the kitchen helping me with some of the pastries for the guests, and I saw her scarf two éclairs, half a bag of potato chips, and then she opened a jar of pickled beets and finished the thing with a fork and a glass of milk."

Jo winced at the thought of how all that would taste together. "That's horrific."

Zoe nodded. "An hour later she was talking about dinner."

Yep, sounded like something was hormonally off with their friend. "I wonder why the secret."

"Maybe she wants to tell us together."

That sounded like Mel. She was the pleaser, and since she was already mother to Hope, probably familiar enough with the whole pregnant thing to know when to tell the world and when to wait.

"So do we play dumb and wait, or do we confront her?"

"Let's wait, see what happens."

Jo shrugged.

They pulled onto the interstate for a brief while before merging onto the highway that would take them home. The windshield wipers flapped against the glass with a steady beat that reminded her of dancing with Gill the night before.

When she'd rolled over in the morning as her alarm rang, she was stunned to find Gill still curled up in her bed.

She couldn't remember the last time someone had spent the night with her. It had to have been before her father had died.

There Gill was, naked, semiaroused, and pulling her close when she tried to slip out of bed.

They'd made love slowly, and then she rushed her shower to make sure she would make her flight in time.

He told her he'd see her before she could miss him.

She told him she never missed men.

"We'll see about that," had been his response.

Arrogant man.

"What is that look on your face?" Zoe asked, glancing her way from the driver's seat.

Jo shook her head.

"Don't even try to keep crap from me. I tell you *everything*."

And Zoe did, from her and Luke's sexcapades to the proper way to cut herbs to retain their flavor. Not that Jo cared, her herbs came from a jar like they should.

Jo let her grin stay. "I met someone."

Zoe's smile dropped. "As in *met someone, met someone* . . . or just hooked up with someone you'll never see again?"

Gill's voice hummed in her head. "You'll see me before you miss me."

"Shauna's partner."

Zoe squealed and pounded the steering wheel in her excitement. "Your someone is Agent McHottie?"

"Yeah."

While Jo gave the short version of Gill, knowing full well she'd have to go over all the details again with Mel and Zoe together, Jo realized Gill was wrong . . . she already missed him.

~

For years, Jo thought her answering machine was a waste of electricity.

When she dropped her bag on her couch and hit the blinking button on the machine, she was shocked to hear she had fifteen messages.

First was Glynis. Apparently the woman had forgotten that Jo was leaving within ten hours of her departure. Glynis stuttered a few times, then laughed at her memory before hanging up. Two of Cherie's neighbors called repeatedly, and one called twice to say she was sorry for bothering her on her *vacation*. The machine cut her off after a few minutes, so she called back to make sure that Jo knew she wasn't upset with her for taking time for herself.

There were several hang-ups, and two calls about the pothole Zoe had told her about. The last call was from Cherie herself, telling her that Deputy Emery wasn't fit to wear a badge.

Jo looked at the time.

A quick shower and she'd manage to get to the station before five thirty, when Glynis left and the place all but closed up. Jo knew she'd have a night of work ahead of her. She didn't remember if she'd had Emery working the day or if it was one of the relief help from Waterville.

Either way, she'd need information on what was being handled and what was handled badly.

The rain had let up when she parked in front of the station.

Glynis had a country radio station playing, filling the silence of the station.

She jumped to her feet when Jo closed the door behind her.

"Jo!"

She caught the woman's hug.

"I missed you. The whole town missed you. I can't believe you were gone for a week. How was it?" Glynis stepped back, the questions kept flying. "Did you see the hole in front of Sam's? I bet today's rain made it worse. Fitzpatrick will be back here anytime. He can fill you in on all the crazy that always seems to happen when you're not here."

"I'm never not here."

Glynis waved her off. "You were gone for Melanie and Wyatt's party in Vegas, and there was that trip to Texas when Zoe was living there . . . now this."

Jo refused to feel guilty about fifteen days off in eight years of service. "I have more vacation time available to me than anyone."

"That's because we encourage Emery to take his time." She lowered her voice. "We like you better than him."

Jo moved around her longtime employee and toward her office. "That may be, but I should be able to take some time off without River Bend falling apart."

Glynis took her place in the chair on the other side of Jo's desk while Jo picked up the mail stacked up with her name on it.

"We didn't fall apart . . . we frayed a little at the edges."

There were bills for the station. A notice from the company that provided the cruisers she and Emery used. She opened that first, saw a recall notice on both vehicles.

"What is being done about the road hazard in front of Sam's?"

"Fitzpatrick spoke with an asphalt guy in Waterville."

Jo looked up from her mail. "A couple bags of concrete won't fix it?"

Glynis blinked a couple times. "You haven't seen it."

No, she'd not driven past Sam's on her way in. "That bad?"

"Swallowed a massive wheel on one of Zoe's production trailers."

That gave Jo pause. "Did the trailer cause it?"

"Hard to say. It was there before the crew came to town."

Something told her that was going to be trouble.

"Luke pulled them out, but it's going to take more than a few bags of anything to fix properly."

"ETA on that?"

Glynis shrugged, motioned toward the back window. "Rain has to let up longer than five minutes first."

The bell from the front door of the station signaled company.

Glynis stood and peeked around the corner.

"Deputy Fitzpatrick, look who's back."

Jo moved around her desk, held out her hand. "Hey, Stan." Stan Fitzpatrick had been a deputy in Waterville for longer than Jo could remember. He'd known her father personally. As it worked out, Stan would step in when her father took a long weekend up at the hunting cabin, or on the very rare occasion he left the area altogether. A few too many fast food burgers sat around Stan's waist, and his receding hairline was peppered with gray.

He knew the people of River Bend, and they liked him. So whenever Jo needed to leave, she asked Stan to step in.

He always did.

"You look rested," he told her.

"That's going to be short-lived from the laundry list I'm being given," she said, waving the mail in her hand.

"The perks of being the big cheese, Jo."

"Yeah, yeah . . ." She moved back to her desk. "Anything happen I need to know about?"

Stan glanced at Glynis, then back to Jo. The look said he had something to say without an audience.

"Glynis, thanks for keeping things going while I was gone. We'll catch up with everything in the morning."

She took the hint and moved to her desk to retrieve her purse. "Great having you back, Jo."

Once the door was closed behind her, Jo offered a chair to Stan. "You have something to say."

Stan lifted his duty belt so he could sit without cramping his weapon. "I'm sure you heard about the whole dog ordeal."

"Yeah. Zoe picked me up from the airport and filled me in."

"It wasn't handled right, Jo. I've pinch-hit here in River Bend since when your dad was alive. That kind of strong-arm stuff is needed in Waterville, but here it just makes enemies."

"Neighbors on both sides left messages for me at home complaining about the noise. Didn't Cherie take the dogs inside?"

"She did. Still Karl jumped in and said he heard excessive noise outside her house and thought he needed to step in for the safety of the animals."

Jo shook her head. "Cherie is the crazy dog lady, but she loves her fur babies. Would neglect herself before she'd cause them any harm."

"Yeah, well . . . now the ASPCA has their eye on her, and they'll be back to make sure she has fewer animals, with the promise to return when those puppies are eight weeks old."

Jo felt the headache travel from the back of her head to the front.

"Even the neighbors who complained thought the punishment didn't fit the crime."

"Making her get rid of four of her pets would be like me asking you to give away one of your kids."

Stan laughed. "Well, my oldest is pissing me off these days. Damn teenagers."

Jo smiled. "Anything else?"

116

Stan told her about a fallen tree that still needed to be removed from the side road past Miss Gina's Bed-and-Breakfast. He did a well check on Mrs. Kate, ate some of her pot roast for the efforts. Said he made a point of driving by her house a few times, made sure none of the local teenagers thought it would be a good time to decorate the town with toilet paper.

She thanked him for that. Seemed picking toilet paper out of trees was becoming a thing. She could only guess teens were to blame.

Jo needed to catch them and introduce them to toothpaste and a toilet . . . and Lob Hill, where she would run their toilet papering asses until they wanted to puke. They'd be too tired to toilet paper her house and maybe stop others from thinking she found it amusing.

Truth was, she had given more than one admiring thought to the culprits of last year. In all her days of toilet papering houses, never once did she consider taking on the house of a cop. That was probably because that would have been hers. But even Emery's house, which wasn't far away, she didn't consider. Now that he was pissing her off, she wished she had.

"Everything else, which wasn't much, I wrote in my log."

Jo stood and walked Stan out. "I can't thank you enough for helping out."

"Did you get a lot out of the Fed training?"

Jo pictured the final simulation exercise, the praise from those who saw her in action. "I learned a thing or two."

"Not sure why you thought you needed to go. You have a quiet town here."

"Oh, I don't know. There's been a fair amount of media vans pulling into River Bend in the past couple years. Even small towns have their problems."

"I suppose."

"Thanks again, Stan."

"Anytime, Jo."

She sat down to her pile of mail and dug in. It was after seven thirty when she left the office and went to Sam's to see the cement pond everyone was so up in their armpits about.

The rain had started in again, making the mess shimmer along with everything else on the road.

"That's impressive," she muttered as she assessed the parameters of the hole. A hole that was worthy of a small town's gossip for months to come.

With her stomach telling her she hadn't eaten since the sandwich she'd grabbed at the airport in DC, Jo stepped into Sam's diner and sat on one of the many empty bar stools at the counter.

She knew the name to every face she saw in the place. Most greeted her with a hello or a welcome back. A few people who were too far away settled with a wave.

"Welcome home," Brenda, the longtime waitress of Sam's, greeted her. She lifted a coffeepot, and Jo shook her head.

"I need to sleep tonight."

Brenda smelled the top of the pot, wrinkled her nose, and put it back on the warmer.

Jo didn't bother with the menu she'd memorized in high school.

"What looks good tonight?"

Brenda set a glass of ice water beside her. "Pot roast. It's Zoe's recipe, and I think Sam finally has it down."

Jo tilted her head. "Has Zoe approved?"

"She tests it every week, says if it gets any better, she'll let Sam put her name on his menu under the dish." Brenda chuckled. "Imagine that, Sam's diner could have a *dish*. Even if it's pot roast."

"I haven't had pot roast in forever. Bring it on."

Jo's phone buzzed in her back pocket. She fished it out to see Gill's name lit up on her screen.

It was a text message. How was your flight?

Jo grinned . . . a silly schoolgirl grin, and promptly looked around the diner to see if anyone noticed.

Uneventful. She texted back.

And did your town fall apart without you?

Jo glanced out the window at the cones surrounding the massive hole in the street. A little.

Nothing you can't handle, I'm sure.

She liked his praise, even if he had little to base it on. Isn't it late there?

Not as late as last night. Some chick kept me up for hours.

Jo bit her lip, her fingers texting faster than when she was a kid.

Shame on her.

She should be spanked. Gill left a smiley face next to his words.

You'd have to catch me first, and I'd bet twenty bucks I'm faster than you.

A series of dot dot dots followed for the longest time. Jo looked around the restaurant again, didn't see anyone watching her.

Challenge accepted.

Jo laughed, and Brenda looked up from where she was putting together Jo's salad.

Good night, Gill.

He followed with, G'Night, Sweetness.

A dinner salad emerged in front of her. When she looked, Brenda grinned from behind the counter. "Must be good."

Jo didn't comment as she tucked her phone away and reached for her fork.

Even Sam's dinner salad tasted better than before she'd left.

Brenda tapped her fingers on the counter. "I like that smile, JoAnne. I haven't seen it in a while."

# Chapter Twelve

Gill looked up from his desk when he saw Shauna walk by. "Burton," he said, catching her attention.

She doubled back. "Yeah?"

"Do you have those files on Jo's case . . . her father's case?"

Shauna regarded him with concern. "I do."

"I'd like to take a look at them." It was Monday, and they'd be working overtime in an effort to find the suppliers of a local high school in the grips of a heroin outbreak. The investigation went beyond the local police due to the number of seventeen-year-olds that were ending up dead. One of whom happened to be the nephew of a local congressman.

Looking at the Ward case would have to take place when he was at home, but he didn't want it to get away from him.

"I'll get them to you. Once you've read them, I'd like to go over a few things," Shauna said.

"Do you see anything suspicious?"

Shauna didn't look convinced. "Seems too cut-and-dry. Like someone put a stamp of approval on his case way too quickly, but I'm not convinced he was murdered."

"You're contradicting yourself."

She walked away. "You'll see."

Gill turned his attention back to his computer and the maps of the high schools involved in his current case. Two of the largest public schools in Eugene took up the majority of cases, and it was starting to leak into the smaller private schools as well. You'd think it would be easier to find a link in a smaller setting, but these were privileged kids who didn't talk, where the public school kids worked a little harder to gain notice and be popular. What Gill needed to do was get inside the heads of these kids. Problem was, it had been fourteen years since he'd walked the halls of a high school. The few friends of his that had kids had young kids, which didn't help him.

He looked through the high school photos of the dead teenage kids.

They looked normal. Painfully normal.

Kids that should be out sneaking beer from their parents' fridges or bumming a joint off a twenty-one-year-old.

Heroin didn't fit.

Gill opened his search engine and requested facts on drug use outside of Eugene but still in the state. It would take time for the information to land in his inbox, so he clicked around to see how many high schools occupied the state of Oregon. It was a really long list.

He scrolled through, not really looking for anything, and found River Bend High. He clicked on the link. The decent size high school taught ninth through twelfth grades, with an average of two hundred students per year. The school collected kids from outside the town of River Bend, which kept the facility in an actual brick-and-mortar building instead of those portable excuses for schools that popped up everywhere.

Just for kicks, he clicked around the high school site, settled on the track and field page, where he paused.

Sheriff Ward, or Coach Ward, as she was labeled on the website, stood beside several students at some kind of meet. One of the alumni from River Bend was quoted on the page, saying, "Coach Ward doesn't hear the words _I can't_. When she's not coaching us, she's policing us, so it isn't like we have a chance to say no."

Another student's quote offered a different accolade. "She's not a coach who makes you run, she runs with you and tells you to keep up."

Gill thought about the text conversation he'd had with Jo on Saturday. Guess he should just give her the twenty bucks now and know he wouldn't catch her if they raced.

He copied a picture of her from the website before clicking off the page.

He pushed from his desk to find some coffee, wondering how soon he would be able to run after the fine sheriff. Then he realized something that smacked him in the face.

JoAnne Ward hung out with high school teenagers every day.

~

Thunderstorms filled every hour of Jo's life for two days and three nights after her return. Because Deputy Emery had pulled in overtime, she was almost entirely on her own. Lucky for her, the list of people she could call for roadside help extended into Waterville. The need to check on the outskirts of River Bend for the elderly that might be stranded due to the poor weather or washed-out roads had her calling in favors from neighbors. And when some of the phones proved to be out of order, she had no problem driving around town asking the business owners to take a drive since she couldn't be in five places at once.

Meanwhile, Sam's Lake, which was what the hole in front of the diner was starting to resemble, grew by the hour.

It was only seven thirty in the evening, but the dark sky made it feel as if it was the middle of the night. At this point, her two-way ham radio worked better than a cell phone.

The radio squawked, and she heard a familiar voice. "Jo, your ears on?"

She lifted the handheld and pressed the button. "I'm here, Luke."

"I'm out past Grayson's farm, about five miles. Pulling Steve out of a ditch." Luke Miller had the only tow truck in town. On nights like this, he patrolled until most of the residents of River Bend were tucked in their beds.

"Need my assistance?"

"He swerved to miss a boulder that came off the hill. You might wanna light it up until I get him home. I'll double back and move it."

"I'm on my way." Jo did a U-turn and rolled through the quiet streets of town before turning off toward Luke's direction. Backcountry roads were notoriously dark, and most often a deer crossing in front of a passing car caused an accident and the need for Luke to tow someone out.

It appeared that all the self-respecting Bambies out there were ducked out of the foul weather, leaving the accidents to inanimate objects.

Jo rolled up on the scene, parked her car beside the boulder that took up half the road, and kept her lights flashing.

She pulled her sheriff hat over her head and tucked her raincoat a little closer to her neck when she exited her car.

Luke was soaked to the bone, and Steve waved at her from the front seat of Luke's truck.

"Looks like he messed up the front axle," Luke said in a voice close to a yell to be heard over the rain and the engine of his idling truck. "I was hoping he could drive it home, but it doesn't look like it."

Jo looked around the dark road.

"Looks like rush hour has passed," she teased.

Luke fastened a chain to the winch on his truck and turned on the motor. Steve's truck slowly rose so it could be towed on its back wheels.

She waited beside Luke and ignored the rain as it tried to find openings in her clothing.

Luke refused her offer of help and worked in silence.

In the ten minutes it took him to secure the truck once it was out of the ditch, not one vehicle drove by.

Jo knew the minute she drove away there'd be a call of an accident, and she'd be right back.

"I need to drop Steve off, then leave the truck at the shop. Take me a good thirty minutes," he said.

"You know where I'll be."

Luke nodded before jogging to the driver's side of his truck and darting inside.

Jo followed suit and huddled in her dry squad car for his return.

She ran the engine and cracked the passenger window a hair while listening to the crackle of the radio. The only other sound was her breathing and the beating down rain.

Times like this she would have liked to have a larger pool of local deputies.

If she received an emergency call from anyone, something would fall through the cracks. Of course, she could put a few flares on the road and hope anyone driving by would take notice. But with visibility so low, the likelihood of an accident was high.

So Jo sat in her car and waited.

The rain slowed from heavy sheets to a steady beat.

Too quiet.

The skin on her arms started to prickle.

She looked out the back window . . . nothing.

As she swiveled back around, she caught something out of the corner of her eye.

With her heartbeat speeding up, she positioned the spotlight mounted outside her car away from the boulder in the street to across the road. Rain and more rain . . . and darkness.

"Lack of sleep and no food," she whispered to herself.

Still, she unlocked the holster on her weapon and kept her eyes scanning the dark spaces surrounding the car.

~

"Details, details, details . . . I want them, Jo," Mel said, waving a bottle of wine in the air like it was truth serum.

Jo looked at her best friends, who stood at her door with sacks full of God knew what, staring at her like she was about to be the center of an intervention. "Do you have any idea how few hours I've managed to sleep since I got home?" she asked them, stepping away from the door.

Mel pushed past her and straight to the kitchen. Zoe followed.

"Zoe said you met someone," Mel chattered as she set up the food she'd brought. "And Brenda caught you staring at your cell phone, giggling, at Sam's the other night."

Jo moaned while closing the door. "Can't this wait?"

"I tried to tell her," Zoe started. "You know Mel, once something is in her head, she's dedicated."

"Okay, okay . . . but I'm giving you the short version. I'm exhausted, and I will fall asleep on you without remorse."

Zoe put her arm around her friend. "You look like hell."

"Thanks, *friend.*"

If Zoe weren't speaking the truth, Jo would have been offended.

"I've been running since I flew back."

Zoe took a dish from the bag and moved to the microwave. "Luke said the roads were a mess."

"And that pothole in front of Sam's is nasty," Mel said. "Wyatt, Luke, and Sam are getting on it first thing in the morning."

Jo knew the town would fix the hole long before she could get anyone from county road services to come in.

"I've had two dozen calls from River Bend's finest at my home to tell me about that damn hole. Like I can miss it." Jo drew in a big breath through her nose and gravitated toward the kitchen. She looked in the microwave.

"Pasta," Zoe told her. "Penne with chicken and asparagus."

Jo's stomach rumbled. "I wasn't hungry."

Zoe didn't comment, took the food from the oven, and set it on the counter.

Mel pulled dishes from Jo's cupboards. "I'm starving," she said.

Both Jo and Zoe looked Mel up and down.

Sensing their stares, Mel turned around. "What?"

"Nothing," Jo said, turning first.

Zoe grinned and pulled a bottle of white wine from her bag. "Mel, can you get some wineglasses?"

Jo watched Mel remove two glasses from her liquor shelf.

Mel looked up. "I'm driving."

"One glass won't hurt," Zoe tempted.

And in the past, Mel had no problem having a glass of wine, so long as she wasn't leaving right away and food was involved. Yeah, their friend had something to share.

"The roads are a mess. Besides, it might start raining again."

The sky had cleared up before Jo turned in for the evening. "Suit yourself," Jo said.

Zoe scooped up portions of food for all of them.

Jo's mouth watered.

From the magic bag, Mel removed foil wrapped garlic bread.

"I'm so glad one of us can cook," Jo said.

"We all have our talents." Zoe grinned and handed her a plate.

They sat in the living room. Mel was cross-legged on the couch, Zoe sat on the floor and used the coffee table for her wine, and Jo kicked back in an old recliner dating back to her dad.

"So dish it out, sister," Mel said.

"This is fantastic," Jo told Zoe.

"Jo!"

"I'm sure Zoe told you the bulk of my story."

Mel talked around her fork. "His name is Gill, he works with that agent friend of yours. You met him in DC and he lives in Eugene."

Jo kept chewing. "Mmm-hmm, that's about it."

Mel rolled her eyes. "What does he look like?"

"I met him at a dive bar and he fit right in. Then I saw him at the federal training center in a suit and tie . . . and he fit right in." Jo pitched a fork into her pasta, spoke right before popping it into her mouth. "I guess you can say he's a chameleon."

Mel was not amused. She glanced at Zoe and said directly to her, "She's dating a lizard."

"Do you have a picture?" Zoe asked.

Jo shook her head.

"You're not helping, Jo!" Mel was miffed.

Jo rolled her eyes. "He's tall, I don't know, six twoish. Thick, cuz well, you know . . . that's what I've always been attracted to. Big and mmmm! He has a five o'clock shadow on his head and a groomed goatee. Is that better, Mel?"

Mel hummed to herself as she ate. "I feel better."

"You're going to see him again. That's the part that has me all girlie with giggling," Zoe said. "I don't remember the last time that happened."

Jo glanced at the ceiling. "Me either."

"I never saw you dating a cop." Zoe sipped her wine after eating only half of the meal she put on her plate.

"He's a Fed, not a cop."

"Is there a difference?" Mel asked.

"Probably not. But hell, I never thought I'd be a cop, so dating one can't be completely outside my new norm."

"When will you see him again?" Mel was like a kid with a new toy.

"I don't know. Eugene isn't exactly next door."

"It isn't crazy far away either."

"I'll be sure and run my dating life past you once I know what it is," Jo teased. "Now enough about me. When is that baby due?"

Mel didn't miss a beat, obviously didn't think before she answered, "November."

Zoe squealed.

Mel dropped her fork and covered her lips as if they had a mind of their own.

"I knew it!"

Jo and Zoe both stared at their friend.

"I wasn't going to say anything yet."

"Why?" Zoe asked.

Mel put her bowl aside, looked down at her flat stomach. "I almost lost Hope in my first trimester. I guess I didn't want to get everyone excited until I was past that."

Jo reached over and touched Mel's shoulder. "If something happened with this baby, don't you think you'd want us around to help? How can we be here for you if you don't let us know what's happening?"

Mel had a tear in her eye. "I guess you're right."

"I'm always right," Jo said, deadpan.

Zoe crawled up to a place beside Mel on the couch, wrapped an arm around her. "You're having a baby!"

Jo joined them in a group hug.

"And Jo has a boyfriend," Mel said.

They hugged again.

"He's not my boyfriend."

"Whatever," both Mel and Zoe said together.

# Chapter Thirteen

Fog socked in, cloaking River Bend in a layer so thick it needed a blowtorch to get through it. Not that it slowed Jo down.

She arrived at the track at six, did her warm-up laps, and waited for the distance team to arrive.

Tim, her team captain, showed up first. Right behind him, Maureen and Tina, her top girls varsity runners, waltzed onto the field, their heads stuck together in gossip.

"Hey, Coach," Tim greeted when he was close enough. "Finally let up enough for us to practice."

Jo smiled. "Not going to do anybody any good breaking an ankle this close to the invitational." The track drained rather well for something that needed to be replaced three years ago, but when it poured like it had, the thing resembled a lake more than a place for kids to run.

Maureen and Tina were still yakking when they hung their backpacks on the spikes of the fence.

Jo looked at her watch and peeked around the bleachers to the parking lot.

Her youngest runner, Louis, was jogging from his mother's car.

The kid was all legs and hadn't yet grown into his years. "Hi, Coach," he yelled from yards away. "I'm not late."

"No, you're not."

The rest had three minutes left. "Tim?" she called out.

"Yeah?"

"You got ahold of everyone about today's practice, right?"

"Texted everyone last night."

"And they all responded?"

"Yep."

Jo removed her cell phone from her armband that housed it when she ran and checked for messages.

From behind her, she heard a girl's voice. "We're here!"

Jo looked up. Ella and Gustavo were running beside each other. Ella was Jo's junior, and Gustavo was the forced recruit that couldn't afford to be late.

The two looked very cozy beside each other.

At exactly 6:30, Tim pulled them all together to stretch them out. At 6:32, Drew, the other varsity senior, rolled in.

Jo gave him _the_ look and raised two fingers in the air.

He didn't argue.

An extra lap after practice for every minute they were late. Those were her rules.

Arguing about the rules resulted in more laps. And as much as these kids liked to run, when they were done with her workout, they were done!

Forced recruits such as Gustavo were given the extra laps and community service. Which for Jo was cleaning up trash on the field, cleaning equipment, and raking the long jump pits. And if there was one thing teenagers hated, it was cleaning up after _other_ teenagers.

"Coach?" Tim caught her attention.

"Yeah?"

"Is Billy coming today?"

"Billy had to take his mother into Waterville for a doctor's appointment."

Tim saluted her and encouraged the rest of the distance team to take their first laps.

Second lap around, she noticed Tina and Maureen avoiding the puddles still accumulated on the track. Instead of calling the girls on it, Jo decided they needed a little off-roading. She joined their third lap and directed them off the field.

The girls moaned, but they got over it once their legs were splattered with mud and avoiding puddles wasn't possible.

As they closed in on the four-mile circuit, her freshman was winded and Gustavo was clenching his side.

"Don't feel like you have to keep pace with the seniors, Louis," she told the youngest runner.

Louis acknowledged her with a nod but didn't try to talk.

Jo sped up a few yards to run beside Gustavo.

"Looks like you lost a little steam during the rain."

He looked at her, frowned. "You said practice was canceled."

"I did. You're right."

They ran side by side a little longer.

"Hey, Drew?" Jo called ahead. Drew was pacing beside Tina. They'd dated on and off since the previous summer. She couldn't tell if they were on again or not.

"Yes, Coach?"

"When I cancel practice, do you still run?"

The girls started to laugh, and Drew turned around to run backward as he answered. "If I don't wanna puke the next time I come out, yeah."

"In the rain?" Gustavo spat out.

"In the anything, dude. Couple miles minimum unless God himself is dumping buckets on River Bend."

"Oh, man."

Gustavo wasn't happy. Then again, he wasn't there by choice. He'd tried to give himself a five-finger discount from the main market in town. The store owner caught him with a pocket full of gum and candy, of all things, and called Jo. It was petty and it was stupid . . . and if Jo had anything to say about it, it would be the last time Gustavo attempted to steal anything from anyone.

He'd been pulled into the cross-country team in the fall and the distance team in the spring. She'd acquit the kid during the summer if she didn't catch or hear of any problems. But this was River Bend. And Jo knew it like sailors could smell an oncoming storm. She knew where to find the teenagers on a Friday night being teens . . . knew how they scored their liquor and where they stashed their weed. Keeping her recruits from year to year wasn't that hard. Some, like Drew, took his extra laps and added time with a shit-eating grin. He played the fence hard, but overall he was a good kid with a smart sense of everything that went on around him, probably a byproduct of being Deputy Emery's son. The kid reminded her a lot of herself at his age.

If she ever received inside information from one of the kids on the team, even if they weren't on the distance team, she kept it confidential and made sure *she* was the one to catch kids in the act of no good.

They all knew, each and every one of them, that they could call her if any situation got sketchy.

And sometimes they did.

So far, every forced recruit finished high school. Which was her goal. Well, that and keeping them from doing something permanently stupid. Three of her kids were given full ride scholarships for their performance on the field. Considering the average income of a River Bend family, she considered those efforts home runs. That wasn't to say she wasn't just as happy with the kids that went to the community college in Waterville and then on to whatever school or trade they decided on to earn their way in life. The best part was, none of her recruits ended up in her jail.

They ran from the wooded trail they'd followed and back onto the track at the high school. They had a couple of cooldown laps where they slowed their pace, and then they'd all go in and grab a shower or rush home to do it before class.

"So, Sheriff?" Drew asked loud enough for all the kids to hear.

"Yeah?"

"Did you learn how to be badass with the Feds?"

She scowled. "Language."

Drew rolled his eyes.

She didn't bother scolding him more. He had parents for that. "I learned a few things."

"FBI training sounds cool," Louis said as he huffed through his final lap.

"Did you shoot a lot of guns?" Tina asked.

"We did."

"I looked it up online," Tim said. "Did you get to drive like a crazy person?"

"We call it defensive driving, Tim. Not crazy person." She laughed.

They rounded the last lap, and the noise from the parking lot told her that the other students were arriving.

"I think it's awesome that our town sheriff trained with the FBI." Tina puffed out her chest like it was her accomplishment.

"It was a lot of hard work, but it was worth it."

"Did they make you run?" Gustavo asked with a laugh.

"No. I made myself run three miles every day." Well, except two, but she wasn't going to admit that.

Gustavo's look of mortification had her laughing.

Tim and Drew raced their last hundred meters, even though they were supposed to be cooling down. Drew caught the first foot over the finish line. With hands on their knees, air moving in and out of their lungs quickly, they sparred each other with words of next time and who was the faster runner.

"Oh, who is that?" The tone of Maureen's voice said she liked what she saw.

"Oh . . ." Tina said on a sigh.

Jo followed their gaze. Her breath caught in her throat and she started to cough.

Gill leaned against the fence. He wore a black leather jacket and jeans. The sunglasses, which weren't yet needed, rested on his nose, blocking the direction of his eyes.

But Jo felt them.

"Hello, JoAnne." Gill's voice was low and sexy. Saying hello sounded like intimacy.

Jo waited a beat, and then she heard it. The low-lying whistle of one of the guys, she guessed Drew, who was ballsy like that. All the girls did the giggle thing.

She took a step toward him.

"He looks a little scary, Sheriff. Might wanna be careful," Drew teased.

She lifted her hand, her back to the kids. With two fingers in the air she said, "Two extra laps, Drew. Let's not make it three."

The kid laughed as he took off to wrap up his punishment.

"What are you doing here?" she whispered once she was close enough so only he could hear.

"I told you I'd come before you missed me."

Jo smiled, tried not to think of the kids who were watching from behind.

"I thought you'd call first."

Gill took off his sunglasses, and yes, he was staring at her. "I was in the neighborhood."

*From two hours away?*

Jo wanted to blush, probably was under the heat on her cheeks. "You're funny. I'm just finishing up here."

135

Gill looked her up and down. "I'll wait."

"Stop looking at me like that."

"Like what?" he matched her whisper.

"Like you want to devour me."

He leaned close, his lips close to her ear. "But I do."

"You're impossible."

His grin screamed sin before he covered his eyes with the glasses and leaned against the fence.

Jo faced her team, who had all stopped to gawk.

"Did you forget to stretch?"

The girls had phones in their hands.

Let the River Bend gossip begin.

~

Did the woman not know how she looked wearing those tiny shorts and the snug top soaked in sweat? Gill couldn't help but wonder if the teenage boys of River Bend High fantasized about their fine sheriff.

Lord knew if he had a coach that looked like her in school, he might have joined track.

He enjoyed making her blush. It was obvious that his unexpected presence tossed her around a little. And if there was something he knew about women, it was that when they were frazzled, they were interested.

JoAnne Ward was completely frazzled.

He'd listened enough to her conversations about her routine to know that she was on the track field with the teens every morning before she went to work. It was safe to say that after all the rain that had dumped on the coast of Oregon since they'd returned from the East Coast, this first dry day would ensure that he'd catch her there.

Gill enjoyed the brisk ride down, made good time on the back-country roads. He never worried too much about speeding tickets, and his bike gave him the maneuverability to get around the objects left behind by the passing storms.

River Bend, or the few roads where the city center was housed, was just as small as Jo had described. Yet the outlying areas, the places that were tucked off the main drags, the farms and larger pieces of property, spread out to her borders. And there was plenty of forest to make up for everything else.

It was quiet. That was the thing that stuck out the most as he drove through. Close to seven thirty and the town was barely waking up.

The high school, Gill decided, was bigger than any other part of the town.

The parking lot wasn't extremely big, but it was filling fast when he pulled in and parked next to Jo's squad car.

A chorus of good-byes caught Gill's attention.

Jo's teens were telling her they'd see her tomorrow. Two of the girls looked his way and quickly started laughing as they walked off.

Gill didn't think Jo had many men around or his just showing up wouldn't have caused this kind of response.

Jo lifted a backpack over her shoulder. "You know what you've done, don't you?"

He shook his head.

"You've started the gossip train."

"What gossip?"

Jo stood toe-to-toe, her head tilted back.

"Only my dad called me JoAnne. And no one, and I do mean no one, has met me by the bleachers that I didn't make run."

He liked the implications of that.

"So using your name, and being here, is gossip worthy, eh?"

"You have no idea." She looked around them.

Gill removed his sunglasses, tucked them in an inside pocket of his jacket. "Well, you know what we should do then?"

Jo turned her attention back to him. "What?"

"Give them something to gossip about." He reached for her waist and pulled her close.

She didn't resist, but then again, the look of surprise said he caught her off guard.

"I missed you," he said, right before he kissed her.

He thought for sure she'd push him away.

She didn't.

So he kept his lips to hers until she moaned, and then he set her back. "There we go," he said. "Something to talk about."

"My badass rep is now shot to hell," she said, licking her lips.

Gill took the backpack from her shoulder. "Have you seen the size of me? Your badass rep just showed up."

~

"I need a quick shower."

"Need help?" Gill asked.

Jo disappeared around the corner of her living room into what he assumed was her bedroom.

"Ha-ha! You show up and I'm late isn't a great combination."

Gill walked over to her fireplace, mumbling, "I think it's a fabulous combination."

Pipes in the walls whistled as Jo turned on the water. "Make yourself at home!"

A framed American flag sat center stage over the fireplace, the plaque under it stated *Sheriff Joseph Alan Ward*, along with the date of his death. To the right of the flag was a picture of Jo as a teenager, her father in uniform, standing beside her.

Gill picked it up to study.

Jo was younger, just as beautiful. There was an edge about her smile, something sneaky she was holding back. Her father squeezed her shoulder close to his, as if her closeness was rare and he wanted to hold her for as long as he could.

A pang of sadness for the man's loss strummed against Gill's breastbone.

The next framed picture was more recent. This one made his mouth water.

Jo stood beside two women, one in a wedding dress, the other dressed identically to Jo. A wedding, obviously, with three great friends. JoAnne Ward cleaned up really friggin' well. A dress, makeup . . . details to her hair, including tiny flowers. He wondered if she hated fluff and the flowers, or did she secretly crave them? She was beautiful, like any bridesmaid should be. Here she appeared less guarded, more relaxed, than she did in the picture with her father.

Gill replaced the photo, craving more.

On the wall hung a picture of her father, again in uniform. This was one that had been taken professionally, one that law enforcement took of their own the day they finished the academy. Right beside it, Jo placed her identical picture.

Gill started to sense a theme.

He moved from the pictures to the house. It felt heavy, dark. A man's home with a sprinkling of female. Like the recliner that sat beside the sofa, it screamed man but had a soft ivory throw tossed over the back of it. The house was neat, not like that of a bachelor, but of a woman living without a husband and kids. The few personal items placed on the coffee table or on the kitchen counter were *placed*, not thrown down and forgotten.

Gill thought Jo would be more of a throw down kind of woman. The neatness surprised him.

He couldn't help but wonder if the neatness was at an OCD level. Gill moved into the kitchen and opened a cupboard. Neat.

He opened another . . . neat.

Gill frowned until he opened the fridge.

The mess made him smile. Okay, so Jo wasn't clinical about tidiness.

"Hungry?" he heard Jo ask behind him.

He closed the door and turned around without explanation.

Jo's hair was wet and pulled up into a knot on top of her head. Her face was clean of makeup with the exception of a tiny bit of lip gloss. She didn't need anything more.

She was half dressed. Well, she had the standard uniform on with her dress shirt unbuttoned, a T-shirt underneath covering his view.

"I am hungry," he said, his voice low.

Jo blushed.

He loved making her do that. Gill slid beside her, stopped her from buttoning up her shirt by pulling her into his arms. "Hi," he said, as if he were seeing her for the first time that day.

"This is crazy," she said before reaching for his lips with hers.

Her gloss tasted like cherries, her kiss tasted like wine. He made the kiss count, tasted every possible part of her mouth open to his and went in for a little more when she came up for air. "I knew you'd miss me," he said.

She wiped his lips with her thumb. "I didn't say I missed you."

"That kiss said you did."

He let her go as she finished dressing. "I have to work."

"I thought as much. I'm sure you won't mind me tagging along."

"It's a boring town, Gill. I hope you brought a book."

He watched her, felt something off. "No book—" His words lingered. "Hey, where is your vest?"

She finished buttoning her dress shirt, tucked it into her pants.

"Vest?"

He tapped his chest.

The placating smile said everything. "It's River Bend," she said as if the name of the town explained the lack of bulletproof protection.

"Nobody in River Bend owns a gun except you?"

Jo came short of rolling her eyes. "You'll see." She disappeared into her room again, returned with her duty belt secured around her waist and her hat in her hand. "C'mon."

Even in the most unflattering pants, with tools of the cops' trade wrapped around her waist, keeping his eyes off her ass as she walked out her door proved impossible.

# Chapter Fourteen

Drew followed the line of cars working their way into the high school parking lot and noticed Tina leaning against her dad's late model Civic. Her tight little running shorts had distracted him all morning, and if he wasn't mistaken, she knew it.

She glanced up when he approached.

"Hey," he said.

"I thought you went home to shower?" she said.

"On my way."

Her phone buzzed.

He glanced down at Tina's phone, saw the same image on every sent section of her text messaging. "Is that the sheriff and that guy?"

Tina opened the image for him to see it clearly. "He's really hot."

Drew pulled his gaze from his coach's ass in the picture to look at the man. "If you like ancient guys."

"He's not old."

Drew rolled his eyes. "He is for you."

Tina pulled her phone away from his sight. "Whatever." She pushed off the side of the car and slid behind the driver's seat.

Drew backed up as she started the engine.

He'd bet money she was still upset he hadn't wanted to go to homecoming. You would think with prom around the corner she'd be a little nicer.

~

Mel refilled the coffee of the guests that had come down to breakfast. Because it was midweek, Zoe wasn't in the kitchen cooking breakfast for Miss Gina. But she had planned the menu and tutored Mel in cooking something other than scrambled eggs and bacon. Not that her culinary efforts would ever give her celebrity status. Still, the banana pancakes and quiche made the guests feel like they were anywhere but home, eating the same old stuff.

Mel felt her phone buzz in her pocket but didn't reach for it until after she'd cleared dishes from one table and refilled juice glasses at another.

She loaded the dishwasher once she returned to the kitchen and felt her phone buzz again.

A text from Brenda at Sam's diner was out of character.

Mel clicked on it to open a picture. She squealed, fumbled, and dropped her phone in the dishwasher.

She muttered a curse and hoped the screen hadn't cracked.

A sigh of relief was quickly followed by another tiny squeal.

Looked like Jo's McHottie was in town.

Mel widened the image. Oh, the man was a perfect fit for her friend. Mel did a silent happy dance, quickly copied the image, and sent it to Zoe.

Once the image said *delivered*, she waited.

"C'mon, Zoe."

Finally, a dot dot dot on the screen had Mel squirming.

OMG, he is soooo Jo!

I know! Mel texted back.

I need to go to the station.
Not without me!

They negotiated a time, and Mel hurried out the back door to find Miss Gina and share the news.

~

Luke dug his shovel into the wet cement and kept pulling air from the mix while Wyatt and Sam continued mixing bags upon bags to fill the hole.

His cell phone buzzed.

Wyatt, bent over a new bag, reached for his back pocket. He grinned.

Luke's phone buzzed again. When he looked, he saw Jo being kissed by a man twice her size by the high school bleachers. "'Bout time," he muttered to himself before returning his cell phone to his back pocket.

Sam reached for the small of his back and bitched. "How many more bags is this gonna take?"

Wyatt glanced around. "Five, maybe six."

"Damn thing is a sinkhole."

Luke nodded. "Sure as hell is."

~

Jo parked in front of the station, like she always did.

Glynis's car rested in her designated spot. She was early.

Gill stood in front of the squad car, looked down the span of the street. "What's going on down there?" he asked.

"Pothole." Jo waved when she saw Wyatt's head pop up.

"Looks like a serious hazard."

"They can take care of it."

If Gill had more questions, he didn't ask.

Glynis jumped the minute Jo pushed through the door, her hand moved behind her back.

"Morning, Glynis."

Her help stared at Gill.

Blushing.

Gossip was already flying. Jo could feel it.

"Glynis, this is Agent Gill Clausen. He works with Agent Burton. You remember her, right?"

She nodded a couple of times. "Of course I remember. You two were partners?"

"Are," Gill said. "We work together in Eugene."

"Oh, that's nice. Uhm, can I get you anything? Coffee?"

Jo smirked. Since when did Glynis play hostess?

"I'm sure I can find it," Gill said. "But thanks for offering."

"Oh, no problem. Any friend of Jo's is a friend of ours."

"Ours?" Gill asked, looking around the empty station.

"The town. I mean . . . I'm not speaking for the whole town, but, well . . . oh, I don't know what I'm saying. Welcome to River Bend."

"Thank you, Glynis."

Jo thought the woman was going to faint for all the color that reached her cheeks.

When Jo moved into her office, and out of earshot of Glynis, she said, "You're going to turn a lot of heads today. Keep your ego in check."

"I'll try." Gill stepped into her office. The size of the man took up quite a bit of space. "How much of this has changed since your dad was alive?"

The question took her off guard.

"Not a lot. He was efficient and wasn't afraid of computers and technology. It wasn't like I had to come in and update his world."

"His world," Gill repeated.

Jo moved around her desk, glanced at the mail from the previous day that she needed to follow up on. "It felt like his world for the first year."

"I would think it still feels like his place."

Jo glanced around the same walls, the same art . . . the same paint. "Sometimes. Little changes around here."

"That should make it easier to investigate a ten-year-old case."

She narrowed her eyes. Hope filled her chest. "Is that why you're here? You think there's something to look into?"

He stepped close enough for her to smell his mouthwash . . . or maybe that was hers.

"I'm here to see you. Your dad's case is a side note, and my case is an excuse." He kissed the tip of her nose.

He was smooth, she'd give him that.

The bell over the front door of the station rang, and Jo heard her best friends greeting Glynis.

"And so it begins."

"What?"

Jo didn't answer, she simply painted on a smile and stared at her office door.

Mel ducked in first, with Zoe close on her heels. Mel looked like she'd run from Miss Gina's kitchen before clearing the breakfast dishes. If Jo wasn't mistaken, there was flour on her cheek. And Zoe . . . in rare form, was wearing yoga pants and a T-shirt. An outfit Jo had seen many times because of their BFF status, but an outfit Zoe didn't wear outside the comfort of her own home.

"Hey, Jo," Zoe said.

Neither of them looked at her, both had their eyes on Gill.

"Oh, my God. Could you two be more obvious?"

Mel walked forward, extended her hand. "I'm Mel, this is Zoe. We're Jo's best friends. You must be Gill."

Gill shook Mel's hand. "I guess it's a good thing you have my name right."

Jo rolled her eyes.

"She described you perfectly," Zoe told him.

Jo wanted to crawl under the table. "I did not."

"You said big and mmmm!"

Gill laughed, moved in to shake Zoe's hand. "I think I'm gonna like your friends, JoAnne."

Mel glanced at Zoe. "He calls her *JoAnne*. Isn't that cute."

"For the love . . ." Jo said. "How did you guys find out he was here so fast anyway?"

"Mel texted me," Zoe said.

"Brenda from the diner texted me, and her daughter, Tina—"

Jo sighed. "I get the picture." She turned to Gill. "Tina is one of my runners that saw you at the school."

"Ah." He shrugged.

"I'm sure half of River Bend has a picture of you two kissing."

"Kissing?"

Mel pulled her phone from her back pocket, showed the image to Jo.

Jo slapped a hand to Gill's chest. "I'm blaming you," she told him.

He looked at the photo, wasn't fazed. "Not my best side, but I'll take it."

"You're killing me," Jo said, sliding into her chair. The day was going to be shot, and the calls would flood in.

"I'm guessing your town sheriff doesn't have many men kissing her around here."

Zoe leaned against the desk. "Not since she was eighteen."

"Even then it was more like Waterville and not River Bend. Right, Jo?"

Jo didn't answer. "Are we really having this conversation?"

Mel waved her off. "You're a federal agent?"

"I am."

"And you live in Eugene?" Zoe asked.

"I do."

"Eugene isn't that far," Mel started.

Jo stood, slapped her hands on the desk. "Okay, enough." She walked around the desk, shoving her friends with both hands toward the door. "I love you both, you know that. But get out of here. You're embarrassing the hell out of me."

Zoe looked over Jo's shoulder. "I can make dinner tonight."

"Get. Out!" Jo shoved until they'd both cleared the door and closed it behind them.

Gill stood by her desk, laughing. *"Big and mmmm?"*

# Chapter Fifteen

The distraction, otherwise known as Gill, made it nearly impossible to work. The paperwork that had been put aside because of the rain had piled up and needed to be taken care of. An hour into her day, Jo decided the only way to complete anything was to move the massive man from her office. Then she'd double-time until she was finished and find a way to incorporate him into her day.

"Okay, Goliath," she said as she grabbed her hat. "Let's go."

"Oh, Goliath. I like that."

Jo rolled her eyes and walked out of the room, expecting him to follow.

"Leaving already?" Glynis said as they walked out.

"I'll be back," Jo informed her.

The woman smiled and waved, her eyes on Gill. "Bye-bye."

Gill kept pace with her.

"So here are the ground rules," she started.

"Rules?"

"Yeah. That kiss that everyone in town has now seen on their phones, no more of that in public."

"Really?" He sounded disappointed.

"I do have to hold some kind of reputation, Gill. The town had a male sheriff for years. It took some of them time to get used to me. If they think I'm all *boy crazy*, who knows how it will go down."

Gill attempted to hold her hand.

She shook him off.

"None of that either."

"No?"

"No!"

"You drive a hard bargain." His smile said he wasn't offended. Besides, they hadn't exactly displayed any affection in Virginia. It didn't need to change in Oregon.

She lifted her sunglasses briefly, so he could see her eyes. "I'll make up for it later."

Gill licked his lips and pushed his hands into his front pockets. "Deal."

"This is River Bend," she said, as if he didn't know. She pointed across the street. "Drugstore. As in, the one and only drugstore. Yeah, they sell the occasional ibuprofen over at the market across the street, but Benson's Drugs sells anything and everything else."

"Expensive?"

"Competitive. Charlie, the owner, knows the dollars in gas it takes to drive to Waterville to pay for your basics and makes it worth your while to buy here. His prices for all prescriptions are the same as if you bought them online, minus the shipping."

"Smart man," Gill said.

"He stays in business. Not to mention his sister makes the best strawberry jam in the county and sells it by the pint seasonally."

Gill grinned.

Jo pointed to the next storefront. "Hardware store. Again competitive, with the edge of farming equipment supplies and seed to offset that which the feed store doesn't always have on hand."

"You have a feed store in town?"

"Just outside town. Close to R&B's."

"The bar I saw coming in?"

"That would be the one," she confirmed.

"I saw a barn . . ."

Jo nodded. "That would be Cody's Feed Store."

"Cody?"

"It's actually Cody's son. But that's how it goes around here."

Gill pointed to the next marquee. "Sam's diner, I presume?"

Jo stopped, spread her hands wide. "Breakfast."

They pushed through the glass door of Sam's and were greeted with the stares of several people from town and more than a half dozen friends.

Luke and Wyatt were a welcome sight. The very men she needed to entertain Gill for a couple of hours.

She approached the counter with a smile.

"Hey, Luke," she said since he made eye contact first. "The road looks like it's coming together."

"It is." Luke eyed Gill.

"Luke, Wyatt, this is Gill."

They were both silent for half a second.

"The guy on your phones. Don't even pretend you haven't got the text. Both Mel and Zoe have already been by the station."

Luke and Wyatt turned in their swivel seats and extended their hands.

"Mel's my wife," Wyatt said with pride.

Luke was next. "I'm Zoe's fiancé."

Gill shook hands with both of them. "Jo and I are hookin' up."

Jo cringed with both eyes closed and prayed to God that Gill's voice didn't carry as much as she thought it did.

Luke stood with his handshake and held on a little long.

"You're a little big to take down, but Jo's like a sister."

The men paused, and for the first time in Jo couldn't remember how long, Luke's sentiment had her heart pinging against her chest.

"Point taken," Gill said before suggesting that Jo sit.

Jo lifted a hand in the air. "I'm good, actually. Just send a bagel my way."

Gill tried to stand.

"No, no, sit. They have a great country fried steak and eggs here. Zoe's gravy recipe." She pointed at Wyatt. "You should show Gill around." She turned to Luke. "Introduce him to . . . introduce him."

"I'm being pawned off." The man was perceptive.

"You," she tapped his chest, "showed up unexpected."

She didn't sit, only waved at Brenda, who made goo-goo eyes at Gill.

"I'll see you at lunch. Miss Gina's, here . . . wherever."

"Who is Miss Gina?" Gill asked.

Jo glanced at Luke.

"I've got it!" Luke exclaimed. "Go." He waved Jo off. "Be the town cop. I've got this."

Gill looked her in the eye, his face softened. For a brief second his lips puckered, almost like he was blowing her a kiss.

And Jo walked away.

~

Jo made the house call she'd put off since getting back to town.

She knocked on Cherie Miller's door and was greeted with a chorus of dogs barking. Jo took a step back so when Cherie looked through her peephole she'd see Jo's whole body in the small viewfinder. Chances were the woman wasn't opening her door to very many people since the pound had been called.

The door cracked open, followed by Cherie yelling at her dogs all at once. "Hush up. Sampson, stay back!"

The woman looked a little haggard, like she hadn't slept much but still managed to shove a shower in and then promptly forgot to blow dry her hair. Luke's aunt had never married. And unlike the normal spinster stereotype, she collected dogs . . . not cats.

"Look who finally showed up," Cherie scolded once she cleared the door and closed it behind her to keep the dogs inside.

Instead of defending herself, Jo smiled and acted as if the other woman had said something pleasant. "Hello, Cherie. How are you doing today?"

"I'm doin' fine, just fine, considering I have to find new homes for my babies."

"How is that going?"

"Going? I'll tell you how it's going . . . it's not. Do you know how many dog lovers we have in this town?"

The question was rhetorical.

"Zero."

"Cherie, that's not true."

"I don't hear my phone ringing with people lining up to help me out while I raise these tiny little pups." As if to prove her point, Cherie opened the door, leaned down to grab the collars of three of her dogs, a trick in itself with only two hands, and motioned Jo inside.

The dogs barked, but didn't do more than sniff once she made it into the house and closed the door. Cherie started yelling out names of her dogs like a mother does for her children.

Everything in the small home centered around the animals. Beds lay on the floor, covering the carpet underneath. A hair-covered afghan sat in a heap on one end of the sofa, multiple bowls for dog food took up space in the three-step hall from the living room to the kitchen.

Cherie let her dogs loose once she cleared the kitchen and reached the covered porch through the sliding glass doors.

Jo didn't pretend to know the names of the dogs that swarmed her. The wagging tails and panting let her know there wasn't a threat.

The screen to the back porch closed the adult dogs on one side, the puppies and their mother on the other.

The distinct smell of puppy overwhelmed her as they stepped into the back room.

"This is Jezebel," Cherie introduced the mother.

Momma regarded Jo for a moment, then licked Cherie's hand in acceptance when the woman knelt to pet one of the half dozen pups curled around Jezebel's legs.

Jo's heart twisted. The tiny fur balls moved around on unsteady legs, their heads too big for their bodies, their little barks as precious as any newborn's should be.

"Tell me these aren't the most adorable things on the planet?" Cherie asked, picking one of the pups up and cradling it in her hands.

"They're precious," Jo told her.

Cherie forced the puppy into Jo's arms. Damn thing mewed, almost like a kitten, then released a bitty bark that made her smile.

"Every one of my dogs were once this tiny little thing, Jo. How do I pick which ones to keep and which ones to let go?"

Jo glanced behind her, saw the bigger versions of fur and bark. She leaned down, put the puppy back in with the rest, and thanked the mom by petting the back of her neck. "I know they're your babies. I understand that. Even parents of children eventually move their kids along."

Cherie opened her mouth to protest, Jo cut her off.

"I'm not happy about how all this came about. But . . ." She took a deep breath. "There is a limit of how many adult dogs one home can house before it becomes unmanageable."

"I'm managing just fine," she protested. "My dogs are fed, clean. My home isn't some cast-off episode of *Hoarders*."

"Dogs bark."

"That's their job. Especially when the pound shows up looking for trouble. And don't even get me started with that deputy of yours. That man hates me."

"Karl doesn't hate you."

Scratching at the back door of the porch caught Cherie's attention. She opened the access without breaking the conversation. In came two more dogs. "The man's missing diplomacy. Marched in here acting like he owned it, telling me this is out of control."

Jo glanced at all the eyes that were watching her. "Do they ever fight?"

Cherie looked at her like she was stupid. "Of course. They're dogs. Sampson is the alpha, he puts everyone in their place."

"Were they fighting when Karl came by?"

"Not fighting, just not happy. They sense danger, and Deputy Emery is that. And those people from Waterville were worse."

Jo blew out a breath, did a quick head count of dogs. "I thought you had eight adults." Jo counted six.

"My old-timers are in my room," Cherie explained. "I can't pawn them off, Jo. It's not fair to push out the old when the babies come in."

"When do you expect the pound to return?"

"They said three weeks."

"All right. Three weeks. We can find homes for four of your dogs in three weeks."

"But—"

"Cherie. I don't like this, I don't. But the law is very clear on kennels, breeding, and residential neighborhoods."

"I'm not a kennel."

Jo made a point of petting the head of the closest dog. "The law would disagree."

Cherie shook her head.

"Sampson is your chief around here, right?" The dog whose name Jo said jerked his head her way.

"Right."

"And Jezebel needs to stay because of the puppies, and your seniors aren't going anywhere."

Cherie caught on to what Jo was doing.

"The way I see it," Jo said. "Those are the four dogs you keep."

"But—"

"Old dogs don't live forever," Jo reminded her. "It's possible that you could end up with one or two of these back before you know it."

The woman looked like she was going to cry.

"And if we find homes in River Bend, you can visit them."

When Cherie sniffed, it took effort to not join the woman in her loss. "We can do this."

"I hate this."

Jo didn't like it either. "And as soon as the vet says it's possible, you fix Jezebel. No reason to repeat this heartbreak."

Cherie walked her to the front door, two of the dogs followed while the others found their beds and curled into balls for a morning nap.

"Jo." Cherie stopped her before walking out.

"Yeah?"

"Sampson's son, Noah, sure would make a good police dog."

The dog at Cherie's left lifted his head to her hand.

Jo smiled. "Let's try and find Noah a proper home first."

Cherie released a long-suffering sigh and closed the door behind her.

# Chapter Sixteen

Gill really wanted to party with Miss Gina. From the smell of the lemonade she was drinking, it appeared she was already ahead of him.

Wyatt and Luke fixed him up at breakfast, introduced him to more people than Gill thought a small town could hold, then brought him out to Miss Gina's, where he'd spent most of the day pulling boxes out of the bed-and-breakfast's attic.

It appeared that Miss Gina held no concern for putting a complete stranger to work within seconds of meeting him.

"Are we looking for anything in particular?" Luke asked, wiping the grime from his forehead.

"I have a box of old photographs, the kind captured on film and not some camera phone. Felix was asking for old images of this place for Zoe's show."

Apparently Zoe was some sort of famous chef who spent a fair amount of time filming her talents for those television food shows. Not that Gill had ever heard of her, or ever watched the food networks. From all the praise he'd heard since arriving at Miss Gina's, Gill looked forward to sampling the woman's cooking.

"If we're looking for pictures, why have I taken ten boxes out to the back porch?" Wyatt asked.

"Since I have three muscle-bound men at my disposal, I'm going to use you." Miss Gina knelt next to a cardboard box and blew dust off the top before opening the thing. Inside sat a bunch of Christmas decorations. "I forgot all about these. Here, Luke, take this down."

"You're killing me, Miss Gina."

"Zoe would approve." She stood and nudged the box with her foot in Luke's direction.

"Is this what you're looking for?" Wyatt lifted a handful of loose pictures over another box.

Miss Gina wore a long skirt and a long-sleeved shirt that belonged back in 1965. The only thing missing was the flower in her long, gray-streaked hair. "Let me see those."

The woman removed the pictures from Wyatt's hands and filtered through them.

She smiled. "Ah, yes."

Wyatt leaned down, picked up the box he'd removed the pictures from. "So we're done here."

Miss Gina glanced around, removed a blanket from old children's toys. Including a creepy-ass doll that belonged in a horror film.

Gill was happy to see the thing made Wyatt shiver. "What the hell is that?"

Miss Gina didn't answer the question. "Maybe we should bring this stuff down, too. Considering there's a baby on the way."

Wyatt took the blanket from Miss Gina's hand, tossed it over the doll. "No kid of mine is going to have that haunting their dreams."

Miss Gina rolled her eyes. "Wimp."

"Whatever." Wyatt lifted the box. "That shit stays here."

"Grab that box, Gill. I'm sure it has more of these pictures."

"Yes, ma'am."

Miss Gina scowled. "Not sure I like that ma'am stuff. I'm not old."

"Treading on thin ice, Gill," Luke warned as he made his way to the pull-down ladder that brought them up to the attic.

He backed down first, and then stood ready to help Miss Gina.

The woman made some crack about Luke looking up her skirt that had Gill chuckling.

"She's quite the character," he said to Wyatt.

"You haven't seen anything yet."

They left the attic, folded the stairs back up where they belonged, and then lugged the remaining boxes out to the back deck with the others. Miss Gina instructed Gill and Wyatt to take the boxes with decorations to her garage to go through later while she and Luke opened a box full of photographs and spread them out.

"So your wife is pregnant?" Gill asked.

Wyatt grinned. "Yeah, crazy."

"Congratulations."

"Thanks. We're excited. She wanted to keep it quiet for a while, but Jo and Zoe figured it out."

"The women seem tight," Gill said.

"They're like sisters. Look out for each other, give each other crap about everything. It's nice." Wyatt pushed the boxes onto a top shelf above the garden tools in the garage.

"How long have you lived in River Bend?"

"Close to eight years now."

"So you didn't know Jo's dad?"

"Nope. Luke knew him, and Miss Gina, of course."

A Range Rover pulled into the gravel drive, bringing with it Zoe and Mel.

The women climbed out of the car. "We have groceries," Mel announced.

Wyatt moved to her side, kissed her briefly before filling his arms with paper bags. "You've met Gill," Wyatt said.

"Yes we have. Is Jo here?" Zoe asked.

"Nope."

"Good."

Gill knew what was good for Zoe was bad for him. "I know a thing or two about interrogation," he told her, removing the bag from her hands and grabbing the last one from the back of the SUV.

"I'm counting on it."

They followed the women inside. "Should I be concerned?" Gill asked, half joking.

"I'm not sure. Jo hasn't dated since I moved here. I wasn't even sure she had a sex drive until Mel moved to town and I overheard them talking."

*She has the drive*, Gill thought but didn't say.

They walked through the Victorian and set the groceries on the counter in the kitchen before moving to the back door.

Miss Gina sat cross-legged on the ground next to one of the boxes of old photographs, reliving memory lane.

"There were concerts in the park in the center of town," Miss Gina was telling Luke.

"I remember a band in the old gazebo before it fell down."

Miss Gina handed the picture to Wyatt. Gill saw an image of a band wearing flared jeans and tight shirts. "You should build this," Miss Gina said.

Wyatt peered longer at the image. "Is this where the play equipment is in the park?"

"Yep. Some asshole thought a playground was better than a place for live entertainment." The woman obviously didn't agree. "Every backyard in this town has a swing set or a tree large enough for a rope and a tire. Not sure why this didn't get rebuilt."

Mel pushed through the back door, a glass of water in her hand. "Wow, where did you find all these?"

A chorus of male voices said, "The attic."

"Do you remember the gazebo?" Luke asked Mel.

"Vaguely." She looked at the picture.

"Looks like there was quite the crowd," Gill said when the picture made it to his hands.

"Of course. Not a lot happens in this town without a crowd. These outdoor concerts were the best."

He handed her back the photo.

She leaned over, pointed to a couple. "That's Joseph and Debora."

The names didn't register.

Mel moved to Gill's side. "Wow, they were so young."

"This was before you kids were born . . . or right after, I don't remember."

"Who are Joseph and Debora?" Gill asked.

"Jo's parents," Luke informed him.

Gill looked again with renewed interest. The couple weren't large on the image, their faces lacked details. But Jo's mom had her frame and the same color hair. Even in the faded photograph. The second look said that Joseph was wearing tan pants and a belt with a holster. He wasn't wearing a hat, and his shirt wasn't more than a button-up variety that didn't scream cop.

"You knew them both?" Gill asked Miss Gina.

"I've known everyone in this town."

He put that information away for another time.

The screen door creaked as it opened. The familiar sound of work boots and leather sliding alongside flashlights and handcuffs made him smile.

"Look who I found," Zoe said beside Jo.

The woman was beautiful. Even tied up in her uniform and the stress it put on her, he wanted to stare at her all day.

"I see you found Miss Gina's."

"Of course he did," the older woman said. "Had to keep him busy while you play cop."

Gill wasn't sure if the comment bothered Jo or not.

Unlike when they were at the diner, Jo moved close and placed a hand on his arm. "Surviving?" she asked.

"This woman is a slave driver."

"*This woman* is sitting right here!" Miss Gina protested.

"She had us cleaning out her attic," Luke told them, still talking in third person.

For a few minutes they discussed the boxes of crap they'd removed and the disturbing doll that hid under the blanket.

Jo leaned close while the others were talking. "You doing okay?"

He kissed her cheek. "You can make it up to me."

She squeezed his arm.

Apparently public displays of affection were acceptable in this particular group.

Gill rested his arm over her shoulders and took full advantage of the new information.

"So, Luke," Jo addressed her friend. "I think the shop needs a guard dog."

Luke blinked a few times. "Oh, no . . . no it doesn't."

"I think it does."

"I take it you've been to my aunt's house."

Jo sat beside Gill on a porch swing and explained the dog dilemma that had plagued her in Virginia. While it sounded trivial then, it sounded spiteful now. Still, it boiled down to bad politics for a deputy and unneighborly for the town. More than that, it sounded as if Jo was taking on the position of matchmaker for four dogs that needed homes.

"Don't look at me," Miss Gina cut Jo off. "I don't need beefy dogs scaring off my guests."

"We already have a dog," Mel said next.

Zoe held up a hand. "Don't even ask. We leave town too much."

"You leave town, Luke doesn't."

It was Luke's turn to protest again. "I'm considering a shop dog, which I doubt my dad will go for . . . don't press two on me. We've been dodging Aunt Cherie's dogs for years."

Jo conceded. "The puppies are really cute."

"Puppies are always cute . . . then they grow up."

Jo groaned. Then her attention moved to her cell phone, ringing in her pocket.

"This is Jo," she said when she answered.

She stood and moved outside of Gill's reach.

The others kept the dog conversation going while Jo engaged in something completely different. "He what?"

Gill kept his ear tuned into Jo's words.

"Hold off. I'll be there in ten minutes. Don't make any decisions yet. I know. Yes." She hung up the phone and turned back to the group.

"What's up?" Mel asked.

Jo looked directly at Wyatt. "Looks like our distance runner might be taking himself off the team."

"What? How?"

"Some practical joke at school."

"We need him," Wyatt said.

Gill had learned at breakfast that Wyatt was the head coach for the high school track team, with Jo helping in cross-country and distance runners.

"I gotta go," she told them.

Gill stood. "I'm going with you."

"You don't—"

"Strictly professional," he told her. "Remember that case I'm working on?"

"Fine," she said, walking down the back steps instead of walking through the house. "We'll be back for dinner."

"Who says I'm making dinner?" Zoe called out.

"Ha!" Jo's comment was met with laughter.

~

Jo walked through the halls of River Bend High as if she was a parent intercepting her own kid who'd got caught up to no good.

In a way, she was. The kids she mentored on the track team were like her own. Except she wasn't old enough to actually have seventeen-year-old kids. In this case, Drew Emery was not only a forced recruit from his sophomore year who turned into a kid that ran because he liked it, he also happened to be her deputy's son. Which made things tricky.

And she liked the kid. He reminded her a lot of herself at that age. He rode the fence on good and bad, tipping the scales on occasion . . . like today.

Jo left her hat in her car and would have liked to remove her belt, too. But that wasn't going to happen in a high school parking lot. She greeted the staff of the high school by name as she made her way down the hall. Gill kept pace beside her, his face neutral. Here he didn't try to touch her, hold her hand, or God forbid, kiss her. She walked right up to Principal Mason's door and knocked twice. Once summoned, she opened the door to find a younger version of herself sitting on the wrong side of the desk.

Drew took one look at her and sighed.

Richard stood when they entered the office, his eyes drawn to Gill.

Jo made quick work of explaining his presence. "Richard, Agent Clausen works with the FBI. He's shadowing me today."

"Shadowing you?"

She waved him off without a real explanation. "I'll explain later." Drew squirmed under her humorless stare. "Tell me again why I'm standing here?"

Richard encouraged them both to sit. "Looks like Mr. Emery here thought it would be entertaining to make Mrs. Walters think there was a ghost in her classroom."

Mrs. Walters had to be close to retirement by now. The woman taught there when Jo was ditching English instead of showing up for class.

"And how did you manage that?" Jo asked Drew directly.

He exchanged glances with the principal. "I downloaded an app."

Jo considered his words, thought he was talking about some kind of ghost sounds or something that might come from a Halloween store.

"An app."

Drew nodded. "Yeah. For the TV."

Now she was confused. Her face must have shown it.

"Every time Mrs. Walters walked by the TV in the room, I'd turn it on with my remote app on my phone. When she'd move to turn it off, I'd turn it off before her fingers touched the set." The image of the old woman freaking out every time the TV went on had Jo laughing hard on the inside.

Gill cleared his throat and placed a hand over his lips.

Jo was fairly certain it was hiding a grin.

"And how long has this been going on?" Jo kept her voice even.

"Three weeks!" Mason exclaimed. "Betty asked maintenance to check out her TV last month. We switched it out, then she started suggesting that something wasn't normal. She even called out sick three days last week, right around the time of your midterms, I believe. Said her room was haunted and she didn't feel safe coming to work."

Jo felt her nose flare, a training technique to keep the emotion from showing on her face. It was a good thing Drew wasn't smiling or she'd probably lose it. The image of Betty Walters running scared from her classroom because of TV-possessing ghosts gave Jo a strange case of pride for the kid in trouble.

To drive his point home, Richard pointed two fingers at Drew. "Mrs. Walters isn't a young woman. This kind of stress can have serious health consequences."

"I didn't think of that." Drew looked down, and that's when Jo noticed the edges of his lips pull into a slight grin.

"Okay." Jo ground her back teeth together to keep from laughing. "Drew, I need you to step outside so Mr. Mason and I can figure out how this is going to affect your track season."

The moment Drew closed the door behind him, Jo's hand flew to her mouth to keep the noise inside. One look at Gill, who sat there silently laughing, and Jo's eyes started to water.

"Don't you dare let him hear you!" Richard said, his own eyes dancing with mirth.

"That's freakin' funny," Jo said.

Mr. Mason's chest shuddered. "Betty was hysterical. I thought the woman was going to have a stroke."

"The prank wouldn't have worked with a younger teacher," Gill said from the sideline.

"Good point."

Jo leaned forward, kept her voice low. "All right. No one was hurt, no property damage."

"The kid shows tech skills that he needs to funnel into something productive," Richard added.

"You can't suspend him from his track season for this. Not only is he good, but he needs the discipline. Imagine what he'll come up with when coupled with idle time."

"I know. Still can't let him go off without some punishment."

"Mowing Betty's lawn every Sunday for the next two months? Pulling some community service for the upcoming reunion?" Jo tossed ideas out there.

"I'll come up with something, Jo. But make sure he knows he skated through this one so he won't try anything else."

She stood, shook his hand. "I will."

Mason looked at Gill. "So you're with the FBI?"

Gill shook Mason's hand with a nod. "I am. Currently working on a case in Eugene where the high schools are getting inundated with heroin use."

Mason's jaw dropped. "You're kidding."

"I wish I was."

"Phew . . . doesn't that put this in perspective?"

Gill grinned. "Sure does. I take it you don't have that going on here."

Mason exchanged glances with Jo. "We always have the occasional cannabis running around. Liquor. Nothing close to heroin."

"Then your problems all have solutions," Gill said. "I wouldn't mind looking around when I'm in town, seeing the teenage dynamics. It might help with my investigation closer to where I live."

Mason nodded like an animated toy. "Of course. Anything to help keep kids off that kind of crap."

With that figured out, the three of them walked to the door, put on straight faces, and made a united front when faced with Drew.

Ten minutes later, in her squad car with only Gill as her witness, Jo let loose the laughter bubbling inside until Gill caught on and they were both grabbing their stomachs.

# Chapter Seventeen

Jo had two very different personalities, three if he was counting properly. She let her guard down around her friends, but even then she wasn't the exact person he'd met on the East Coast.

The whole person slowly came into focus.

They'd returned from the high school after giving poor Drew the riot act on what he should and shouldn't do. Gill was convinced that the kid knew their number. He knew they were all secretly laughing along with him and it was only a matter of years before they'd laugh about the whole thing over drinks.

There were a couple more hours at the station, along with a drive through town and the city limits. When the clock was officially off, he and Jo returned to Miss Gina's, where Gill had a culinary experience he'd never matched before.

He had no idea who Zoe Brown was, but he had every intention of looking her up when he was back home.

The woman could cook.

Miss Gina managed to bring out a few photographs of all three of the girls when they were tweens in lanky bodies and identical haircuts.

He liked them. The whole lot.

They were a strange kind of family that didn't share blood. For some reason that made it even sweeter.

He followed Jo into her home and watched her routine as she walked through the house, shedding her uniform, and with it the personality she'd adopted because of it.

Gill watched her from the doorway of her bedroom. Her bed was made, but without a lot of fluff. No massive stack of pillows for Jo to have to deal with every day. There was a book on her bedside table, one he couldn't see the title of from where he was sitting. He'd have to check it out before he left. There was a lot to be learned about a person by their reading material.

"You've seen every end of River Bend twice," Jo said from the adjoining bathroom. "What did you think?"

What did he think? "I'm actually kinda surprised it's survived the last decade's failing economy."

Jo pulled the band from her hair, letting it fall on her shoulders. "We've actually grown. And with the new homes going in between here and Waterville, we've had a larger demand on commerce and traffic. The business owners love it." She looked at him through the mirror as she pulled a brush through her hair.

"If the town grows, won't your budget afford another full-time deputy?"

"There is already talk of another part-timer."

"So it's you and Deputy Emery?"

She nodded as she left the bathroom, sat on the edge of her bed, and unlaced her shoes. "Yep. Deputy Fitzpatrick helps out part-time, comes in full-time whenever Emery or I take time off."

"Both these men worked with your dad?"

"Yeah."

"Did one of them want your job?"

She toed off one shoe, started on the next. "I think Karl did. He took over for a while after my dad, but the town wasn't excited to push him on to being the town sheriff. They weren't happy to elect someone they didn't know either."

Gill moved to the bed and sat beside her as she shed her shoes. "So who was sheriff between you and your dad?"

"Karl stepped in as interim, but overseen by the Waterville department."

"Then you graduated from the academy and the town elected you."

"In a nutshell, but it wasn't that easy. I had some serious groveling to do while I got my feet wet in Waterville."

Gill leaned back on his elbows and watched as her mind worked through the details for him. "Groveling?"

"I wasn't the poster child for propriety growing up. I skated the line every time I found the damn thing and crossed over it whenever no one was looking."

The woman was too hard on herself. "You were a teenager."

"I was rebellious and bucked everything."

"Did you graduate from River Bend High?" He already knew the answer to that but wanted to make a point.

"Skated through."

"Did you go to jail?"

"My dad put me in a cell once to prove a point."

"But were you arrested?"

She lowered her head. "No."

"Did you do drugs? Spend every weekend wasted?"

"I was forced onto the track team, or that's how it would have worked out. We found our share of liquor."

Gill reached for her hand and made her look at him. "At seventeen I was arrested for assault. Bloodied the nose of a kid hitting on my high school girlfriend."

Jo tilted her head. "Well—"

"Drunk in public at twenty-one," he continued to list his crimes. "Should have been nailed for drunk driving at twenty-two. Back roads of my hometown, it was late, but that isn't an excuse. Joined the marines and spent the next four years eating sand and praying for rain."

Jo linked her fingers with his, watched his face while he spoke. "How did the FBI come in?"

"I trained in intelligence and investigation when I wasn't armed in the service. Took two years on the other side of the service to earn my degree, and the FBI was right there asking me to work with them."

She smiled. "Sounds like you figured your shit out."

"So did you. We're not a whole lot different." He stroked the side of her arm, enjoyed the softness of her skin.

"You ended up with the better job."

"I *picked* a different job. You can always pick something different, too. Nothing is stopping you."

She looked like she was about to argue, then changed her mind. "You know," she said as she trailed her free hand down his chest, "I've been talking about River Bend, my job, and my life for hours when all I really want to do is help you take this off."

The look in her eyes meant trouble. The kind he liked to see. Gill lifted both his hands above his head and lay back on the bed. "Do what you have to do."

Jo climbed over him, straddled his hips with her thighs, and ran both hands over his chest.

Everything south of his belt line heated. Breath caught in his throat when Jo dug the tiny bits of her fingernails into his skin. She bent over, brushing her breasts against his chest, and brought her lips to his.

Then someone pounded on her front door.

She stopped all movement and waited.

"Jo?"

The voice was male, not one Gill recognized.

"I know you're home. We have to talk."

Jo blew out a breath, rested her head on Gill's shoulder for a brief second before pushing away.

"Who is it?"

"Karl Emery."

"Your deputy."

"My deputy."

Gill placed both hands on Jo's slim hips and plucked her off his frame.

"Jo!" More pounding.

"Persistent, isn't he?"

She grabbed a rubber band off her dresser and tossed her hair up into a ponytail before meeting the noise beyond her front door.

~

This was ridiculous. It was as if the town had a radar on her life and knew when she was trying to find some kind of balance.

She opened the door with enough strength to show she wasn't happy for the late call. Karl was dressed casually, with his gun belt around his hip. He was on duty this time at night, but it wasn't as if he needed to patrol River Bend, just take care of any calls that might come in and call her only when he needed backup. Which didn't happen very often.

"I hope this is important," she stated after opening the door.

"You were in the principal's office with Drew today."

So this was personal. "Yes, I was. As his coach."

"Why wasn't I called?"

Jo felt Gill walking up behind her.

"I assumed Richard called you."

"He didn't. You should have."

Karl took that moment to notice Gill standing behind her. Karl's eyes flared and then narrowed.

Jo stood back, giving him room to enter her house. "Let's take this away from the neighbors," she told him.

Once inside, she lifted both palms to the men. "Karl, this is Gill, my friend. Gill, this is my deputy, Karl."

Gill extended his hand, and for a moment it didn't appear that Karl was going to shake it. When he did, it was brief and no words were exchanged.

"I shouldn't hear from my son's girlfriend's father that my kid was nearly suspended today."

"It wasn't that bad," Jo protested. She took a moment to give him the short version of what went down. Not that it appeased the man.

"When a cop is called on my kid, I need to know about it!" Karl wasn't letting it go.

"Coach. I was there as his coach. Richard wanted me to drill home to Drew that if he continued doing this kind of thing, he would be kicked off the team. I thought for sure he'd call you and Caroline to discuss the situation."

"Well, he didn't."

"Then you need to be on his door, not mine." Jo looked the man directly in the eye and didn't back down.

"I guess you've been too busy today to bother dropping over one block to let me know what happened." His eyes lingered on Gill.

Her teeth ground together, his implications clear. "Yes, Karl. I was a little busy today. Trying to find new homes for dogs and patching city streets and getting out squad cars scheduled for maintenance. It has been a busy day."

"Not that the sheriff needs to justify her day to you, *Deputy*." Gill expressed her thoughts in a deep voice that made Karl turn his twisted ego on the other man in the room.

Karl leaned forward. "I'm here as a *citizen* of this city asking the *sheriff* why I wasn't notified of her presence in a situation regarding *my* son." Jo could cut the bitterness with a knife.

"Your beef is with Richard, not me."

"I work with you."

She conceded. "And had I seen you, it would have come up." She needed to decompress the situation. Working with the man wasn't optional, it was mandatory. "I'll stop by tomorrow and talk with both you and Caroline about the whole thing. It really wasn't that big of a deal, but Drew knows he messed up."

Karl's breaths slowed down. "You should have called me."

"Your point is taken, Karl. Now if you don't mind, it's been a busy day." She reached behind him and opened the door.

He left without a backward glance.

She closed the door and leaned her forehead against it.

Gill came up behind her and slid his arms around her waist to gather her close.

"I am so done."

He kissed the space between her shoulder and her neck and whispered in her ear. "I know, sweetheart. Come on. Let me help you forget about all this for a few hours."

Jo reached around and held his arms close before turning her head toward his. "A few hours?" she teased.

"I'll do my best."

He lifted her in his arms and walked them back into her bedroom.

# Chapter Eighteen

Gill moaned when Jo woke at the ass crack of dawn and put on her running shoes.

"You can come with me."

He reached for her, pulled her completely clothed body on top of him. "I'd rather bench press you."

She gave his bicep a love bite. "The only bench press we have is at the high school, and even then, I doubt it would be much of a challenge for these."

When she pushed away, he released her. "I'll find a Harley to swing around."

"Like the one you drove here?"

"I'd probably drop it." He wouldn't. It was his most prized possession. The small house he'd bought in Eugene could go up in flames, but his bike . . . now that was another story.

"Today is a wash and repeat from yesterday."

He was starting to see her frustration. "With less drama, I hope."

"That would be nice."

He leaned up on one arm, watched her gather her keys and a windbreaker. "You know I've been going over your father's files."

Jo met his gaze. "I know. I assumed you hadn't come to any conclusions or you would have told me."

"I haven't. But I'd like to see the cabin. Mind if I go up there today while you're working?"

Indecision swam in her eyes. "I don't go up there."

"You don't have to go with me. Miss Gina said she knew where it was."

Her half smile had an edge of vulnerability.

"There's a swing on the porch, to the right of it is a statue of a dog. The key is hidden under the dog."

He had to laugh. "Where everyone would know to look."

She smiled. "Yeah. My dad wouldn't say no to someone needing to use it anyway."

Gill swung his legs out of bed, walked his naked body next to hers.

Jo's lingering gaze made him stand a little taller. She didn't hide her appreciation of his body and wasn't shy with her own.

"I'll see you this afternoon."

He kissed her briefly.

"Don't expect dinner on the table," she said.

"I saw frozen pizza. We won't starve."

She unclipped a set of keys from her keychain. "For my Jeep. The roads up there aren't maintained, and the recent rain might be difficult on your bike."

"I don't think Miss Gina would appreciate the Harley."

Jo barked a laugh. "Miss Gina would give her right boob for your bike. Problem is, she would be propositioning you for that and more after an hour on it."

Gill blinked a few times, then squeezed his eyes shut to remove the image of Miss Gina getting turned on by his Harley. "Bad image," he moaned.

176

"She's harmless." Jo kissed him again and slapped his bare ass. "I'll see you later."

~

The road was a mess.

Miss Gina held on and didn't complain once. In fact, she grinned the whole time they were on the road.

"I haven't been up here in years. Too bad, too. Sure is beautiful."

Gill's eyes were on the holes, ruts, and rocks that had slid down to make the path to the Ward hunting cabin nearly impassable.

"Jo said she doesn't come up here."

"She doesn't. After Joseph's death, once we had it all cleaned up, she did. And a few times once she became our sheriff." Miss Gina looked out the window. "Too many memories for her."

"Her dad dying up here can't help."

"See those trees?" She pointed to a patch of maples. "Turn right."

Gill slowed down. "Is this a road?"

"More or less."

More like less. Gill turned right, managed to get through a thicket of trees and then out into an open field of green and wildflowers. Jo's Jeep laughed at the excuse of a driveway as they inched closer to the lone house that overlooked the small thicket below.

Gill stopped the car at the base of the stairs and looked through the window. "Wow."

"It's a man's cabin. Off the grid one hundred percent," Miss Gina told him. She swung the door open before he managed to turn off the engine. Outside, the woman lifted both arms to the open air as if sucking it in. "I could use a joint," she said, tossing her head back.

Gill couldn't help but laugh. "The sixties were good to you?"

"The best days ever." She opened one eye to regard him. "No joint?"

"Fresh out," he told her.

"Shit. Okay." Her arms fell to her sides and she took the steps one at a time.

The log cabin was made from real logs and not some facade that mimicked the real thing. From the outside, it looked like the entire place was less than six hundred square feet. The outside had a small deck, one that ran the length of the home, with a two-person swing that filled the majority of the porch. Gill found the faded statue Jo had told him about and then the key.

Miss Gina leaned on the rail and looked below. "I keep waiting for Jo to have an easier time with her father's death to ask if I can get up here once in a while."

"She'd probably be okay with it." From what Gill had learned about the woman, she wasn't attached to the place but couldn't bear to part with it either.

"Not until she finds her father's killer. Then she'll be ready."

Gill hesitated before twisting the key in the lock. "She told you her theory about her dad?"

Miss Gina shook her head. "No. I know she's mentioned it to Mel and Zoe. Not a word to me."

"It could have been an accident," he said.

The humor faded from Miss Gina's face. "Joseph Ward was murdered."

"How can you be sure?"

"Same way Jo is so sure. The man was meticulous about his weapons, anal about how he cared for them. Borderline OCD when it came to that stuff. Him accidentally shooting himself would be like me accidentally lighting my inn on fire with a blowtorch and gasoline."

"If you were so sure, why not make people listen back when he died?"

Miss Gina looked at him like he was a little short on brain cells. "Look at me."

She wore loose pants, a top that hid her aging belly, and that same long, gray-streaked hair blew in the breeze. She looked like a woman who never left the sixties. "Half this town thinks I'm a little crazy. The kids in this town have always used my place as a safe haven when they had nowhere to go. Put those things together and then have me crying foul when Sheriff Ward ended up with a hole in his head, and something tells me I'd find myself in all kinds of trouble. Besides, I did smoke pot back then. And it wasn't legal."

"Not every questionable character is a bad reference."

"If an agency had come around, asked the right questions, I would have made sure they knew my feelings. But they didn't. And when Jo returned and took over for her dad, I knew she was looking. I figured it was only a matter of time before she found something."

"Only she hasn't found anything."

"That's cuz she's too close. There are things about her father she doesn't know and might not be receptive to hear if they came out."

Gill stared at Miss Gina. "What kinds of things?"

She smirked. "I'll tell you, but I'd like to see just how good of an FBI agent you are, Mr. McHottie."

He laughed. "McHottie?"

"That's what the girls call you." She swept his frame with a smile.

He was more than a little creeped out.

"I'm going inside," he said, twisting the door handle.

Miss Gina laughed.

~

Jo glanced at her watch. They'd be up at the cabin by now. Walking on the memories of her father's life. She should be there, with them.

The place tore her up. Letting Gill see her like that would open her in a way she wasn't ready for. No, it was best he was there without her bias, the one thing she couldn't remove from her sideline investigation into her father's death.

While Gill and Miss Gina climbed the mountain, Jo drove the short street over and one block down to speak with Karl and Caroline while Drew was in school.

She should have called Karl the second she left the school. If it were her son, she'd have asked for the same courtesy. Having Gill in town was a distraction, proven by her lack of thought. Even if Karl was continually making her job harder, Drew was his son, and he had the right to be pissed at her actions.

Jo knocked on the Emerys' door, stood back, and waited.

Caroline answered. In her midfifties, she could have passed for her early forties. She had the gift of good genes and an organic diet, according to the things Glynis had told Jo over the years. At five foot five the woman didn't have the history of walking a runway of *America's Next Top Model*, but she was known to turn heads. Unlike Karl, Caroline had a kind face that the people in town loved and respected. Not that the town didn't respect Karl . . . but in his case, they had no choice but to.

"Hi, Caroline," Jo said when the woman answered the door.

Her sheepish smile and quick study of the ground told Jo her presence there made Caroline uncomfortable. "Hi, Jo."

"Is Karl here? I'd like to talk with you both about what happened yesterday."

"C'mon in."

Jo followed her into the house, her belt making noise as she walked.

Caroline yelled Karl's name before turning to her. "I'm sorry Karl bothered you last night. I told him it could wait, that if anything terrible had happened you would have come to us right away."

"Thank you for that, Caroline, but I should have come to you anyway."

"Damn right." Karl stood behind her, leaning against the door frame leading into the family room.

"Karl!" Caroline's voice held a friendly warning.

"Can we sit down?" Jo asked.

"Of course." Caroline switched into hostess mode, asked if Jo wanted something to drink, sat when she declined.

"I need to apologize," Jo started, staring directly at her deputy.

He waited.

"I'm sorry. I should have called you when I left the school."

Karl stared.

Jo kept the conversation going. She explained what Richard had told her, what Drew confirmed. ". . . outside of Betty believing there are ghosts at the high school, there really wasn't any harm done. Mason pointed out that Betty isn't in the best of health, and that was the concern that should have been thought of."

Caroline tilted her head to the side and placed her hand over Karl's. "It's not a big deal."

Karl and she exchanged glances, and some of the edge over his features softened. "That was for us to decide."

The man wasn't letting Jo off the hook. "It won't happen again," she assured him.

He conceded with a nod and Jo left without another word.

~

Running Lob Hill sucked ass. Drew's dad wasn't talking to him, and Coach Ward drilled him hard with extra laps and zero sense of humor.

Drew knew the sheriff had been hiding a smirk at least once during the confrontation in Principal Mason's office the day before, but today it was narrow lines on her face and attitude. You'd think he'd been found getting stoned in the gym bathroom.

He hated River Bend more every day. How his parents had landed in such a small town and stayed there wasn't something Drew could find a logical reason for. Maybe if his dad was together enough to have been elected sheriff, his desire to live there would make sense. But his dad wasn't the sheriff, he was the deputy. And hell, his dad could be a deputy anywhere.

Drew pushed through the remaining three hundred meters of the Lob Hill climb, tagged the tree that had been touched by hundreds of teenage hands in the past, and made his way back to the school. His thoughts shifted to the weekend. A weekend free of a track meet, which meant he could party. He could really use a break. Adults weren't the only ones to have stress. Between school, track, his parents, Tina being entirely too hard to get, and constantly having the question "What's going to be your major in college?" thrown out at him . . . Drew was a walking nerve. The only stress relief was rigging the TV in Mrs. Walters's room. That shit had made him this side of famous for the senior class at school. The CIA should be hooking him up, he decided.

Drew slowed his pace as he ended the hill run and found Coach Gibson.

He rested his hands on his knees to catch his breath. "I'm done," Drew told his coach.

Coach Gibson stood with his arms crossed over his chest, his eye following the sprinters as they ran their drills. "Coach Ward has you running that hill for the next week."

Drew rolled his eyes. "I know." And mowing lawns. Good thing Mrs. Walters liked her flower garden, so the lawn he needed to mow this weekend wasn't that big.

From the corner of Coach Gibson's mouth he heard, "So that app you used to turn on the TV . . . what was that?"

Drew took a moment for the question to register. "Uhm, there are a few of them. Depends on your phone. I used Gizmode."

Coach Gibson's head nodded a couple of times. "On the app store?" he asked.

"Yeah."

"Good to know." The coach glanced at the stopwatch in his hands and walked away without more questions.

# Chapter Nineteen

Nerves swam like a school of fish chasing the leader in circles. Jo left the station early, made sure Glynis had the calls forwarded to her for the night.

Gill had dropped Miss Gina off and pulled in the driveway shortly after Jo.

Jo grilled, she didn't cook. Outside of a couple of steaks and some vegetables she could toss on the barbeque, they'd have to do without. Doing the whole domestic thing was like trying to wear two left shoes. Uncomfortable.

"I have beer, water, or milk," Jo announced once Gill had returned from her backyard, where he had heated up the grill.

"Milk is for breakfast."

Jo handed him a beer, twisted the cap off of one for herself.

"Your dad's cabin is every hunter's dream."

"Are you a hunter?" she asked, wanting to get the pleasantries of his trip out of the way so she could determine what he'd learned.

"No. From what I saw, your dad didn't dedicate all his time up there to searching for venison."

"He'd bring back a deer once in a while. It wasn't a big priority for him. The cabin was more a place to get away without going too far."

"Because he was married to his work." Gill's statement made her pause.

"After my mom, yeah."

Jo seasoned the steaks while they spoke.

"Does everyone in town know about the cabin?"

She nodded.

"Even the kids?"

"Not sure about those that have grown into their teenage years since his death, but yeah. Growing up, everyone I hung out with knew about the place. I wouldn't be surprised if it was used by kids hooking up."

Gill looked at her over the neck of his beer. "But not you?"

Jo's skin crawled. "That place was always my dad's. The idea of getting naked there with a boyfriend was about as appealing as having sex at the station."

She lifted the platter with the food and encouraged Gill to follow her outside. Once there, Gill took the food from her and proceeded to take over the cooking detail.

Jo let him.

"On the report from your dad's file, it listed more than a dozen names of men he'd been known to go up to the cabin with to hunt."

"My guess is the list is short. Just about everyone with a shotgun went up there with my dad at one time or another. There were a few regulars, which is what the list is referring to."

"His death was ruled accidental from the start."

She nodded. "I made a stink, and because he was the sheriff, they made a second pass at the cabin, but by then there had been so many hands and eyes going through the place the prints they found were all accounted for."

"Was your father a clean freak?"

"Define freak."

"Everything has its place, spit shine and polish everything after it's used?"

"He was neat," Jo said. "Bleach clean . . . no. Not completely. He hated clutter but wasn't big on using the vacuum obsessively."

Gill flipped the steaks, lowered the flame on the gas grill. "That weekend he was up there alone, no visitors?"

"I was living in Waterville at the time. But that's what Karl gave in his report. He'd asked Luke's father to join him, but the garage was unusually busy, probably because of the class reunion."

Gill tilted his beer back and then asked, "Class reunion?"

"Yeah, every year, within a couple weeks of my father's death, there is a River Bend High class reunion. The ten-year reunions are always at the school gym."

"What about a twenty-year, or thirty-year?"

Jo shook her head. "The school makes the effort for ten years, it's up to the alumni to manage anything beyond that."

"Was there a twenty that year?"

Jo scratched her head. "I'm not sure. I'll have to ask."

"Miss Gina didn't know of a back way in and out from the cabin, do you know of any?"

Jo shook her head.

Gill shuffled the veggies on the grill a few times, kept his eye on their steaks. "At face value, I would have to agree with the original investigation, Jo."

Her nose flared. "Face value?"

"Yeah. But there is something that bugs me about the whole thing."

That, she wanted to hear. "Which is?"

"It was too easy."

"What do you mean?"

"Everyone knew when your father took time off, right?"

"Right."

"And most knew exactly where he was going to go during his time off."

"Yep."

"So if your father had an enemy, they'd know where to find him alone and have an easy explanation for his death unless there was a struggle."

Jo didn't like the sound of it, but yes.

"There wasn't a struggle," Gill said as he removed their dinner from the grill.

"Which means the person who murdered him knew him." Jo had already come up with that conclusion. "My dad didn't have enemies."

Gill gave her a sideways glance. "Everyone has enemies."

A lack of outside furniture moved them both inside, where they dished up their food and sat at the small kitchen table. "Ask around town, Gill. Everyone loved my dad. Pillar of the community, respected."

Gill cut into his steak, pointed a piece of meat at her with his fork. "If you believe he was murdered, he must have had an enemy."

"I haven't figured out who that is," she said.

"Someone familiar with that cabin. Someone he trusted completely."

"That would be just about everyone. Sure, there are a few people in town that stepped out of line over the years that needed my dad to reel them in. Zoe's father was one of them, but he was in jail at the time of my dad's death, and he wouldn't have trusted Ziggy with a second of his time."

Gill paused, started to laugh. "Zoe's father's name was Ziggy?"

Jo waved him off. "Long story."

He spoke around his food. "What about Zoe's mom, was she upset about her husband's arrest?"

"The arrest happened long before my dad died. From what Zoe tells me, right after Ziggy went to jail, her family finally relaxed and learned to smile once in a while. The man was a real dirtbag," Jo informed him.

She took the first bite of her steak, hardly realizing that she wasn't eating. "You grill a good steak."

"Meat is my only cooking talent."

"Great, mine, too. Malnourishment might be in our futures."

That didn't stop him from putting more in his mouth.

"I'll continue looking, Jo. I'm not sure I'll find anything."

The fact that he looked was enough for her. "Thank you."

Gill's cell phone rang in his back pocket. He swallowed his food with a swig from his bottle and answered. "Hey, Shauna."

Jo listened to the one-way conversation between Agent Burton and Gill, watched Gill's body language. His smile moved to a frown, his brows pinched together, and he looked at his watch.

"When is this starting?" he asked.

Jo took another bite.

Gill pushed back from the table.

"I'll be there."

The steak in Jo's throat went cold. As would Gill's dinner, if she wasn't mistaken.

He released a sigh as he placed his phone in his back pocket. "I have to go."

"I thought as much. What's going on?"

"The kids we've had our eye on have organized a rave-style party."

"So you're crashing a rave."

He laughed, looked down at his broad chest. "I don't blend, JoAnne. But surveillance will give us something, with any luck."

Jo followed him into her bedroom, where he gathered the small bag he'd brought with him holding a change of clothes and a toothbrush.

"I'm sorry I have to rush out."

"Don't be. I completely understand." Even if she was a little disappointed she wouldn't be cuddling with the man that night.

Gill wrapped his arm around her waist and pulled her close. "I'm going to miss you."

"You're a distraction," she told him, not committing to the *missing him* words.

He kissed her with a smile, warmed into the kiss before letting her go. "Okay, going now."

She walked him to her garage, opened the door so he could pull his bike out. "Be safe."

He pulled his helmet over his head, tucked his fingers into riding gloves, and kicked the bike over. With a wink, he backed out of her driveway and waved as he drove away.

She watched until his bike disappeared completely, waited another minute before the noise of the Harley faded. When she turned to go back inside, her skin prickled, and she twisted around. None of her neighbors had stepped outside, but she was fairly certain someone watched.

~

Mel had roped Jo into doing some crafty crap for the upcoming reunion all day Monday, and then Zoe came over to add her ideas . . . then there were cocktails, as in more than two, which was rare for Jo when in town. Mondays were routinely her day off, and since she'd met Gill, she was reminded to have a life of her own. If he could escape his duty with the FBI, she certainly could manage a day without carrying her gun or wearing her uniform at all.

By Wednesday she was into her routine, her morning run over, the afternoon planned, which included a trip into Waterville with her squad car for the recall. Something about brake failure after fifty thousand miles. There had been enough cars in their fleet to warrant a recall for officer safety. Fitzpatrick was on call, and Emery was at the helm.

All her plans went to hell with one frantic phone call.

"Someone stole her. My Jezebel. Oh, my God. You have to find her."

Cherie was borderline hysterical.

The call came in as Jo was passing R&B's. She hit the brakes, which were not yet faulty, to take the call. "Cherie, calm down. Start from the beginning."

"Someone stole her, Jo. I let Jezebel outside to do her thing. She's never long. I leave the back door open for her. She's gone. Gone!" Cherie spoke in short bits and spurts. "The puppies are barking. She never ignores her babies."

"How long has she been gone?"

"Half an hour."

Jo checked the time. Chances were the dog chased a squirrel or some such animal and ended up on the other side of the fence. In light of the dog issues, she couldn't leave without checking around the neighborhood.

"Keep looking for her, I'm on my way over."

By the time Jo arrived at Cherie's home, which was on the other end of town, the timeline of the dog's disappearance ran on forty-five minutes.

From inside the house, Jo heard a couple of the dogs barking at the excitement. She walked around the back instead of knocking on the door. Cherie kept her fence secure; the automatic closing arm and heavy spring couldn't be manipulated by the dogs.

Cherie was at the far end of the yard, calling the dog's name.

Making sure the gate was closed behind her, Jo walked along the fence toward Cherie, looking for places the dog could have escaped.

The woman was close to tears. "This isn't like her. Even before the puppies, she wasn't the one to run off."

Jo placed a hand on Cherie's shoulder. "We'll find her."

They walked the fence together. Toward the south corner of the yard, a second gate gave access to the field beyond. The latch was secure. "How often do you use this gate?" Jo asked.

"Daily. I take the dogs on walks out in the woods to avoid my neighbors."

A path ran from the gate to a patch of trees. "Have you checked out there?"

"To the tree line. I didn't want to leave the puppies or miss it if she came back."

"She'll come back," Jo assured her.

"This isn't like her at all. I know my dogs. This is her second litter, and she's a very good mom. Cried when I found homes for her last puppies."

Jo didn't care for the sound of that. "Do any of the dogs wander off to a neighbor's?"

"The neighbors who called Deputy Emery on me? No."

Those same neighbors had called Jo, but she wasn't about to tell her that.

Jo opened the back gate. "You stay here in case she shows up. I'll search the woods."

"Okay." Cherie reached into the pocket of the windbreaker she was wearing. "Here, a treat for her."

Jo took the dog food and put it in the front pocket of her pants.

It was spring in Oregon, which called for cloudy skies and misty weather most days. This one had a breeze that bordered on brisk. Under the cover of the pine trees, it was downright cold.

Jo walked through an obvious trail, calling the dog's name. Twenty minutes down the trail, Jo doubled back without luck.

Cherie was on her back porch, the alpha at her side.

"I called my brother."

"Good. I'll drive around."

Cherie wiped a tear from her eyes. "I need to feed her babies."

Which meant bottles for the puppies and hours of time and effort. It was in the middle of the school day or Jo would solicit some of her runners to help.

"You take care of the puppies, I'll find their mom. Dogs don't just disappear."

Only Cherie didn't look convinced.

~

Drew walked behind Tina, her ass keeping the attention of his eyes and the hardness in his dick. Not that he needed a visual for that. He was seventeen, the damn thing had a mind of its own.

He placed both hands on her hips in a playful tickle.

She laughed and skirted out of his reach in a playful way.

He took the action as a positive sign.

"We're supposed to be looking for a dog."

The entire distance team was asked to run in different parts of town, in pairs. They could train and try to find a missing dog.

Drew actually liked dogs, and the searching in pairs thing was a complete win when Tina was playing nice.

"We are looking for a dog." Drew blew a whistle. "We're also sup-posed to be running."

"Yeah, well . . ."

Tina sat on the fence of rebellion. With a little work, the girl could be a perfect mix of naughty and sweet. But the naughty part also gave her an edge that sometimes turned on him in a negative way. She was one of the prettiest girls in school and she had a decent rack. And Drew liked boobs.

Thinking about those boobs had him shuffling his legs in an effort to not embarrass himself with a raging hard-on.

They were a good two miles deep in the woods, the backyard he'd grown up in and an open space between the dog lady's property and his parents'. Everything connected eventually, but this part of the open space that surrounded River Bend happened to be the center of Drew's childhood. Tina lived on the other side of town, where the houses were a little bigger and the people had a little more money than the rest of them.

Tina whistled. "Here, doggie."

"Bet the thing is on the road to Waterville," Drew said.

"Yeah. Probably. But Coach Ward doesn't ask us to do this kind of thing very often."

Girls liked guys who liked animals. "It's probably scared." He dipped his voice, pretended he really cared.

Tina gave him a coy little smile. A grin that told him he was working it.

"Maybe we should split up," Tina suggested.

"That's not a good idea. It's easy to get lost out here."

Tina stopped, looked around. She pointed behind them. "That's the way back to your house."

Drew moved beside her, captured her hand, and moved it a foot. "More like over there."

"Oh."

When she dropped her hand, he kept a hold of it. Before too long, Tina laced her fingers with his.

Holding hands was nice, but what he really wanted to do was make out, maybe get a little further.

They walked a few more feet, neither one of them acknowledging their hand holding outside of a smile.

"Prom's coming up," Drew said.

Tina squeezed his hand. Her voice trembled a little when she spoke. "I know."

"Looks like it will be fun."

He noticed the color rise to Tina's cheeks, the sparkle of hope in her eye. "It does."

"It could be lame, too."

She frowned.

"Prom can't be lame."

"Oh, I don't know. It would be lame if you didn't go. Sitting at home on prom night when everyone else is dressed up and having fun."

Tina narrowed her eyes. "You can always go to prom, even without a date."

"Who said anything about a date?"

She was frowning now.

Drew kept a straight face, turned away, and whistled for the dog.

As if reminded about their task, Tina called for "doggie" again.

A few more feet and still holding hands, Drew tested the waters. "Do you have a date for prom?"

Tina shook her head. "No, do you?"

"No."

That seemed to make her happy.

He waited a few steps, then asked, "If I asked you to prom, would you say yes?"

She stopped. "If you asked me?"

Drew stepped in front of her, looked down. "Yeah, *if* I asked you."

"*If* you asked me, I *might* say yes. Depends."

"Depends on what?"

"How you asked me."

"How?"

Tina shrugged. "Yeah, like will you ask me with flowers? Or will you put a sign in the school gym asking me? Make a big fuss during a track meet? You know, *how* you ask."

Drew cussed all the guys before him that had started the traditions of grand gestures to ask a girl to prom. "You know all the guys who do that already know the girl is going to say yes, right?" He made that up but hoped he'd said it in a convincing enough way that Tina would believe him.

"Really?"

He turned, her hand still in his, and kept walking. "You can't tell your girlfriends this. It's part of the guy code."

"Oh."

"Yeah. So the guys who do all those crazy things wouldn't do it if a girl is going to turn them down. When was the last time you saw that?"

Tina mused that over for a moment. "Never."

"See."

"Hmm." She walked, obviously weighing the truth in his words. "Ask me," she finally said.

Drew smiled. "Okay, I will."

She stopped. "No. Ask me now."

He took both her hands in his. He'd seen that in a late movie once. "Tina, will you go to prom with me?"

Straight teeth flashed. "I'd love to go to prom with you."

Drew licked his lips and made his move.

They'd made out before, at the beginning of the school year, but somewhere along the line Tina freaked out and stopped wanting to be with him.

They were both a little older. Six months in high school made a difference, at least in his head. He wasn't sure if Tina had been practicing on her pillow or watching some kind of porn on her phone, but her kissing had improved.

He was raging within seconds of their tongues touching, but he kept his cool and let her get used to him being in her personal space.

Tina wrapped her arms around his back and he had no choice but to move closer. The contact of his boner touching her stomach used to make her jump. Not now.

He wondered why, but then she pulled back for air and kissed him harder.

Tina had definitely changed. When he ran his hand up her back and touched the side of one of her boobs, she didn't stop him.

This was worth a trip to prom.

Drew took it further, a full palm with a full boob. His hard-on screamed.

It wasn't until he reached for the edges of her shirt and lifted it up that he felt Tina hesitate.

He backed off. Disappointed but hopeful. "Too much?" he asked.

"A little." Her sheepish smile was a little adorable.

"Can we still make out?"

She nodded and lifted her lips to his.

Drew backed her up to a tree, like he'd seen in that movie.

Tina seemed to like it.

He went back where he was, kissing her, one hand on one boob until he felt her nipple under the fabric tighten. Then he moved to the other.

Tina kept her hand on his back until he pushed one down over his ass. At first she just let it sit there, and then she squeezed.

He thought he was going to come, right there in the woods, completely clothed. He stopped kissing her.

"What's wrong?" she asked.

"Nothing." He saw stars. "This is really good."

When his hips pushed her into the tree, the light in her head must have turned on.

"Oh."

"Yeah. Sorry. I can't help it."

His words must have relaxed her. "I know. It's okay."

There she was, looking all adorable at him. "We should probably stop. I don't want to scare you."

"I'm not scared. Just not ready."

"We don't have to rush." How he wanted to rush, but he wasn't stupid. Prom was over a month away. A lot could happen in a month.

"Let's head back," Tina suggested. "That stupid dog isn't out here."

They walked, hand in hand, for about a mile. Then decided to run so it looked like they'd followed all of Coach Ward's instructions.

About a half a mile to his house, Tina's shoe came untied.

They used the last bit of hiding in the woods to practice their kissing. Drew went straight for her boobs, and she grabbed his butt without him suggesting it. When they broke for air, his body protested, but his head knew he was getting there. They dodged off the path, taking a shortcut that would bring them out of the woods a few minutes later.

They ran by a fallen log, and something caught Drew's eye.

He slowed down. "Tina, hold up," he yelled.

Drew stepped over the log and around the trunk of a big tree.

He froze. "Christ!"

"What is it?"

Drew turned so fast he nearly fell over the dead tree on the ground. "Don't look," he yelled.

But it was too late, and Tina started to scream.

# Chapter Twenty

"Half the town was looking for that dog, Karl."

What a mess. What a fucking mess. Drew was holding a hysterical Tina in the backyard of one of the Emerys' neighbors. Nearly every distance runner at River Bend High had shown up and needed to be kept back. Luke and Zoe were sitting with Cherie, keeping her from breaking down as much as they could. And Karl Emery stood beside Jo, hands on hips and words flying.

"You shouldn't have told the kids to look for the damn dog."

"Keep your voice down!" she said in a rough whisper.

He stepped closer.

"You're overstepping your position, and now my kid is going to have nightmares for God only knows how long."

Jo's eyes skirted over to Drew. The kid looked like he was keeping it together. Probably for Tina.

Mr. Miller, Cherie's brother, arrived with a giant bedsheet and proceeded to tack the thing up around the scene.

Every time Jo's sight landed on the dog, her stomach twisted.

Jo put on her bitch voice, made sure Karl heard it. "Quit your pissing match, Karl, and put your cop hat on. I need my deputy right now, not a pissed off father of a nearly eighteen-year-old son. This is a clusterfuck of a mess, and the last thing we need right now is the town seeing us at odds." Jo nearly never pulled rank, but she did now. "Put your personal feelings aside and do your job or gather your son and walk away." She'd already put in a call requesting Stan to help with the investigation. He was less than thirty minutes away and didn't have the personal connection with Cherie Miller, her dogs . . . or have any children on her track team that she'd asked to help look for the dog.

If Karl walked away now, she'd encourage a weeklong vacation for the man. Considering he'd been the one to make the dog mess bigger while she was out of town, he wasn't on the top of the list of compassionate neighbors.

Karl glared, obviously torn.

"Jo?" Mr. Miller called her over to help block the scene from lookie-loos.

When they were done, Jo forced her eyes on the scene. She needed her camera. If this were a person, she'd need to call in forensics from Waterville, or maybe Eugene. She considered it, even though the dog wouldn't be considered a homicide. Animal cruelty and a misdemeanor if the culprit was found. That would be the extent of charges filed.

The damage went way beyond that.

It took a special kind of sociopath to steal a dog and hang it from a tree. The kind she didn't want roaming among the citizens of River Bend. Knowing who was capable of this crime had become her number one priority.

"Keep anyone from coming back here," she told Karl. "I'm getting the camera."

She walked through the backyard of a home and to her car, parked in the street.

Neighbors watched and muttered among themselves.

By the time she returned, the number of people standing around had doubled.

She needed to do this quickly. Snap a few pictures, remove the dog from the woods, question the neighbors, Tina, and Drew.

Jo waved off approaching bystanders and moved to get the hard stuff done first.

Karl waited, hands on his belt, anger in his face.

She moved around the sheet and aimed her camera. Blocking out the image, she moved around the brush, snapped pictures of the ground.

"This is awful," Mr. Miller said by her side.

Karl stood with his back to them.

"Who could do such a thing?"

"I don't know, but I'm going to find out," Jo insisted.

"Hi, Stan. You didn't need to rush over," she heard Karl greet the man before Stan walked around the sheet.

A hand moved the sheet aside, and Stan froze. "Holy shit."

Jo met his eyes.

"What . . ."

"More like who," Jo corrected him.

"Is this one of Cherie's dogs?"

"Yeah."

Stan glanced behind him. "Who found it?"

"A couple of my track kids. I asked them to fan out and search for a missing dog. This isn't what I thought they'd find." She'd not make that mistake again. Even finding the dog deceased on the side of the road would have been a better outcome than this.

He motioned to the camera in her hand. "Are you done with the pictures?"

Jo looked around, snapped a couple more. "I'm good."

"Okay. Let's get her out of there."

Stan was tall. He removed his utility knife from his belt and proceeded to cut Jezebel down. The weight of the dog hit the ground with a thud.

Jo hoped no one was close enough to have heard it.

Mr. Miller winced.

Jo took a few more pictures, rolled the dog over, and took a few more.

Then she laid her hand on the head of the animal and gritted her back teeth together.

"Did you call animal control?" Stan asked.

"What for? The dog's dead. This was done on purpose. Cause of death is irrelevant. Animal control will simply lay pressure on Cherie to move her dogs faster. We'd be better off calling in a doctor to prescribe the lady some Xanax."

"I have black collection bags in the back of my car, I'll get one. I can take the dog to Waterville if you'd like, make it easier on Cherie."

"Get the bag, I'll talk to her."

In her years as sheriff, Jo had never needed to tell a loved one that someone had died. The benefits of a small town and a population that normally took care of one another. Although Cherie knew her pet was gone, the circumstances of the dog's death were horrific.

Talking to Cherie about her dog left Jo raw and at the same time pissed her off to the point of seeing red.

~

"You found what?" Gill was on the phone with Jo. They had gotten in the habit of texting or calling at the end of their day. On occasion he'd send a flirty text midmorning, followed up with something sexy by the afternoon . . . and then on to a *how was your day* conversation by the evening.

"My dog problem has turned criminal," Jo said.

"Someone hung her?"

"From a tree not far from where the owner lives."

Jo's strained voice told him a lot.

"People who torture animals are a special breed of monster."

"I know. I talked to all the neighbors, the ones who complained in the first place . . . you know what I got?"

"Tell me."

"A round-the-clock feeding team for the puppies that no longer have a mother. And neighbors willing to step up and house the dogs until permanent homes can be found."

"They don't sound like your suspects."

"No, they don't."

"I know you have this, but if you need to talk it out, I'm here."

He heard her sigh over the phone. "Do you ever get that sixth sense thing going . . . the one that tells you something is way off?"

"I get it all the time."

"Do you ever ignore it?"

"Never."

"Me either." Jo sighed again. "Tell me about your day."

He and Shauna had two more small-time dealers they were following in hopes of finding their source. Gill kept the details short, not used to talking about his cases with anyone but his partner or his boss. He knew he could speak in confidence with Jo but always worked in some sort of silence to avoid possible leaks in his cases.

"What are your weekend plans?" Gill asked, hoping to lure her in his neck of Oregon for an overnight stay.

"Starting guns and timers," she said.

It took Gill a minute for her words to register. "Track meet."

"Yeah. River Bend High has an annual invitational that brings in about a dozen teams to compete. It's our big fundraiser. I'll be helping with setup on Friday, and the meet is all day Saturday."

"Looks like I'll see you Sunday morning."

"You don't have to drive all the way—"

He cut her off. "Teenagers party on Friday and Saturday nights. Sunday is better for me."

"Gill, it's a long way."

"Jo, I want to see you."

"But—"

"Do you know when the last time I drove two hours for a date was?" he asked her.

"No."

"Never."

There was a pause on her end. "Why now?"

"Walk into your bathroom."

"What?"

"Just do it. Walk into your bathroom." He waited for thirty seconds. "You there?"

"I feel stupid."

She was there.

"Are you looking in the mirror?"

She sighed . . . an annoyed sigh that translated over the miles.

"Now take your hair out of that rubber band."

"How do you know my hair is in a rubber band?"

"Is it?"

She sighed again.

Gill laughed.

"I need a haircut," she said.

"Haircut aside, look at yourself. Tell me what you see."

Women never saw what men saw. He was fairly certain of how she'd answer his questions.

"I see a washed-up thirty-year-old with dark circles under her eyes."

"You know what I see?"

Jo barked out a laugh. "A washed-up thirty-year-old with dark circles under her eyes and a rack."

The thought of her rack warmed his belly. "I do see your rack."

Jo laughed.

"I see," he started. "I see your smile under sexy, tired eyes that dilate into a deep, soulful blue when I'm kissing you. I see a woman who works hard and isn't afraid to sweat for all the right reasons. I see a firm body with a soft rack that turns me on in ways I didn't know existed."

"Gill—"

"I'm not done. I see a caring woman who is pissed off she cares so much and doesn't know how to control it. I see compassion, integrity, and loyalty."

"Gill—" Her voice was soft.

"I see," he didn't let her finish, "all the qualities in a woman a man like me can want." He hadn't meant to be so open about his own feelings but left them on the table.

There was a long pause before Jo said anything. "Two people in our profession getting together is a recipe for disaster."

"Good thing we like danger."

"You should find some demure debutante who needs you to take care of her."

He thought of an ex-lover and quickly shook that memory away. "You need me, you just don't know it yet."

"Is that right?"

"It's okay, you'll catch on."

Jo laughed, and he could see the smile on her face if he closed his eyes.

# Chapter Twenty-One

"I'm being cheated out of my Jo time."

Jo listened to Mel's complaint over a stack of colorful paper, scalloped scissors, and glitter that they were using to make name tags for the upcoming reunion.

"I don't know what you're talking about."

"Your off time is either on the field at track meets or in the sheets with Gill."

Instead of denying the truth, or what had been the truth for the better part of a month, Jo poured glitter over the wet glue edging the paper she was working on. It smudged everywhere.

Glitter and glue were not her thing.

"You'd deny me my hookin' up time?"

Mel rubbed her still flat belly. "No."

Her denial was unconvincing.

Jo made another attempt at glittering paper. "Why are we doing so many extra of these?" Yes, she was whining, no, she didn't care.

"It's not extra."

"How is that possible?" The count was triple the normal graduating class.

"The kids from Waterville were bused in because of the fire, remember?"

The information rang a bell. "That's right." She attempted to flick glitter from her fingers, failed miserably. "Zoe would pick this week to go to New York."

Mel took another stack of papers and lined them up to cut. "If it makes you feel any better, she's agreed to help with the food."

"That's her thing. She cooks. Glitter isn't my thing. I'm a cop, I cop."

Mel frowned. "You're a friend, you friend."

Jo scowled. "You're pushing the friend card."

Mel blew her a kiss from across the table and nudged the glitter closer to Jo's side.

She pushed it back. "How about I write the names on these?" Jo removed the list of names of the graduating class that would be attending the reunion.

"I've seen your penmanship. You should have been a doctor and not the sheriff."

No matter how Jo spun that statement, there wasn't a compliment to be found. She eyed the names on the list and only recognized a third of them. There had been a lot of traffic in and out of River Bend the year her father died.

"Are you going to supervise the prom?" Mel asked.

Jo cringed. "No one wants me hanging out at prom."

"You were the shit at our prom."

"Yeah, well, now I'm *just* the shit. I'm getting used to it."

"You don't have to be."

"Yeah, Mel. I do. I can't look the other way when a responsible kid is doing something he shouldn't do. Even if I don't think it's going to screw him up. Even if that kid is doing exactly what I did at their age."

"Like drinking."

"Like all of it." Jo lifted her hand, made an invisible line in the air. "Everyone needs to be right here. Congenial, friendly . . . keep the conversation going, give everyone the opportunity to voice their thoughts, opinions. But the minute I give someone an inch . . . like Cherie and the freakin' kennel she's been running, look what happens."

"That wasn't your fault."

"I'm not blaming me. It's just hard. I don't want to be the hard-ass all the time. I wanted to laugh when Principal Mason dragged me into his office to discipline Drew for connecting his phone to the TV as a remote."

Mel's eyes lit up. "Wyatt downloaded that app. Works great."

"See? Kid was smart, and that shit was funny." Glitter and glue forgotten, Jo sat back from Mel's kitchen table, which doubled as a crafting zone.

"You're up for election next year. Maybe you should reconsider running."

She had, more times than Jo could count. "The thing is, I don't mind being a cop. And now that I have someone in my life occupying my thoughts, it's even harder to do my job."

"I would think it gave you some stress relief."

"How so? I haven't left town since I got here. I can't even get my car in for the recall. This weekend is the meet in Eugene. The first time I'll have an opportunity to see how Gill really lives."

"That's a good thing."

"I have to squeeze in a personal life. Even then I've gotten some slack from the fine churchgoing women in town asking me about my *male friend*."

"Oh, no." Mel had given up on the crafting.

"Oh, yes. Complete with enough snide comments to let me know that my father wouldn't approve of me *living in sin*."

"They didn't use that term."

"They did, and do. Part of the problem with my being everyone's *friend*. I suppose they'd still call me out if I wasn't. I'm not sure how my dad did it."

"Your dad was a widower, it was different."

"My mom died fourteen years before my dad. He'd celebrated his fifty-fifth birthday the fall before he died." She stopped to think about that. "A forty-one-year-old widower . . ."

"I can't even think about how that felt."

"I remember him crying the day of my mom's funeral. It all feels like a black-and-white still frame in my head. I remember hurting, and sleeping next to him for about a month. Then he forced me to my room."

"Probably for the best."

"Yeah. But still, forty-one. He never once brought a woman home."

Mel stared at the wall across the room. "He must have really loved your mother."

"He did. He talked about her all the time. But he was still a man."

Mel moved her eyes to Jo. "What are you getting at?"

"I'm thirty and get turned on hearing Gill's bike driving down the street."

"You always were the wild one."

"That's not what I'm getting at. How long did you have between lovers?"

"Nathan was an ass. And I had Hope by then."

Jo lifted her palms to the air. "That doesn't mean you didn't find the time to have sex at some point."

"Yeah. But not often."

Jo did the math in her head. "So you had Hope, were still with the ex-asshat for a while after. By the time you were back in River Bend and hooked up with Wyatt, Hope was seven, right?"

"Right."

"And in between there was one, two lovers?"

"About."

The details didn't matter . . . the math did. "Even I managed a few as sheriff over the years, now Gill."

"What are you getting at?"

"What is the likelihood that my dad didn't have one single hookup in fourteen years?"

Mel leaned forward on her elbows. "You think he had a lover?"

"My dad was kinda hot." Jo cringed when she said it, but Mel knew it was true.

"He was."

He didn't have tattoos, but he had been a big man who wasn't afraid of hard work and building muscle. "If he had a lover, someone had to have known about it. It makes sense that he had someone. Even if it was casual."

"Your dad didn't strike me as a 'casual' guy."

"Then finding his lover that was less than casual shouldn't be that hard," Jo said.

Mel made a whistling noise. "Finding a lover of a decade past, one who didn't come out of hiding when he died, isn't going to be easy."

"It's a small town. People talk. Gossip is a pastime best spent with a cold beer or cheap wine. Someone has to know something." And if not, why was it such a secret? And if her father could keep it hush-hush, then there might be a link to how he died. It was the only new thing itching in her head in ten years, and Jo needed to follow the lead.

Mel stood and crossed the room to the refrigerator, pulled out a beer as if Jo was making a suggestion. Though Jo had to admit, a beer while talking about her dead father's sex life was a fabulous idea.

"Why would he keep it secret?" Mel opened a bottle of sparkling flavored water for herself while Jo popped the top of her beverage.

"That's easy to answer." She took a drink. "This town is full of conservative individuals that feel as sheriff I shouldn't be keeping the company of men."

Mel's look of astonishment should have been recorded. "I'm having a hard time with that."

"Yeah." Jo went on to give Mel names of the neighbors who'd approached her and those who said nothing with their mouths but everything with their eyes. "It's only a matter of time before their respect of me drops in the toilet."

"People can't expect you to be Virgin Mary."

"They want it hidden. Even Josie told me that when I stopped by R&B's yesterday."

"Josie thought you needed to hide your relationship with Gill?"

"No," Jo corrected Mel. "She said in her years as a single woman in this town, she'd been told more than once that she shouldn't be seen keeping men overnight. And she runs a freakin' bar." Jo pointed to her own chest. "I'm the sheriff. Next to Minister Imman's family, I'm up there for censure."

"That's stupid."

"Might be stupid, but it is what it is. I doubt it was any better ten years ago when my dad was alive."

"It was probably worse. Your dad was a single father raising a daughter."

"I didn't think about it that way. I bet he had a lot of women telling him how to parent."

Mel leaned back, placed her feet on an opposite chair. "Maybe one of these moms from Waterville who was in River Bend shuffling their kids was the lover?"

Jo glanced at the list again. "How many of these kids had single moms?"

"Or unhappily married moms?"

Jo shook her head. "An affair? That wasn't my dad."

Mel stared her down. "I wouldn't close my eyes to that if I were you. If there was a lover, she didn't come forward when he died. Why would a woman stay hidden?"

"Maybe she didn't want people judging her."

"Okay . . . or?"

Jo did not like the fact that Mel had a point. "I still think someone had to have known about a romantic relationship, if my father was having one."

"What about Karl?"

Jo swallowed some of her beer. "Even if he did, the man wouldn't tell me. Especially this month."

"Would Glynis know?" Mel asked.

"Glynis can't keep a secret. If she knew something, I'd know something."

Mel's foot did this nervous twitch thing when she was thinking. "Josie? Everyone talks to the bartender."

"Maybe."

"I always talk to my hairdresser. Did your dad go to Russell's barbershop?"

"Back when Russell Senior cut hair."

"Worth a shot to ask around."

Jo had to admit that Mel had some great ideas of places to start the search for the woman her father had some kind of involvement with.

"We could be wrong. Your dad might have just sworn off women," Mel said.

"I'm craving Gill and it's only been a week."

Mel smiled. "Wait until you're pregnant. Everything funnels right down here." She made hand gestures to her groin and squirmed in her seat. "Pregnant women shouldn't be this horny."

"I bet that makes Wyatt a very happy man."

"As long as he leaves my boobs alone, we're golden. My girls hurt."

They talked about the changes in Mel's body and the liberation of married sex. Later, with a list of the graduating class of a decade past in her hand, Jo walked the few short blocks to her house in thought.

Her father hiding a woman in his home wouldn't have happened. Wherever he might have gotten his engine started, it had to have been somewhere else. And since he didn't leave town often . . .

Jo looked at the houses surrounding hers with renewed interest.

Someone had to have seen something.

But who . . . and who in River Bend could keep a secret?

When her eyes swept the neighborhood a third time, Jo paused.

"Miss Gina," she whispered to herself. Miss Gina could carry a secret to the grave.

# Chapter Twenty-Two

"Who was my dad sleeping with?" Jo stared Miss Gina down and jumped right to the point.

"Are we having this conversation without alcohol?"

Jo pointed to the badge on her chest. "I am."

"I have guests. Let's take this out back." Out back referred to Miss Gina's porch, which covered the span of the house overlooking the backyard and guesthouse that Gina herself used.

Her skin prickled, like it did when a knock came to your door at two a.m.

Instead of sitting, Jo leaned against the banister and took several deep breaths as Miss Gina made herself comfortable on a cushioned Adirondack chair.

"Let me start by saying I don't know who she was, just that there was someone."

Disappointment hit.

"What do you know?"

"You were in middle school. That preteen walking mess made worse by a lack of a woman in your life. I remember the first time Zoe convinced you to stop here. Something had upset you enough to make your friends want to take care of you. I soon learned that wasn't the normal pattern."

Jo wasn't sure about that. Seemed Mel and Zoe were watching out for her those last years in school.

"How does this timeline play into my father's lover?"

"I paid attention at that point. For all I know it was going on before then, but after, I was certain."

"I'm listening." Jo tried to remember that time in her life. Her mother had been gone long enough that she'd strained to remember the sound of her voice, the smell of her perfume. Puberty had hit and her father understood nothing. Looking back, he'd done his best, but he had been rather clueless.

"When you, Mel, and Zoe started to come around, Joseph started stopping by with some regularity."

"You said he did that after I moved away."

"He did. There was a time when he'd already deemed me safe and didn't bother hovering over you here. I agreed to call him if I thought you were in trouble."

"So my father watched me through you."

"A little."

When Jo was a teenager, she would have felt betrayed. As an adult, not so much.

"I'd always known your father. We'd have a conversation or two over the years, but as a respected citizen of River Bend, one that didn't need to be escorted out of R&B's, we didn't cross professional paths. Outside of when your mother passed and I invited guests at her funeral to stay overnight."

"But you managed to get to know him after."

"I did. He never came right out and told me there was someone, but when I hinted that he was a little more relaxed than normal, he'd give me that grin that said both . . . *yes*, and *what are you talking about?*"

213

Jo knew that look well.

"How is it possible you never figured out who she was?"

"It wasn't my business. I didn't pry, didn't look around with a magnifying glass."

"Why would he keep it secret?"

"Maybe it wasn't serious."

"How long did this go on?"

Miss Gina narrowed her eyes as if searching her memory for a clue. "Your dad was really uptight when you were in high school."

"Frustrated," Jo said.

"Probably."

Frustrated meant he wasn't getting it. She knew that feeling well. Or he could have been fed up with her behavior and sex had nothing to do with it. "Do you think he took a woman up to the cabin?"

"Could have. It wasn't like anyone drove up there to check."

There hadn't been so much as a tube of lubricant up at the cabin to indicate a sexual rendezvous.

Jo turned around to look at the line of trees surrounding the property. She hadn't needed a cabin when hooking up as a young adult. Her father may have had higher standards, or maybe not. It wasn't like she could ask him now.

"You think this lover was connected to his death, don't you?"

"I think his lover is the only new thing I have to go on to figure out what really happened. My father's death wasn't an accident."

Jo half expected Miss Gina to deny her allegation.

"I agree."

"I'm not sure they are connected, but if my father could keep something as transparent as a girlfriend, lover . . . or whatever she was a secret, what else had he been hiding?"

"Well, if there is anyone who can figure that out, it's the woman who stepped into his shoes. You live in his house, have his friends, his colleagues, his office . . . hell, you're sleeping in his room. You live his life."

"Until lately," Jo mumbled. Gill's presence and the desire to get out of River Bend and find something to occupy her world outside of potholes and barking dogs was a complete departure from life as she knew it.

"What about the year he died?" Jo turned to watch Miss Gina's face.

"I think he was itchy. We'd sit right here on this porch, drink my lemonade, and he'd get that look in his eyes."

"What look?"

Miss Gina pointed a finger at Jo. "That one. The one that said he wasn't happy and wanted a change."

"So why didn't he leave? My mom was gone, I was gone."

"That's the ten thousand dollar question."

Twenty minutes later, Jo stood over her father's grave. The image of him that had always come up when she closed her eyes started to become less of a memory and more of a snapshot. Like a photograph without animation. An image without scent or feelings. A stone protruding from the ground in place of a life.

Her throat clogged. "What were you hiding, Dad?"

The answer was there. Jo knew when she found it everything would fall into place.

She bent down, pulled a dandelion, and ran her fingertips over his name. In contrast, she turned to the site of her mother's resting place with less attachment. She hated that. Would have loved to have known her mother better before the car accident that took her life. Her entire family sat in one place. Two dead, one alive. Her maternal grandparents sent cards at Christmas, the occasional birthday sentiment. Her paternal grandfather had passed before her father, his mother had died shortly after. Burying her son wasn't something Nana Ward had taken well. She'd had a stroke shortly after, and then fell and broke a hip. It was over after that. That left Jo. There were cousins, but none that had kept a close relationship and none that lived anywhere close to River Bend.

Her friends were her family.

Jo straightened and closed her eyes.

The phone in her pocket buzzed, breaking her concentration. Gill's name flashed on her screen.

"Hey," she answered.

"Is this a bad time?"

"No. It's fine." She turned away from her parents' graves.

"What's wrong?"

She smiled, attempted to pull the cloud that had blown over her out of her voice. "Nothing."

"You don't sound like it's nothing."

"Just one of those days. I'm fine." It was nice that he cared enough to ask. "What are you doing?"

"Nothing pleasant."

Jo glanced around the cemetery. "That makes two of us. Guess what I found out."

"That my name is Gaston and I'm really a French spy."

Some of her cloud lifted. "Can you even fake a French accent?"

"Wee, wee."

It sounded like a kid telling her he needed a potty. It felt good to laugh.

Jo turned and took a final look at her father's grave. "My dad was having an affair . . . or had one prior to his death."

Gill paused. "You didn't know that until today?"

"You did?"

"I assumed. Did Miss Gina tell you who she was?"

Jo shook her head. "Wait, how did you know Miss Gina knew anything?"

"She tested me up at the cabin. Told me if I was worth my weight I'd figure out one of your father's secrets."

Jo noticed another weed, reached down to pull it. "She told you before saying a word to me."

"She didn't tell me anything. Not really. Do you have any idea who the woman was?"

"Not a clue."

"Was there a face or name that came to you when you realized there was someone in his life?" Gill asked.

"No. No one. It's disturbing."

"Disturbing because he had a lover or because you can't think of who it was?"

"I could only hope my dad found something after my mother. He wasn't an old man. I should have realized there had to be someone in all those years before now."

"You're his daughter. It's hard to think of our parents being sexual people."

She hadn't really thought about the whole thing on a physical level. The thought made her cringe.

"He never left town. We'd go up to the cabin when I was young. Once in a while we'd visit my grandparents, but that was so seldom I don't remember the color of their house. His whole life was this town."

"Not his whole life, hon. There was someone at some point. And from what I can determine from your father's profile, the man was Mr. Commitment."

"He was that."

"So if he was a serial monogamist, then he had few lovers, and those he did have he felt some kind of connection with."

"Who? I can't figure out who."

"Evidence is somewhere."

"I've searched the house for anything to clue me in on his life. I've never found a photograph, a letter . . . anything."

"Maybe it's not in the house. Or it's so hidden you've yet to find it."

She tossed the weeds onto the grass. "It's frustrating."

"Most investigations are."

"This is personal."

"I know," Gill said. "Makes it even harder to see the truth."

Her head was too full, full of information, full of what she didn't know. She shook it all off. "I'm looking forward to this weekend." She was driving into Eugene a few hours before the track team for the meet taking place in Gill's city.

"I'm starting to think you like me," he teased.

"I wouldn't go that far," she said with a smile.

She heard him chuckle. "Will I jeopardize your reputation if I show up at the track meet to watch?"

"Don't you have work to do?"

There was a pause. "If you don't want me there—"

"I didn't say that."

"So you do want me there."

Jo rubbed the bridge of her nose. "Since when do you sound insecure?"

"Just trying to get my girl to ask me to come."

*His girl?*

"Manipulation."

"I wouldn't say that," he said, quoting her.

"I would." Jo looked up from the grass she was studying during their conversation and scanned the empty cemetery. Her eyes landed back on her father's name. "You're not a secret in my life. If you want to watch a bunch of kids run, jump, and throw heavy objects, knock yourself out."

"I'll see you at noon."

Jo's skin started to itch. She turned a full circle, scanned the edges of the cemetery. "Noon."

"Are you okay?"

She pulled the phone away from her ear briefly, thinking she heard something that sounded out of place.

"Jo?"

The dead were silent, the birds scattered from tree to tree, and bees buzzed in a tree a few yards away. She shook off the cold that had washed over her.

"I'm here."

"What's going on?"

"Nothing. Just distracted."

"You sure?"

Another glance to her left, then to her right. "I'm sure."

"I'll see you this weekend."

Jo disconnected the call, did another full circle scan before walking to her car. Once inside with the engine running, some of the cold dissipated, but the hair on her arms continued to stand on end.

# Chapter Twenty-Three

Drew lifted his leg up along the fence and leaned over it to stretch. The week sucked. Outside of Tina, there wasn't one redeeming hour to remember. The week before was forgettable, too.

"Drew?"

He glanced over his shoulder and noticed Parker, a rival from Eugene, walking toward him. They'd often alternate between first and second in the one mile, ending with handshakes and *better luck next times*.

"Hey."

Parker placed his leg along the fence for a similar stretch. "Wanna bet on who is going to win today?"

"Is that kid from Sheraton here?" Sheraton High sat in South Eugene.

Parker shook his head. "No. He's out for the season."

"Injury?"

"I heard drugs."

Drew switched legs. "It's hard to run and smoke pot," he said.

"I heard it was something bigger." Parker stretched his hamstrings.

"Really?"

"Someone said prescription stuff, then I heard morphine . . . or was it heroin?" Parker shook his head. "It wasn't good, whatever it was."

"Jesus, what was he thinking?"

"No clue." Parker finished his stretches, leaned against the fence. "Sure you don't want to bet on who is going to win?"

"With my running luck, I'd lose, fall, and break something and end up banned by CIF for betting. I've had a really crappy week."

"Yeah, I heard about the dog."

Drew figured he'd be part of the rumor mill. "It sucked."

Parker was quiet for a minute. "So you didn't do it?"

"Do what?"

Parker shifted his feet. "Nothing."

The hair on Drew's neck stood up. "What do you mean?"

Parker glanced around the busy field. Drew followed his gaze. Runners in ten different uniforms gathered in clumps of the same colors, awaiting their event. The starting gun went off and the girls in the three hundred hurdles took off running.

"I knew it had to be bullshit," Parker said.

"What is bullshit?"

"Someone suggested you planted the dog to scare your girlfriend."

The air in Drew's lungs collapsed. "What the fuck."

"I didn't think that sounded like you."

Drew looked over the field as if whoever had repeated those words would be standing there with an arrow pointing down at them. "Who did you hear that from?"

"Someone from North."

Drew didn't know anyone from North. "Any idea who they heard it from?"

Parker shook his head.

There were some rumors Drew had no problem suffering, but not this one. "This sucks."

"Sorry, man."

The adrenaline pulsing through his veins, Drew would use to win his race, then he'd find who was starting those rumors and beat the crap out of them.

~

It was cool and damp and Jo was wearing some kind of yoga pants that hugged her tight butt and firm legs like a second skin. On her head was a baseball cap embossed with the school logo, her hair in a ponytail poking out the back. She could have easily passed for one of the students and not their thirty-year-old coach. Their thirty-year-old *hot* coach who turned heads when she walked by clusters of kids from the opposing school.

Gill watched her from the stands while pretending to pay attention to those running the races.

He'd only been in the stands for ten minutes before the weight of his stare penetrated her armor and Jo searched the bleachers with her eyes.

He smiled when they finally landed on him.

Even from several yards away, he saw her grin. Then someone pulled her away, and off she went, playing coach.

"Someone playing stalker?"

Gill shaded the sun from his eyes with the palm of his hand to find Mel standing over him. "More like bodyguard." He patted the space beside him.

Mel sat. "I can't stay long, I have two vaulters competing with the varsity team."

"You're the pole vault coach?"

"You sound shocked."

"Impressed."

Mel blushed a little. "I didn't do too bad when I was in high school. Since my husband is the head coach, it wasn't like I had a choice in helping out."

"I'm sure the fact that River Bend isn't a major metropolis with tons of high school track coaches helps out, too."

"I'm sure it does." Mel turned to the field. "What makes you think Jo needs a bodyguard?"

"Have you seen how those horny high school kids are looking at her?"

Mel started to giggle. "They looked at her like that when she was in high school, too. It works now about as much as it worked then."

"She wasn't interested?" Gill was surprised a second time. He thought for sure Jo was the outgoing dating type when she was younger. And by dating, he figured she was one to set her own rules and run through boys quickly.

"She didn't date many kids from our town. I'm sure her daddy being the sheriff helped with that. Kinda like if you were a dad. Chances are your daughter would be in a chastity belt hidden in an ivory tower."

The mention of him being the father of a little girl raised the future guardian in him. "Third story with a locked bedroom door, if nothing else."

"With you to get through. Jo's dad wasn't as big, but he was just as protective."

The starting gun shot through the air, directing their attention to the field.

"Which race is this?" Gill asked.

"Two mile."

A herd of teenage boys took the first turn. Most of the uniforms were of the opposing team, a few of River Bend's colors filtered in with the runners leading the pack. "These are Jo's kids, right?"

"Yep." Mel stood. "I've gotta go. Will we see you in town tomorrow?"

"No. I'm kidnapping your sheriff instead."

Mel leaned down and whispered in his ear, "She likes handcuffs."

"Information to hold close to my heart," he said with a grin and a wink.

"You pass the smell test, Gill," Mel told him.

For effect, Gill lifted his left arm and sniffed.

Mel walked away laughing.

From his vantage point, Gill could see the runners and hear their teammates yelling out times as they passed a certain point on the field. Jo stood back from the finish line with a stopwatch in her palm. The runners were on their second lap and looked to be settling in for a long run when Gill noticed a woman encouraging one of the runners to pace himself. The kid looked familiar, even from the sidelines, sitting a couple of benches up on the bleachers.

He found himself watching the last lap on the edge of his seat. The announcer, one that sounded like he'd take a spot on a television show if given the chance, called out the last names of the top three runners. The name Emery stuck out in his head. Jo's number one runner was neck and neck with the runner from Eugene. The third in line was another River Bend local. The last hundred meters of the race had the stands cheering. The home team advantage screamed encouragement while the kids of River Bend stood on the sidelines, screaming at the two in purple and gold.

Gill dashed his eyes to Jo. She screamed. She yelled. She held the stopwatch in the air like it would somehow will the runner to make the right time and cross over before the opponent.

When the first foot crossed the finish line, inches away from the other, the stands sighed in short disappointment since the winner was from River Bend. The minority cheered, and all three of the top winners patted the others on the back as they held their hands to their knees in an attempt to catch their breath.

Jo stepped into the striped lanes to congratulate her winner.

~

Drew allowed himself to be pulled into a hug from his coach.

Crossing the finish line first and exceeding his personal record by half a minute sealed his position to compete in the finals. His rankings in the state were in the top ten, his chances of going to state championships almost a given. Which meant he'd have his pick of colleges far away from River Bend.

He couldn't wait.

"Finals and then state," Coach Ward said, clasping Tim's hand. "I can't believe I have two runners going."

"You forgot the Masters meet."

Coach Ward waved Tim off. "Semantics."

"Coach, let me get a shot."

Drew caught his breath long enough to see a camera pointed at the two of them.

Without pause, they both straightened toward the camera and smiled.

"Drew!" his mom called from the sideline, her hand waving frantically in the air.

He smiled and waved back.

"Go say hello." Coach Ward shoved his arm. "She drove all the way here."

He looked beyond his mom.

"Your dad volunteered to take the shift," Coach Ward told him.

Drew sucked in his disappointment. Fitzpatrick could have stepped in. Had in the past. His father had barely spoken to him for a month. Between the stunt with Mrs. Walters and finding the dog. Drew shivered. Thinking about the animal made his stomach twist.

He ran across the track to the fence line to talk to his mom. The short fence allowed her to reach over and hug him, sweat and all.

"I'm so proud of you."

"Thanks, Mom."

When she tried to hug him a second time, he pulled back. The mom hug after winning a race was a onetime thing.

"Do you want to ride home with me or take the bus with your friends?"

The bus sounded smelly, but Tina hadn't run her race yet, and sitting next to her with his hand on her thigh sounded better than listening to mom music all the way back to River Bend. "I'll go on the bus. You don't have to stick around."

"I don't mind."

She probably didn't, but he wasn't going to be the reason she was stuck in the bleachers all day.

"Is Dad still mad?"

"He's fine, honey. He'd be here but someone had to work."

That wasn't how Drew saw things. "Whatever."

"He tries."

"Sure." He called bullshit on that. Drew looked over his shoulder, saw the kids lining up for the next race, and used that as an excuse to walk away. "I'll see you at home."

She lifted her hand in a wave as he turned.

For a brief moment he wondered if his father would bother visiting him when he went to college . . . or would it just be his mom?

~

Pizza and teenagers . . . because everything was better with melted cheese.

The team had taken up several tables. Wyatt and Mel sat with several other kids, and a couple of the parents had stuck around to join the pizza party. Jo and Gill sat with her distance team.

River Bend had an excuse for a pizza parlor that had changed hands multiple times since she was a kid. Jo knew there was no way out of joining the team after the meet for pepperoni and sausage. Gill, on the other hand, had no idea.

He was handling it well, considering the amount of attention he was getting from the team. Once the boys learned that he'd served as a marine, talks about state finals and prom ceased.

"That is badass."

Jo didn't call Drew on his language.

"It's a job." Gill downplayed his role.

"I think it's brave." Maureen sighed into the word *brave*.

Tina jabbed an elbow into Maureen's side, helping the girl snap out of her moony look in Gill's direction.

When Gill squirmed, Jo hid a laugh behind her soda.

"What made you join?" Drew asked.

"It was the right fit for me at the time. Are you thinking about joining?"

Drew shrugged. "I dunno."

Jo listened intently. She thought Drew was headed for college. The military wasn't something he'd ever talked about.

Tina leaned into Drew's arm. "What about school?"

"My dad's a cop. Seems the military might work for me. It isn't like I'm staying in River Bend."

"I don't know, dude. Having people shoot at you doesn't sound fun," Gustavo said.

"Do people really shoot at you?" Tina asked.

"In war." Gill picked up a slice of pizza, shoved half of it in his mouth.

"People shoot at cops, too, Tina."

"I know that. But Drew doesn't want to be like his dad."

"No one shoots at the cops in River Bend," Tim added.

Gill exchanged glances with Jo.

She thought of her father, hoped no one noticed the tension she felt inside.

"The only time Coach fires her gun is when she's target practicing, isn't that right?" Drew asked.

"That's the goal," Jo said.

Wyatt walked up to their table. "We're headed out in ten. Next bathroom is in Waterville."

Tina and Maureen scooted back and took the hint.

"You'll be back tomorrow?" Wyatt asked Jo.

"Afternoon," she confirmed.

Tim leaned over to say something in Drew's ear. They both snickered. The guys were worse than the girls.

She pointed her finger in their general direction and narrowed her eyes.

"I didn't say nothin'," was Drew's response.

"Let's keep it that way."

A few minutes later Jo was shuffling kids out of the busy pizza joint while Gill pulled his bike close to her Jeep.

Tina stepped up beside her as kids filed onto the bus.

"Hey, Coach?"

"Yeah?"

Tina held out her hand. In it was a homemade business card. "A girl in the bathroom handed this to me."

Jo peered closer.

*Finals?* with a question mark was written in a fuzzy font. *Let me take away the pain.*

There was an Instagram ID under the caption.

"A tutor?"

Tina took the first step onto the bus. "She looked strung out, practically shoved this in my hand."

*Drugs.*

"What did she look like?"

"I don't know . . . like a teenager." Tina boarded the bus without any details.

Drew was behind her.

"Have fun, Coach."

Jo felt a smile she couldn't hide. "Can't stop yourself, can you, Drew?"

He laughed and followed his girlfriend.

The roar of Gill's bike followed the doors closing on the bus and it pulling away.

"Ready?"

She was going to follow Gill to his place since she didn't know the way. "Not yet." She turned back to the pizza parlor.

"You're still hungry?" He swung his leg off his bike, the size of him standing beside her a welcome comfort.

Jo handed him the card. "Someone gave this to one of my girls. Sounded like something you'd be interested in."

She waited while he read it.

"Take away the pain." Gill took in the parking lot while Jo relayed what Tina had said.

They walked back in together, one of the kids behind the counter saw them. "Forget something?"

Jo smiled. "Yeah." Without elaborating, she walked toward the restrooms while Gill pretended to check out the table where they'd been sitting.

The women's bathroom was empty. She checked both stalls and poked through the trash.

She caught Gill's attention and shook her head. They both scanned those left in the place. A few families. A group of guys, somewhere in their midtwenties, filled a booth.

Jo searched for a strung out teenage girl and came up short.

Outside, they walked around the back of the building and then met at her Jeep. Gill had his phone in his hand. "The Instagram account is private."

"It's probably nothing."

"I don't know. This is exactly the kind of thing these dealers are moving these days. Social media has given them access to lots of clients." He started typing into his phone, took a picture of the card. "I'm sending this to Shauna. Her fake account will request access to this person."

"Shauna has a fake Instagram account?"

"We both do," he said, grinning. "It's easy to be a teenage kid looking for dope online."

"Or a sixty-year-old pedophile looking for prey."

Gill shoved his phone into his back pocket. "Exactly."

"Can we do anything else here?"

Gill lifted his hand to hers and pulled her close when she grasped it. "I'm pretty sure what I want to do is frowned upon in pizza parlor parking lots."

The feel of his hand wrapping around her waist made her sigh. "And what do you want to do?"

He buried his lips in her hair, whispered in her ear, "It involves handcuffs."

The thought shouldn't have shot a thrill down her spine. The handcuff thing was a joke that had started when she took the badge. Jo squirmed. "Who said I like handcuffs?"

The deep grumble of his laugh gave promise to the evening. "That didn't sound like denial."

She smoothed her hand over his hip, pinched his ass. "You first."

# Chapter Twenty-Four

Jo was aware of soft lips on the back of her shoulder.

*Gill.*

Even through closed eyelids she could tell the sun had barely started to rise. She moaned and burrowed deeper into her pillow.

Gill's teeth scraped her shoulder.

*I can get used to this.*

"You're not asleep."

"Yes, I am," she muttered.

He kissed her again.

She opened one eye, peeked over the shoulder he was claiming. "You're dressed."

Gill rested his chin in her shoulder, the freshness of his breath, the soap on his skin told her she'd slept through him getting up and taking a shower. "I have to leave."

"Why?" She rolled over, didn't try to cover herself when the sheet slipped to reveal her naked breasts.

Gill's gaze wandered. "That Instagram account hit a hotspot. I'm meeting Shauna in twenty minutes."

Jo moaned, more than a little disappointed to have to share him.

"Sorry." He leaned down, kissed the top of one breast.

"I understand."

"I don't know when I'll be back."

She glanced across the room at the digital clock on his side of the bed. "It's okay."

"No, it's not. I wanted to spend the day with you."

"I have things to do at home anyway. No worries." She didn't, but letting him off the hook felt like the right thing to do.

He sat taller on the bed. "Take your time."

She closed her eyes and grinned. "I'm going to find your little black book and erase all the numbers," she threatened.

When he didn't tease her back, she opened her eyes to find him staring, his expression endearing.

"What?" she asked.

Gill didn't say a thing. Instead, he bent down and touched his lips to hers, made sure his kiss reached the depths of her soul before pulling back.

Aroused and missing him already, she asked, "What was that for?"

"For being here."

Jo reached up and touched his cheek.

He leaned into her palm.

"Be safe."

He kissed her palm and stood from the bed.

She leaned onto her elbows, watched as he tucked his service weapon into the holster inside his jacket. "Good luck finding that black book," he said when he reached the door.

"Oh, I'll find it."

Gill shook his head once and paused. "I threw it away in Virginia, when I knew I'd see you again."

And then he was gone.

Jaw slack, his words sank in. And in a completely girlie fashion, Jo flopped back on the bed with a silly grin on her face. Her fingers landed on a pair of handcuffs on his side of the bed. Images of the previous night had her giggling.

And Jo never giggled.

~

"You know what the problem is with these puppies?" Zoe asked.

Jo had lingered in Gill's space longer than she thought she would. For fun, she left a few notes throughout his house saying she'd searched the drawers or the cupboards for his black book, when in fact the only thing she'd done was clean up after them and make his bed. She'd deny sniffing his pillow if asked. Now she sat on the floor with a litter of puppies and the small bottles needed to feed their hungry mouths. "What's that?"

Zoe petted the head of the puppy she was feeding. "They grow on you."

"You're caving."

"I don't need a dog."

Three of the animals were sleeping, sprawled on top of each other, while the others were bouncing about, one particularly noisy since it hadn't been fed.

"Good thing they are off to Luke's parents' tomorrow."

The puppies had made the rounds. Every family member, every friend, even the neighbors had taken turns with the furry bundles. Cherie couldn't look at them without crying. No one in River Bend was willing to make her look at them. The older dogs were taken in by Luke's parents, and animal control had backed off once word got out about Jezebel's demise.

Zoe cooed. "I don't need a dog."

She was a goner.

Jo refused to let the tiny tongue that was licking her hand affect her emotions. Even when the owner of that tiny tongue crawled on her lap and circled three times before nestling into the crook in the back of her knee. No. The animal had no effect on her.

None whatsoever.

"You don't need a dog," Zoe said, laughing.

Jo glared. "*We* don't need dogs."

"I'm so screwed."

Jo laughed.

"Tell me about Gill. Take my mind off my doom." Zoe cuddled the animal that had her name on it.

"I'm not sure I can. He's . . ." Jo blew out a breath. "Unexpected."

"Elaborate, please."

The map of their relationship sat before her and she still couldn't figure out where she stood. She looked for the space where an arrow pointed, stating "you are here," and she couldn't find it. "I'm not like you . . . not like Mel."

"In what way?"

"I'm not a serial monogamist."

Zoe blinked a few times. "Serial what?"

"I'm not a relationship girl. I don't know that I can truly say I've ever had one. Not with any regularity."

Zoe looked to the ceiling for answers. Didn't find them. "What about after high school? Wasn't there someone in Waterville?"

"Do you remember his name?"

Zoe shook her head.

"Exactly. I had . . . there were a couple of guys. None stuck. Once I turned into River Bend's finest . . . there was less than that."

"That's sad."

"It's true."

"Doesn't make it less sad."

"Then Gill slips into my life like a knife in butter and I'm sitting here daydreaming about the man."

That had Zoe smiling . . . all toothy like. "What's wrong with that?"

"It can't last." The reality of that hit hard.

"Why not?"

"We're both cops. Kinda."

Zoe stared. "What does that mean?"

"Do you know what the divorce rate is for those with a badge?"

Zoe's stare turned into a grin. "Did he ask you to marry him?"

"Oh, good God, no." Jo almost choked.

Her friend's smile fell. "Then why are you worried about divorce?"

"I'm not. I'm saying . . . it can't last. Even the way it is, it can't last."

"Why the hell not?"

*Why the hell not?* Jo closed her eyes, saw her father . . . smelled the distant memory of her mother's perfume. Then she pictured Gill. He stood in the suit she saw him in that first day in Virginia. He was standing in a parking lot, one like that of the pizza parlor. From nowhere, shots fired.

She flinched.

"I think you're coming up with excuses."

"Cops die, and marriages fail. It just won't work."

When Jo opened her eyes, she took in Zoe's. In them were tears.

~

"When did you know Consuela was the one?"

The question sat in the air for a good minute before Lee answered. "Is she the one?"

"Christ, Lee . . . how do you know?"

Gill's best friend laughed over the phone. "You could do a lot worse."

"Don't I know it." The images of countless others swam before him. Blondes, brunettes . . . and the redheads. Lord knew they were all wrong. Right for right then but wrong to be left alone in his home. Wrong for being stuck in his head like an endless loop of a love song he couldn't shake.

"If it's any consolation, I like Jo. She's a little guarded, but that's to be expected."

"How so?"

"She's an orphan, Gill."

The word *orphan* never entered his head. Yet when he thought of it, he saw a child standing on a street corner, looking around for someone to take care of them. "I never thought of her that way."

"That's because she's an expert at hiding it."

Gill sat looking at one of the half dozen notes Jo had left throughout his home, her handwriting burned into his memory. *Your kitchen is a mess . . . do you ever cook?* He'd laughed when he found that in his cupboard. He remembered when he'd gone through her kitchen and found it overboard neat. Remembered how happy he was to see her sloppy in her refrigerator.

"She doesn't fake anything."

"I didn't say fake. I said hiding. Faking is on purpose, hiding is defensive. One is protective, the other is deceptive."

"How the hell did you become so perceptive?"

Lee laughed. "Do you know how many people look past you when you're in a wheelchair? I have more opportunity to study people than anyone else."

Gill sighed. "You didn't answer my question."

"Which one?"

"When did you know Consuela was the one?"

Another long pause. "Why are you and Jo working?"

"Well, the sex—"

"You can get sex anywhere."

Lee was right about that. "I don't know . . . she's the right amount of angel, the perfect amount of she-devil. She likes the Harley and carries a badge for reasons bigger than her."

"Reminds me of someone I know."

"I'm not an angel."

"Why do you wear a badge?"

Gill didn't have a reason like Jo's. "It's what I know."

"The case you're working on . . . what's the name of the last victim?"

"Pete Shafer." His answer was immediate. The image of the kid who would never see his eighteenth birthday swam in his head.

"Your Pete is almost like Jo's father. Jo's might be personal, but they are both just as important. That is what makes Jo attractive to you."

"Jo's a knockout without any of that."

"I'm not going to disagree. But looks are temporary. The part of Jo that has you coming to me asking what made me realize my woman was the one is staring you in the face."

"I thought opposites were supposed to attract."

"Balance, my friend. She reminds you of your rebellious nature, and I'm guessing you do the same for her."

Gill couldn't help but laugh. "My rebellious half wouldn't have spent the last ten minutes talking about relationships."

"Mr. Rebellion rushes forth and does things, Mr. Responsibility spends time burning your friend's ear about girls."

# Chapter Twenty-Five

Jo rested her head against the crook of her arms on her desk. The statements of Drew, Tina, and Cherie swam in her vision like the drops a doctor put in your eyes to dilate them. Only these drops didn't make her see better . . . they blurred and diffused everything.

She'd questioned the neighbors, the very people who had complained about the dogs barking.

Every one of those neighbors had offered support to Cherie after Jezebel had been found. Not one of them was capable of taking a pet's life as a vendetta.

So who held the grudge?

Footsteps at her office door had her jumping.

Glynis was out for lunch and the sound wasn't expected.

"Karl?"

Her deputy stared from the doorway. "When are you going to butt out of my kid's life?"

"What are you talking about?"

"Drew is talking about joining the service . . . the marines. Sound familiar?"

She opened her mouth only to have Karl cut her off.

"Looks like your boyfriend talked him into it. Caroline is beside herself. Cried all night."

"Hold up. Gill told all the kids about *his* time in the service, I wouldn't say he talked anyone into anything. When Drew said he was considering it, I was just as surprised as you."

Karl wasn't listening. With hands on his service belt and attitude in his scowl, Jo would have been concerned if she didn't know the man. "That's not how I heard it. Seems every time I turn around these days, my son is talking about the influence you have on him."

"I'm his coach, Karl. And up until recently, I thought I was a friend to his father." She placed both hands on her desk. "It appears that I'm wrong about the latter."

"Drew was going to college. Not joining the military."

"What's wrong with the service?"

"Boys from small towns always come home in a box. I don't want that for my kid."

Jo shook her head. "You're exaggerating."

"If Drew wants to join, he should finish college and enlist as an officer. Not go in as a grunt."

"Have you told him that?"

"He didn't listen. Just went on about your boyfriend and how *badass* he is."

*Badass* had been tossed around a lot.

She stood and attempted to change the conversation. "What is all this really about, Karl? You've been riding my ass like you're my boss and not the other way around."

Karl's nose flared. Jo was sincerely grateful that looks couldn't kill.

"Your hand in my personal life isn't wanted. Lately, you haven't been doing your job here either."

"Excuse me?" That was one hell of an accusation.

"You pick and choose which laws you're going to enforce, make criminals run laps instead of doing time."

"None of that has changed since my father was here."

"I didn't much like that when he was alive either."

It was time for Jo to glare. "Then why don't you do yourself a favor and put your name on the ballot next year when I'm up for reelection. If you're unhappy with how I run things, have the good people of River Bend vote you in."

"I just might do that. Seems I'm not the only one around here concerned about how things are being handled."

Jo's heart kicked hard in her chest. She knew there was some grumbling about Gill and his occasional sleepovers. She assumed the gossip stopped there. "Is that right?"

"Yes, it is. Only people can't come to you with their concerns, can they?"

She'd never closed the door of communication with anyone in town. Then again, she'd never had to.

Jo stewed in her own thoughts before lifting her hand to him, palm up.

"What?"

"The keys to your squad car."

He paused. "What for?"

Oh, how she would love to be taking the car away from him for good. But he'd just put her in check on a game of chess. If in fact he was going to run against her during the next election, her taking his position away as deputy now would appear deeply unprofessional. She'd need more than a personal gripe to remove his badge.

Like maybe finding out he was responsible for Cherie's dog.

Jo hated that she'd thought he was capable, hated that she didn't see anyone else remotely close to being the culprit.

"I'm taking it into Waterville for the recall."

He rolled his eyes. "I'm capable of taking my car in."

"Fine. I'll deal with mine, then."

His sinister smile didn't go unnoticed.

"I have Fitzpatrick coming in to cover for me."

"That isn't necessary."

She looked him straight in the eye. "I wouldn't want the people of River Bend thinking I'm putting too much on my deputy, now would I?"

"We wouldn't want that."

~

Jo couldn't remember being this angry in her work. In all her years as sheriff, the early ones had given her the most trials. Now it seemed she was having to prove herself again.

Was Karl trying to get under her skin or were there legitimate complaints outside of the personal nature of her relationship status?

Glynis returned from her lunch, giving Jo an opportunity to stretch her legs. She should probably find some lunch for herself, but the thought of eating anything made the anger in her belly churn.

Jo stood in front of Miller's Auto Repair in hopes of finding Luke's father. When she breached the metal doors of the garage and heard country music instead of blaring rock and roll, she knew she was in luck. Another scan around the place told her Luke wasn't there.

She walked to the short hall that smelled of tires and oil and found Mr. Miller reading the Waterville paper while drinking coffee. A pink box of donuts sat in its usual location by the door.

Jo knocked twice on the open door. "Anyone home?"

"Jo!" Mr. Miller removed his reading glasses from his nose and stood.

"How are you?"

"Fine, fine . . . what brings you in? That Jeep of yours acting up?"

She refused with a shake of her head. "Something a little more personal."

Mr. Miller's ready smile wavered. "Come in. Sit down. Can I get you some coffee?"

She glanced at the pot and the black liquid in the carafe. Shop coffee was about as good as that at the station. "I'm good," she told him, sitting.

"Any luck finding more on Cherie's dog?"

"I wish I had something to report."

"Disturbing. Has people locking their pets in at night."

"And locking their doors."

"That's probably for the best anyway."

Jo sighed. "I guess."

"So what can I do for you, Jo? You look a little stressed."

No use pretending she wasn't. "I am."

Mr. Miller frowned and Jo continued.

"I have been informed by my deputy that there have been complaints about me."

"Complaints?"

"Apparently. He didn't elaborate, but he did make it sound like more than one. He went on to suggest he might run for my job next year."

Mr. Miller sat back, the reclining desk chair groaning under his weight. "Karl doesn't have what it takes to be River Bend's sheriff. He didn't cut it after your father passed and couldn't do it now."

As much as Jo liked to hear this, she couldn't let one man . . . a man who was the father of one of her best friends, assure her he was right.

"He's a good cop."

"He's an okay cop. His diplomacy needs CPR, and his attitude is in constant need of adjustment."

"He still does his job."

Mr. Miller pinned her with a stare. "Do you think he can do yours?"

"No."

"Glad we have that figured out. Now what can I do?"

"Keep an ear out. I'd ask Luke, but I doubt anyone would talk trash to him. Or to Mel or Zoe. I don't need names, just want to know if there is something I could improve."

"Of course, Jo. Now, how is this man in your life? He treating you well?"

The question hit her in the chest. "He is."

Mr. Miller smiled again. "I'd like to meet the man. You bring him around for Mrs. Miller's pie next time he's in town."

"I'll do that."

The weight of the day shifted on her walk back. Stan's squad car was parked in the street. He was early, which was just as well. She'd like to get to Waterville and back, if at all possible, before dark.

She found him leaning against Glynis's desk, telling a joke.

Jo walked in right at the punch line.

They were both laughing.

"I missed a good one."

"I can repeat it," Stan said.

"Later. I need to head out. Just came to get the keys."

"Glynis said you're taking your squad car in for service."

"Brake recall."

"Good thing. Nothing like your brakes having issues."

"I'm sure they're fine. I don't need mechanical problems on top of everything else."

Stan followed her into her office while she grabbed her keys. "Any progress on the dog ordeal?"

"Nothing. It's been quiet since."

"Maybe it's an isolated thing."

"Is that your gut talking?"

"My gut says whoever did this has done something like it before and will again."

Gill had said as much, too.

"No more dead animals, please!"

"Or worse."

Jo swallowed hard. She'd thought about that, too. Sociopaths tortured animals and often moved on to bigger challenges. She'd request help from Gill's people if more turned up.

Stan followed her out the back door to the small parking lot. "Drive carefully. I'll handle everything here."

"I appreciate it."

# Chapter Twenty-Six

Shauna slapped a piece of paper on Gill's desk and did a little happy dance.

"What's this?"

"My divorce will be final on the twenty-first."

"Congratulations?" he asked, a little surprised at her enthusiasm.

"Hell, yeah. That bastard tried to go after half my retirement. Like he earned it by snoring in my bed for three years."

Gill had seen the full cycle of Shauna's turmoil. First there were tears, then anger . . . now this. "I'm happy for you."

"Me, too. We need to celebrate."

Gill glanced at the paper again, the date ringing in his head. "I'll be in River Bend on the twenty-first. Promised Jo I'd be around for the class reunion."

"I'll be celebrating for a month. After?"

"Of course."

Shauna swiped the paper from his desk. "Marriage is overrated."

"Is it?"

She paused, curbed her excitement. "Except for Jo. I mean, Jo's perfect for you. I knew that long before I sent her to Marly's."

"Sent her?"

Shauna batted her eyelashes in fake innocence. "You didn't think that was on accident, do you? If I told Jo I knew a guy that would be perfect for her, she would have never given you a chance . . . meet her on *accident* . . . and boom!" She patted his head and bounced off like a woman half her age.

He'd been played . . . by his own partner. Gill smiled, happy with the outcome.

When he couldn't get Jo out of his head, he left his desk and found a quiet bench outside the building and dialed her number.

The fuzzy connection told him she was driving.

"Hey, good-looking."

"A friendly voice," Jo said.

"I thought everyone in River Bend was friendly."

"Not hardly. How are you?"

"Perplexed."

"Oh?"

He told her of Shauna and her divorce. "It's strange to see someone waving sparklers around after a marriage falls apart."

"Shauna was really unhappy. Best they figured it out before they had kids. Mel's parents split the day she graduated high school, and that was devastating."

"My parents are still together," he told her.

"Yeah, well . . . mine died, so who knows if they would have worked out."

"Were they unhappy?"

"How would I know? I was finger painting and counting to ten when my mom died."

Jo's voice told him she'd gotten over this loss long before now. "Where are you?"

"On my way to Waterville. Squad—recall—waited long enough."

"You're going out on me, say that again."

Jo yelled into the phone as if that would make the connection better. "My squad car has a recall. I need to get it in."

"Got it."

"How is your case?"

"We're getting close. Found the girl at the pizza parlor. Definitely hooked. Second-level seller."

"You're looking for her connection."

"Exactly."

"Let me—I can—hello—shit—" The line went dead.

Gill tried calling her again. Her phone went to voice mail. On his third attempt, he left a message. "Lost you. Call me when you get to Waterville. Miss you."

$\sim$

Gill was perched in a car, a high-powered lens of his camera aimed at the Eugene High School senior parking lot. Rachel, the girl from the pizza joint, was easy to spot. Her profile on Instagram had pictures of her at a party, red cup in hand. Like the other girls her age, her long hair went halfway down her back, her eyes heavy with makeup. Chances were the makeup was an attempt to add color to her washed-out skin.

He snapped a picture of her and the girl she was walking with.

The girls separated when Rachel's attention diverted to a low-riding Subaru. The car had been modded to the point where it probably wasn't street legal.

Gill zoomed in on the license plate, took a picture.

She leaned into the car like a hooker, ass in the air.

Not her dealer, Gill decided. Someone dealing wouldn't drive around in a car easily pulled over by the local police. Not if they carried any stash.

Gill waited, was fairly sure a deal had just gone down in front of him. Busting her now would do no good. And it would alert her higher-up that she'd been tapped.

Rachel moved to another car as the parking lot started to empty out. This car was a modern variety import. Nothing fancy, nothing that stood out. He zoomed in on the license plate, then the driver's side. Looked like a mom . . . maybe Rachel's, Gill didn't know.

His cell phone rang. Not recognizing the number, he let it go to voice mail.

A few more pictures of the car and Rachel and her driver were gone.

Gill skimmed his photographs and called them in.

He'd have the name of the legal owners of the cars within an hour . . . maybe less.

His message light blinked, and he listened to the recorded voice.

"Gill, it's Zoe."

The hair on his arms went on alert. He glanced at the time. He hadn't spoken with Jo in a few hours. She was supposed to have called when she reached Waterville.

"It's Jo. There was an accident."

He hit "call back" without listening to the rest of the message, his breath short and his head spinning with worry.

"Hello?"

"Zoe, it's Gill."

"Oh, good. You got my message."

"How is she, is she okay?"

"All things considered."

"What things? Where is she?" He turned over the engine of his car and pulled out of the apartment complex parking lot he was hiding in.

"Waterville Community Hospital. She's in radiology."

"Jesus, is she okay?"

"Her car bounced, slammed into the side of the road, and spun. A tree kept her from taking a dive off the cliff. She's really lucky."

"I'm on my way. Tell her I'm on my way." Gill tossed the phone aside, placed a light on the top of his car, and let the siren fill the air.

~

Son of a bitch . . . her head pounded, her body ached. One minute she was losing her connection to Gill on the phone, the next she was staring down the side of a cliff with a twentysomething search and rescue pulling her out of her mangled squad car.

Lights, ambulance . . . doctors asking questions. And everything hurt.

Her back teeth hurt.

She'd hit the brakes. Nothing happened. Panic and then nothing.

"Sheriff?"

"What?" She thought she was shouting, but only a sigh of a breath asked her question.

"How are you feeling?"

Jo didn't open her eyes. The woman's voice an unknown source. "Like shit."

A chuckle. "Do you know where you are?"

The smell of antiseptic, the dinging sounds of monitors. "Hospital."

"Good. Rest."

Okay . . . rest. Great plan.

"Jo?"

The voice was familiar.

"You're a mess."

The second voice was familiar. She tried to open her eyes. Light blinded her. "Screw you."

A chorus of tiny laughter, the kind that people released when they were nervous, filled her ears. Then there was silence.

She woke slowly. The bed under her was soft, not hard like the one before. That Jo remembered. The noise of the room was quiet. A tiny beep every few seconds was like a reassuring heartbeat, letting the person listening know they were alive.

Someone was holding her hand.

With a dry mouth, she moaned.

The hand in hers squeezed.

"Talk to me."

"Gill?"

"Oh, baby."

Jo looked down to see Gill, his forehead rested on their clasped hands. She tried to move, something on her left side stabbed her in the chest.

"What the hell . . ."

"Don't move, sweetness. Let me get the nurse."

Every breath was painful. Jo looked around the room. It was small, private. Someone she didn't know in a uniform stood beyond the door.

Everything flooded back. The call, the brakes . . . the trip in the bumpy ambulance. Even the bouts of nothing. "Mel, Zoe . . . Zoe?" They were there. She knew they were close.

"Sheriff?"

"Yeah?" Jo opened her eyes, barely realized they had closed.

In zoomed a nurse. The stethoscope and caring smile clued her in. "I'm Cathy. How are you feeling?"

"Like I got ran over."

Cathy laughed. "Not quite. You were in an accident."

"I figured that out." Jo tried to move again, felt the stabbing pain in her left side. She looked down. "What's that?"

"A chest tube." Cathy punched buttons on the monitor above Jo's head, spoke on autopilot. The woman had done this many times before. "You arrived to the ER with a collapsed lung. Side impact on the car. I was told a few feet in any direction and you wouldn't be with us."

Chest tube? That couldn't be good. That explained the crazy pain in her side. "It hurts."

The nurse laid a hand on Jo's shoulder—even that hurt—and offered a smile. "I'll get you pain medication."

Much as Jo wanted to deny the need, the pain in her entire left side stopped her.

Cathy left the room, leaving Gill standing in the doorway.

"Hey."

He crossed and took her right hand in his. "What time is it?"

"Ten."

"At night?" Jesus, she'd been out for hours. How was that possible?

"Jo?" Mel and Zoe stood at the door.

"I'm fine."

She wasn't, she felt like shit, but she wouldn't concede to her pain with her friend looking down at her.

"You're such a dork," Mel said.

"You looked better the night after Mike's graduation party," Zoe reminded her.

Jo closed her eyes. "That was an epic night." Followed by a wicked hangover.

Closing her eyes helped the pain.

She felt a hand on her leg, looked up to see Mel attempting to smile.

"That bad?" Jo asked.

"You don't want to look in the mirror," Zoe told her.

Cathy returned with medicine, and Jo closed her eyes. When she woke again, it was late in the night, and Gill was at her side, asleep . . . his hand in hers.

~

Gill joined Jo's friends in the waiting room while the nurses cleaned Jo up for the day.

"Is that coffee?" he asked, eyeing the box they'd brought in from a local Starbucks.

"Go for it."

He'd hardly slept, and when he did manage a few winks, one of the staff in the ICU stepped in the room. When he was awake, he watched Jo breathing. The bag hanging at the side of her bed that was connected to her lung glared at him. Without any details of the accident, and only the worry over Jo's recovery to keep him occupied, he'd aged a year overnight.

"You're looking a little shot, Gill." Luke patted him on the back.

"I'm not the one lying in a hospital bed."

Mel's hand shook when she reached for the coffee after Gill was finished. "She's really lucky. Did you see the car?"

"No."

Mel removed her phone from her purse and opened the pictures.

Gill's insides froze. The space where Jo had been sitting was smashed into the center of the car. No wonder her lungs didn't take the impact without protesting. She was lucky to have escaped with a broken clavicle, two ribs, and a dozen stitches in various parts of her body.

"According to Karl, the car was in for a recall on the brakes. It's safe to say the recall came a little late." Wyatt removed the coffee from Mel's hand and encouraged her to sit. Worry clouded this group of friends, even though Jo was officially out of the medical woods; Gill could see the distressed lips, the tight fists.

"Did Jo say the brakes were slipping?" Gill asked any one of them with an answer.

"No. When she told me of the recall, I took a quick look. I didn't see anything to warrant a tow to Waterville for the fix. Obviously I was wrong." Zoe placed an arm over Luke's shoulders. The man blamed himself.

"Recalls are usually bogus. A problem affecting a small percentage of cars. Chances are the issue isn't something that can be determined until it fails." Even as Gill said the words, he questioned them. He wanted more details. "Jo's a hell of a defensive driver. She passed her training at Quantico like a champ."

"According to the rescue team, she'd aimed for the side of the hill, bounced, and went over."

It was the second time he'd heard that report.

Jo's day nurse found them in the lobby. "Two at a time, please. We're working on a private room to accommodate Miss Ward outside the ICU."

"Is she stable enough to leave the unit?" Zoe asked.

"She is."

Zoe and Mel took the first turn, disappeared behind the doors.

Gill sat on the uncomfortable couch, the coffee had yet to penetrate his brain. He needed a change of clothes and a shower. And as soon as he was convinced that Jo was on recovery road, he wanted to set his eyes on her car himself.

He smoothed the sides of his beard before running a hand over his head.

"How are you holding up?" Wyatt asked.

Gill offered a nervous shake of his head. "I hate feeling helpless."

"Amen to that," Luke said. "Good thing Jo is durable. She'll be barking to get out of here before long."

"Not with that tube in her chest."

"It won't slow her down long."

Gill gulped his lukewarm coffee and couldn't sit still. Shauna could bring him clothes. She had a key to his place. "I'll be right back." He stepped out of the waiting room, aware the other men watched his exit, and made a call.

~

"Wow, you look like shit."

Jo didn't want to laugh. It hurt. "Always telling the truth, Zoe. Lie to me, will ya?"

"Can't do it." Zoe sat at the foot of Jo's bed.

"The track team wants to visit. We told them to wait," Mel told her.

"Tell them to run instead."

"Kids with a cause. Keeping them away won't happen, we'll just have to deflect until you don't look like you had a one-on-one with a grizzly."

Jo lifted her right hand. Even with the IV sticking out of it, it hurt far less than her left one. "Give me a mirror. It can't be that bad."

Zoe produced a pocket mirror from her purse.

"Damn." She did look like crap. Crude stitches stuck out of her hairline on the left side of her face, bruises around both eyes were spreading out. Her neck was red and her lips were swollen. "I'm guessing the airbag went off."

"The car was trashed," Zoe told her.

"You saw it?"

"We all did as we drove past. Karl called us from the scene."

It was all fuzzy. "I don't remember."

"By the time we got there you were already on your way here. Karl was shaky. I don't think I've ever seen the man so upset."

Jo tried to take a deep breath and winced. "Both our cars were recalled. He probably pictured himself in my position."

"Maybe," Mel said.

"I need to have his car towed here. Karl can't drive it." She pictured the recall notice on her desk, hoped Glynis could find it in her pile.

"I'm sure he's figured that out."

"Can't leave it to chance." She handed the mirror back to Zoe. "Give me your phone."

Zoe looked at her like she was crazy. "Woman, stop. You're in the hospital."

"Karl's a father and a husband. He might be an asshole these days, but this can't happen to both of us." Jo made grabby motions with her hand.

"I'll take care of it," Zoe said.

Jo didn't fight. "Make sure you do."

Zoe saluted her. "Ma'am, yes, ma'am."

She laughed. "Don't. It hurts."

Zoe leaned down, tried to find a place to kiss her head. "I'll send Luke in. Make your phone call."

"Love you," Jo said, closing her eyes. She'd only been awake for two hours, but her body felt like it had been running for a week.

"Can I bring anything from your place?" Mel asked.

Jo licked her dry lips. "Chapstick."

She opened her eyes to a knock on the open door. Luke frowned. "You look like—"

"Crap, I know. Thanks."

At least they were laughing about it.

Even though laughing hurt like hell.

~

"I want out."

Gill protested. "You've barely started walking the halls."

"It's a prison. Complete with a guard."

Gill glanced at the door. One of Waterville's finest had been bedside since Jo arrived. The protocol of police protection 24/7 when one of their own was in the hospital should have come as a comfort. Not for Jo. She hated the attention.

"Prisons don't have this many flowers."

The room was a florist's dream. Every shade and shape of flowers, balloons . . . and even a massive poster handmade by the track team had sentiments and the occasional tongue-in-cheek joke about Jo's driving, which hung across one wall of the private room.

"Everyone has put their life on hold. The sooner I'm in my own bed, the better."

"Let the doctors determine when you leave."

Jo glared. "You wouldn't be saying that if you were in this bed."

"That's not the point."

"Ha!" She flinched, held her side. The tube had come out, but Gill could tell every time pain reminded her that it had been there. "Break me out of here."

"Not gonna happen."

"I'm going to remember this."

"When we're eighty, you can repay the favor."

She smiled. "I'll leave your sagging ass hanging out of a hospital gown for everyone to see."

He faked a frown. "Who says it will be saggy?"

"Everyone's ass is sagging at eighty."

"I'm going to rock an eighty-year-old butt."

Jo rolled her eyes. "C'mon, Gill. I'd leave myself if I could drive."

Gill leaned down, kissed her forehead. "Tomorrow."

# Chapter Twenty-Seven

"Coach Ward wants us training. So we're running like she's here riding our ass." Drew didn't expect an argument, and he didn't get one. They'd slacked the first two days Jo was in the hospital. A few of them camped outside the hospital, waiting for permission to visit her. She looked as bad as everyone said she did. Worse.

Drew gave her shit about her driving skills and had her laughing. Making her smile was the only reward he wanted.

It didn't escape him that the car she'd been driving had the same recall as his dad's. It could have easily been his father in that hospital bed. Drew hated that for a brief second he'd wished it was.

The feeling didn't last. Especially when his father acted guilty about the whole thing. When they'd visited Jo, his father was visibly upset.

"Let's take Lob Hill," Tina suggested.

Gustavo moaned.

"Bite me. C'mon. Lob Hill, then our normal. We'll send her a picture of us up there and make her proud," Tina said.

Drew liked the way his girl thought.

"She's going to ask what we were doing to all be up there."

Tim was right. Coach Ward would think they'd been out partying. Which none of them dared this close to state.

"Whatever," Drew said. "I'm in." And they started to run, grumbling Gustavo and all. At the top, they snapped a picture and sent it to Jo's cell phone.

Drew paced beside Tina during their normal run through the woods surrounding the school.

"I hope Coach Ward can be here for prom."

"I bet she will," Drew said.

"Did you rent your tux?"

He smiled. "Nope, gonna wear jeans and a T-shirt."

Tina slapped his arm.

"C'mon." Drew picked up the pace.

"Overachievers!" someone yelled from behind them.

Drew flipped them the bird and kept running.

Later, when they were cooling down and finishing with a stretch, the morning football practice took over the field.

Drew and the others skirted off the fifty-yard line to give them room.

"There goes dog-killer's son," he heard someone in the crush of football jocks say.

Drew swiveled around.

"I heard Dad jacked the car, too."

He clenched his fists. "Who said that?" He started toward the football team.

Tim and Gustavo jumped up from their stretches, grabbed Drew's arms.

"Ohhh, looks like someone wants to defend *Daddy*."

Drew's eyes burrowed into the voice. Freddy. The kid deserved to be on Coach Ward's track team for all the partying he did. His daddy kept him in football even though he'd never make it past high school in the sport.

"You have something to say, douchebag?" Drew asked as he attempted to pull away from Tim and Gustavo.

"Everyone knows your dad wants Sheriff Ward's job. What better way to get it than to off her?"

Drew saw red.

By now the remaining track team had joined them and faced off with the football team.

"That's fucked up, Freddy." Gustavo's grip on Drew's arm loosened as he spoke.

Just when Drew was ready to make Freddy eat his words, Tina jumped in front of him. "Don't do it. You punch him and there's no prom, no state. He's just an asshole." Tina forced his eyes to hers. "Please."

His back teeth ground together, his fists dug holes into his palms.

He wanted to punch something.

"He's not worth it," Tina pleaded.

Drew's breath came in short pants. "Fuck!" He turned away.

Behind him, Freddy laughed. "Dog-killer's son is a wimp, too."

Drew didn't move fast enough.

Gustavo did. He had a mean right fist, and it connected with Freddy so fast the kid didn't see it coming.

The football coach jumped in before Freddy could get to his feet.

Gustavo shook out his fist, turned to Drew. "I hadn't planned on going to prom or state."

~

Miss Gina's idea of playing nurse when it was her shift—Jo's friends had mapped out a schedule of who was with her day and night—involved marijuana and vodka. Neither of which Jo took her up on.

Jo didn't mind. She'd blown out of the hospital after six long days and five nights. Three too many, if anyone asked her.

No one did.

Gill refused to let anyone else drive her home other than him.

She wasn't sure how he was managing to avoid his day job while he played nursemaid. Shauna had visited twice, both times bringing Gill up to date on the case. Jo envied their working relationship.

Jo couldn't help but think of the tension between her and her so-called partner. Through the years, they had managed to work well, but in the recent past things had become seriously strained.

Still, she was ecstatic to be home.

Miss Gina sat on Jo's couch, a plate of one of the many dishes Zoe had made and stocked her refrigerator with warm in her lap. "So much better than hospital food," Miss Gina said between bites.

"You act like you were the one in the hospital."

"Am I wrong?"

Jo had eaten half her meal, put the rest aside. "Nope."

From her bedroom, Gill emerged fresh from the shower, his chest bare, his hips holding up his jeans.

"Well, that's a damn fine sight." Miss Gina hummed over her fork as she stared.

Gill paused. "I feel strangely violated."

Miss Gina kept teasing. "That can be arranged. Pretty sure I can take Jo out in her current condition."

Jo laughed, held her side with her good arm. The left sat in a sling, more for the broken collarbone than anything else. Overall she was feeling pretty good. Didn't mind taking the pain meds before bed but stuck with the over-the-counter stuff during the day. Even if that meant feeling the pain with every chuckle.

Gill ducked back into her room, returned with a shirt covering his broad chest.

"So not cool," Miss Gina muttered.

The doorbell rang. Miss Gina jumped to answer it.

Mrs. Miller stood in the doorway, a pie in her hands. "Hello, Gina. Taking care of our patient?"

Miss Gina shrugged, opened the door wide.

Mrs. Miller smiled at Jo, glanced at Gill, who had sat on the arm of the recliner Jo was perched in.

"Looks like you're on the mend."

"Thank you. My friends keep telling me I look like crap."

Mrs. Miller cocked her head to the side. "Well . . ."

Jo glanced at Gill. "Will someone please lie to me!"

Gill stood and extended a hand. "I'm Gill."

Mrs. Miller smiled and handed the pie to Miss Gina. "A pleasure. I've heard a lot about you."

"You have me at a disadvantage," Gill said.

"I'm Luke's mother."

"Ah." Gill eyed the pie. "I've heard about your pies."

"I suppose it could be worse." Mrs. Miller crossed the room and leaned down to Jo's side. "How are you feeling?"

"I have a marathon scheduled next week. I'm in."

Mrs. Miller smiled. "I'm not staying. Just wanted to stop in. You call if you need anything." The woman kissed Jo's cheek.

"I will."

After Mrs. Miller left, the parade began.

Once the fourth neighbor had stopped by and left, Gill excused himself, said he wanted to see how everything at the station was running. Considering how much she'd talked about her job, about the cars . . . about Karl's desire to vie for her job, stress ate at her sleep almost as much as the pain.

Gill noticed.

~

The station was an excuse. He had every intention of stopping in, make sure that Karl knew Gill was paying attention, but not before talking with Wyatt about his cloaked text. Gill agreed to meet him at Miller's

Auto. Since the mild weather was holding out, Gill took the opportunity to walk through town.

Each step felt more familiar than the last.

When he passed the station, and then Sam's diner, he found himself waving at the waitress through the glass. He'd forgotten her name but remembered she'd been kind.

Hard rock pumped through the doors of the garage. He found Luke and Wyatt shooting the crap around an old pickup that looked like it was twenty years past its prime.

They shook hands, went over how Jo was doing now that she was home.

"What's going on?" Gill jumped to the point.

"There are some significant rumors going around," Wyatt told him. "Beyond gossip."

"I'm listening." Gill crossed his arms over his chest.

"It's starting at the high school. One of my track kids ended up suspended for the last few days for fighting. Apparently he was defending Drew Emery."

"Karl's son?"

"That's the one. One of the kids alluded to the possibility of Karl being behind the dog."

"You're kidding."

"There's more," Luke said. "With Karl taking a position for Jo's job, there's talk of him tampering with the brakes."

Gill uncrossed his arms, looked over his shoulder, down the street to where the station probably housed the man right now.

"Gossip or reality?"

"Hard to say. I'd like to know what the mechanics find on the squad car," Luke said.

"Karl's dislike for animals isn't rumor."

"These are some serious accusations."

Wyatt shuffled his feet. "Karl is taking point on Jo's job now with her laid up. An accidental death . . ." He let his words die in his mouth.

"Like her father's?" Gill asked on a breath.

"We all know how Jo feels about that."

Could it be that simple? Could Karl be that man?

"Jo can't take this right now."

"Which is why we're talking to you," Luke told him.

"If it is Karl, why wait until now to make a move?"

"Too suspicious to happen on the heels of her father? You're the FBI agent, you tell us."

Wyatt had a point.

"I don't like how this smells."

"Neither do we."

# Chapter Twenty-Eight

"How is it you're still here?" Jo asked on her third night home.

"I'm the night shift," Gill told her as he tucked her into the crook of his arm once they climbed into bed for the night. "You have to admit, I'm a decent pillow."

"You're hard as a rock."

He kissed the top of her head. "You love it."

"I do. But seriously, you have a job, a home."

"Shauna has it covered."

Jo wasn't convinced. "I can't keep you away forever."

"Yes, you can."

She looked up at him. "Gill."

"My boss understands. Everything is okay." He closed his eyes.

"You wouldn't lie to me, would you?"

Gill nodded without apology.

"Gill!"

"It's okay."

She hated being placated. "Gill!"

He opened his eyes and sighed. "Okay, here's the truth. You ready for it?"

The tone of his voice suggested maybe she wasn't. She said yes anyway.

"I told him the woman I've grown to care about more than life itself needed me. And that if I had to take a leave of absence to watch over you, I would."

Gill's words stole her breath.

"You know what he asked?"

She swallowed.

"He asked if he was going to be invited to the wedding."

Jo felt dizzy. "What did you say?" she whispered.

"Only if he granted me time off." Gill was slow to smile. "Then he told me of his fondness for wedding cake."

If she'd been taking pain medication, she'd swear she was dreaming. "Wedding cake is just like any other cake."

He didn't agree. "No, it's sweeter than birthday cake, because birthdays happen once a year, weddings happen only once."

"Not always," she found herself saying with worry.

Gill kissed her forehead once again. "For us. Only once."

The conversation scared and thrilled her equally. "Gill—"

"Shh." He pointed two fingers at her head. "Let all that cook in there for a while. It's taking time marinating in mine."

She snuggled back in his arms, the silly grin he'd put on her face threatening to stick. She licked her lips, thought of cake.

*Sugar.*

"Gill?"

"Yeah?" he asked in the dark.

"Is there any of Mrs. Miller's pie left?"

~

"I want a prom picture," Gill said as he straightened his tie.

"You're kidding me."

He poked his head into the bathroom, smiled at Jo through the mirror. "Does this look like my kidding face?"

Gill pinched his lips together. And when Jo laughed, it didn't hurt like it had the week prior.

The doctor had given her the go-ahead for desk work. Which she'd already been cheating with. A few more weeks and her bones would be mended enough for her temporary disability to lift.

She couldn't wait.

Now she just needed to convince Gill to go back to work.

"One picture."

"I'm holding you to it."

She pointed to the back of her dress. "Help me."

Gill zipped her up, kissed the back of her neck before standing back. "I don't think I've ever seen you in a dress."

"It doesn't happen often."

He slid a hand down her waist, lifted the edges of her dress until the length of her thigh was exposed. "Dresses have an advantage."

She leaned back. "As much as I'd like to explore that idea . . ."

Gill dropped the dress. "I know. Three weeks."

The doctors had warned her against moving too soon. From running to sex. The frustration building between them was thicker than a twenty-eight-ounce steak.

Jo had to close her mind to the thought.

"Three weeks."

Gill kissed her neck and nibbled on the lobe of her ear. "We can make out. Like in high school."

"I doubt you stopped with kissing."

"I can."

She closed her eyes when his teeth grazed her neck. "I can't."

∼

The high school gym was glowing with white twinkling lights and silver balloons. The theme was "Reach for the Stars," and the associated student body, along with a few parent volunteers, had done a brilliant job of taking the gym space and making it feel small and intimate. It might have been considered the senior prom, but that didn't stop freshmen and sophomores from attending.

"Take a good look," Jo told Gill. "The same decorations will come out for the reunion."

"River Bend goes all out."

"Hey, we'll have a bar."

"Big-timers."

They were both laughing when Jo heard her name. "Coach Ward!"

Tina and Drew were walking toward them, hand in hand.

"You both look spectacular." And they did. Tina wore a strapless black dress that hugged her waist and stopped just below her knee. Drew's tux looked like he was born to it. They both were so grown up.

"I'm so glad you came," Tina said, giving her a one-arm hug, careful of her arm still stuck in a sling.

"You wouldn't be saying that if I hadn't had the accident."

"That's not true."

The town sheriff was a killjoy at a high school party.

"You clean up rather well, Drew."

He tugged on his tie with a grin. Something about his action rang in her head.

"How about a picture?" Gill suggested.

Drew and Tina flanked her. Drew placed his arm around Jo's shoulder, and Tina leaned in. The moment was frozen in time. One that Jo knew she would keep for years.

"Going to be a couple busy weeks. You both ready for graduation?"

"I am." Tina had already committed to the University of New Mexico. Drew had been accepted to a few colleges but had yet to say where he was going.

"Drew? Any more thought on school versus military?" Karl wouldn't like that she asked, but Jo couldn't bring herself to care.

"I honestly don't know."

"You'll figure it out," Jo told him. "Either way, I'm proud of you."

Drew looked deep in her eyes. "Thanks, Coach."

Jo waved them off. "Now go on . . . I'm sure standing around talking to the sheriff isn't your idea of how to spend your night."

"No way," Drew said, taking Tina's arm. "We have an epic party out at Grayson's farm."

Jo knew she scowled.

"Kidding!" Drew laughed. "No one parties out there anymore."

Jo warned him with a look. "I did."

"Yeah, we know that," Tina said before they walked off.

Gill slid into the space the kids had left behind. "They have your number."

"I'm going to ignore that they said that."

"Probably a good idea."

She glanced over her shoulder, saw Drew pull Tina into his arms to dance.

"How about that prom picture?"

～

Drew kept half an eye on Coach Ward while dancing with Tina. "Do you think we should skip the senior prank this year?"

Tina followed his eyes. "It's a tradition. TPing the coach's house on reunion night never fails."

"Yeah, she'll probably feel left out if we don't do it."

The slow song switched to rap. They both danced until breathless. And when it wasn't too obvious, Drew pulled Tina outside for air.

He kissed her as soon as they were alone.

Tina kissed him back, completely into it.

"How long do you wanna stay?" Drew asked when his body raged. "An hour?"

An hour . . . he could do an hour. "And then?" They'd talked about taking the next step. He knew he was ready, was fairly certain she was, too.

"And then . . ." Tina's coy smile answered his question.

"You sure?"

"I'm ready."

His dick jumped and he kissed her again. "This is going to be the longest hour of my life."

~

Jo's first day back to work was Gill's first night away from River Bend. She forced the issue.

Glynis celebrated her return with a candle in a donut.

The bruises had faded, the stitches removed. Jo put on her uniform and her belt. She'd removed some of the weight but kept her handcuffs, her gun, and her extra clip. Everything else was sitting on the dresser by her bed. Desk duty, she reminded herself.

She'd gone to the high school in the morning and watched as the remaining seniors that were going to state paced themselves. Drew and Tim rounded out her distance runners, and the relay team was there, too.

It felt good to pull the moist morning air into her battered lungs.

She stayed long enough to pitch a few pointers to Drew and Tim. They didn't need her at this point, both of them hungry for a spot on the podium.

Oregon was a hard place when it came to track. Some of the best schools in the sport were there, and the competition for a state title was fierce.

Still, they had a chance.

She was proud either way.

With a half-eaten donut and a cup of coffee, Jo took her place behind her desk. It was surprisingly clean.

"Glynis? Where is all the mail?"

"Most of it was taken care of."

"What?"

"Deputy Fitzpatrick stayed on top of things. I have the papers that need your signature."

Jo wasn't sure she liked being replaced. "Where are they?"

Glynis moved to the filing cabinet behind Jo's desk. "In here."

Jo peered into the cabinet, felt her heart skip. "Where are all my files?"

"Archived. Anything over seven years. I've been scanning and shredding."

"You've done what?" Jo's voice rose an octave.

"It's okay. I scanned everything. I've let it slip the last couple of years. Deputy Emery told me I should make room."

"Is that right?"

"Is something wrong?" Glynis asked.

Jo ran her hands over the files, opened the next drawer.

Gone . . . everything around the time of her father's death was gone. "I want to see the scanned documents."

"Of course." Glynis scurried off, and Jo slammed the file drawer.

"Welcome back, Jo."

Jo tried to keep her cool as she turned to see Karl in her doorway.

"Thank you." She didn't make eye contact.

"It's been quiet without you here."

A snarky comment about how quiet it would have been had she tumbled off the cliff sat on her lips.

She kept quiet.

"Listen, Jo. I'm sorry."

She found his eyes.

"I was shitty before the accident. Said some things I didn't mean."
He sounded sincere. "You don't want my job?"

"Not at your expense. I admit it's been hard at times. I remember
sitting in this office, talking with your dad about your crazy teenage
years. To have you take his place wasn't the easiest thing for me."

"I thought we were past all that," Jo said.

"I thought I was, too. Sometimes the past comes back to haunt us."
Karl shook his head as if removing thoughts. "Anyway. You might not
believe me, but I'm glad you're back."

Not sure what to make of his words, she decided mutual ground
was best. "You're going to Drew's state meet, right? I'll make sure everything is covered here."

"Fitzpatrick has done a lot already."

Jo wanted to scream at the man. "Karl. I'm talking as a friend, not
as your boss. Drew wants you there."

"I don't know. After the incident at the school I think my being
there will just make it worse."

"What incident?"

Karl shuffled his feet. "Nothing."

"Sounds like something. Spill."

"Someone on the football team said something. There was a fight."

"What?" She hadn't heard of any fight. "Drew?"

"No. Almost, but no. That little Tina is good for him. Gustavo
threw the punch."

Jo hadn't seen Gustavo since the team's trip to the hospital to visit
her. "What on earth for?"

"Apparently there's some shitty gossip going around town. I've
pissed off all the dog lovers in town, and some think I strung up Cherie's
dog."

To have her concerns vocalized by the man she herself had begun to
blame was either brilliant on his end to drag her off his scent or stupid
for putting himself on her radar.

"Jesus, Jo . . . not you, too."

"No," she denied too quickly. "Of course not."

"Right. I need to go before I say something crappy and undo all the fence mending I'm trying to build."

Jo stood a little too quickly, felt the pull in her side. "Karl, please. It's been a stressful couple of months."

"Yeah. You have no idea." With his parting words, he turned and left.

Jo rested her head in her hands and silently cussed the universe.

~

Gill stood over the mangled mess of Jo's car. It scared him every damn time he looked at the seat she'd been in.

"Agent Clausen."

"Mac?"

"Right." They shook hands. Gill had been in contact with the mechanic in charge of investigating Jo's accident.

"You have something for me?"

"I do. I started with the brake recall. The ABS actuator damaged O-rings, which decreases the brake fluid pressure . . . causes a delay in the ability to brake in time."

"I know how brakes work," Gill told the man.

"Right. Anyway. You said Sheriff Ward reported a lack of brakes altogether. That hasn't been reported on this recall. In fact, other than this accident, there hasn't been anything other than a fender bender."

"So were the O-rings damaged?"

Mac shook his head. "No."

"So what caused the brake failure?"

Mac waved Gill over to a computer and pulled up a magnified image. "What am I looking at?"

"Brake line. Front right tire."

As with any image magnified a zillion times better than what the naked eye could see, it looked frayed. Gill knew better than to think the entire tube was faulty.

"This is normal." Mac pulled up another image. "This one is off the line in the back right tire. Smooth, perfect. The left lines were shot from the wreck." He flipped back to the first image.

Gill looked closer. "What's this?"

"That," Mac paused, "is a hole."

"From what?"

"Ten thousand dollar question. Looks too smooth to be organic."

"Organic?"

"From a rock on the road, an animal biting it."

"Big enough to cause the brakes to completely fail?"

"With enough time the leak would bleed the line and malfunction. But I didn't like what I saw, so I looked again." Mac pulled up another image. This tube was a dark gray, larger.

"Power steering line."

"You're good," Mac praised him. "Either River Bend has vampire mice puncturing holes into lines or we have someone trying to kill your sheriff."

Gill left the auto shop with the phone to his ear.

He called Luke first. "Don't let Jo drive anywhere."

"Why, what's going on?"

"Her accident wasn't an accident."

"What? Does she know this?"

"Not yet," Gill said, jumping into his car and heading straight to his office. "I'll be back in town tonight. Confiscate her Jeep, take the battery out of the squad car. Just don't let her drive."

"I'm on it."

"And don't tell her anything."

"But . . ."

"Trust me. Someone close to her did this, and the only people in town I trust right now are you, Wyatt, and your ladies."

"Jo's smart, she's going to figure out something's up."

"I'll tell her. Just wait for me to get there."

Gill blew past his colleagues when he entered the office after being gone for two weeks.

"Shauna?" He poked his head into her office, motioned her to follow him.

"Hey, stranger." She scrambled to catch up with him. "What's up?"

Gill blew past his superior's secretary. "Reyes in there?"

"He's on the phone."

That didn't stop him. He knocked once and let himself in.

Reyes looked up from his phone call. "Right . . . okay. Listen, something just blew in. I'll get back to you." He hung up. "Clausen . . . Burton."

"I have a new case." For the next thirty minutes Gill explained the situation. From Jo's nonaccident to the questionable death of her father ten years prior. One too many coincidences pointed to foul play and murder. The holes in the lines of the squad car were attempted murder of a sworn officer. And no one wearing the uniform was okay with that.

"You're too close to be objective," Reyes said once he agreed there was a case.

"I'm the only one close enough to investigate this. A new player in this town will scare off our suspect."

"And you think this deputy is our guy?"

"He stands to gain if something happens to Jo."

"Feels too neat," Shauna said.

"I have to agree with Burton."

"Still think you're too close, Gill."

"Send someone else if you need to, but I'm going in. I'll tell Jo I'm taking a vacation. Shauna can come visit. Be a second set of eyes."

"Our heroin case?" Reyes asked.

"I'm a day away from the warrants being signed," Shauna told him.

"We need hard evidence."

"I'm not new. I'll get your evidence."

Reyes stood. "I want a daily report."

Gill offered a tight smile. "Done."

"Go. Get out of here."

Gill didn't need to be told twice.

# Chapter Twenty-Nine

Jo sat across from Gill, her kitchen table separating them, and listened.

Before he was finished, she felt sick to her stomach. A serious desire to empty what dinner she had managed to eat sat close to the surface.

"Maybe the mechanic is wrong."

Gill held her hand. "He's not wrong. I saw the lines with my own eyes. The holes were large enough to warrant leaks, not big enough to dump all the fluid in one sitting. It was deliberate, Jo."

"Why?"

"We're going to find out."

Someone had tried to kill her. The sling holding her left arm and her inability to run a block, much less the five daily miles she'd run before, were evidence that whoever that someone was, they'd nearly succeeded.

"When I was in the academy, the other cadets would talk about wearing a badge, how it was a target just asking for someone to aim a weapon at them. I never felt like that. I figured my father's death was isolated. Something that involved him . . . not this badge."

"There's no way of knowing if they're connected," Gill told her.

"No way of knowing they're not either. Seems a little too convenient to have my father 'accidentally' shoot himself and for me to bite it going off a cliff." Jo pictured the cemetery where her parents lay and for a brief moment saw another flag-draped casket.

"You didn't bite it." His eyes were large orbs of worry.

"How are we going to find this person? They've been hidden for ten years."

"They're not hiding now."

Jo shook off the chill. "I've felt like someone has been watching me for close to a year."

"Probably have. Which tells me that whoever this is, they're local, or local enough."

"They climbed under my car. They would have to know about the recall, my schedule." A long list of names filled Jo's head.

"So write those names down. No matter who they are."

"I know it isn't Luke or Mel . . ."

"But Luke is a mechanic, and maybe he said something to his father about the recall."

"Mr. Miller is like my second dad," she protested.

"Mr. Miller runs an auto shop. He might have said something in passing to Joe Blow from outside of town."

She hadn't thought of that.

"Every name."

The list in her head doubled. "How am I going to trust my car?"

"Playing post-traumatic stress might be the best way to handle that right now. River Bend is small enough to walk. It's almost summer."

"That can't last forever."

Gill squeezed her hand. "Honey, I'm not waiting forever to nail this bastard to the wall."

She brought their clasped hands up to her lips and kissed his fingertips.

～

Gill liked working with as few players as possible. He and Shauna were a pretty good tag team for that very reason. Shauna would network as the social one, and he would sit in parking lots and snap pictures.

Bringing in Jo's friends was unavoidable. Especially when Gill himself had called Luke to make sure Jo wasn't driving before he could make it back to town.

Outside her small circle of friends, no one was eliminated from the suspect list. When he'd suggested Glynis, Jo laughed him out of the room. But her name stayed on the list. She knew about the recall, had access to the car, was removing files.

When he'd pointed these things out, Jo still laughed.

In Gill's head, the number one suspect was Jo's deputy, Karl Emery. The man didn't pretend to be completely charmed, but he wasn't a total asshole either. He sat on the fence, and he watched both Gill and Jo a little too hard.

Gill had the list of activities Jo was on point to attend. Events that everyone in town would be aware of.

The state championship competition for her runners. That would take place in Eugene. They agreed to make it sound like she was driving her Jeep to the event, and at the last minute they would take the van with the kids.

The senior graduation was less than a week after state, and then the class reunion back at the school gym.

Jo would have a personal bodyguard at every event.

Gill knew he'd driven his point on her personal safety home when he witnessed her putting on her vest before her uniform.

~

Life couldn't get much better.

Thanks to all things Tina, Drew passed his chemistry class. Something he knew he'd never use again in his life.

Thanks to Tina, he'd found the meaning of his sexual life. Not just once, either. She was into it, and he was constantly on the lookout for places they could duck away and learn something new. They used condoms and she told him she was on the pill. He'd thought about saying the *L* word but wasn't completely sure he was. Besides, she was going away to college, and he was going away somewhere too. Even though they were temporary, neither of them brought that up.

Then there was state. He'd made it, along with Tim. Together they hoped to bring home a respectable place. Coach Ward had told them both that they'd already earned a spot at River Bend's hall of sports fame, but they both wanted to bring home number one.

Either way, Drew's senior year had been worth the long runs, and late night study sessions. He missed parties between his dad and Coach Ward. He could hardly wait until he could come home from wherever he ended up and buy Coach Ward a drink.

He'd come to terms with the fact that he and his dad were never going to be the tight ends on any team. Drew realized that part of the reason he wanted to join the marines was because his father was so against it. He was also smart enough not to jump at this final shot at rebellion. He might be better off getting a tattoo instead.

Drew would make a decision after state, after graduation.

He skipped through the door, shouting to the house. "I passed!"

His mom yelled from the kitchen, "I'm in here."

Drew smelled cookies. "This day is getting better and better."

Wearing jeans and a T-shirt, his mom looked like just about every other mom in River Bend. She didn't wear a lot of makeup, had shoulder length hair that he thought maybe she was dyeing these days. He made a point after she'd been to the hairdresser to say she looked nice, but that was usually followed by a request for twenty bucks for a movie or something.

And there were cookies.

He took one from the top of the pile. It was warm.

"What about washing your hands?"

Drew snorted. "Germs help build your immunity to crap. I learned that in chemistry . . . which I passed."

His mom smiled. "One more final and that's it?"

"English."

"You better hope Mrs. Walters doesn't hold a grudge."

"Way to dash my hopes, Mom."

"Yeah, well . . . pranks like that happen after the person you're pulling them on is no longer in charge of your academic life."

He immediately thought of the stash of toilet paper he and the seniors had in store for Coach Ward's house.

"Any more decisions about what you're going to do after next week?"

She was asking about the service.

He shrugged. "I don't know. I'm not sure college is right for me."

"You told Oregon State you were interested."

"I am . . . but only because of track. I realize I'd be throwing away a free education if I said no, but what if I hate it?"

"What if you love it?"

He leaned against the counter, shoved a second cookie in his face. "Would it be so bad . . . me joining the marines?"

He hated the stress he put on his mom's face but needed her to know that he was serious about the option.

"I'd be scared every day."

"Every day if I were shipped off."

She attempted to smile and failed.

"Dad is a cop, don't you worry about him?"

"It's not the same here. Maybe if we lived in New York or something."

"What if I wanted to be like Dad?"

She sighed. "I'd be proud of you either way, Drew. I know your father would be proud of you, too. It's your life and your decision to make."

He knew her words were hard for her to say. Drew leaned in, kissed her cheek, and went in for his third after-school snack before turning to walk away.

"Nice decoy," she told him. "Now take out the trash."

Oh, yeah . . . every day after school . . . you'd think after eighteen years he'd remember.

Well, he probably didn't do it when he was two.

He bundled up the plastic bag full of kitchen garbage and headed out the back door.

The cans on the side of the house were full and starting to smell in the warm weather.

He shooed away a dozen bees before opening the blue barrel.

Something on top of the white plastic bags attracted the buzzing insects. The stench had Drew choking back his cookies.

He peered closer and gagged.

~

"I think it's a rabbit." From the little bit of fur Jo noticed on the thing.

"Been dead a day or two," Gill said.

"You took the trash out yesterday, right?" Karl asked Drew, who still looked green.

"Yeah. That wasn't in there."

Caroline stood to the side, a finger under her nose.

Jo was at the station when Caroline called Karl about the dead animal in the trash can. Not just a dead rabbit that may have come to some unfortunate demise and then been tossed into a garbage can, but one that was staged with missing parts.

"Who is doing this, Dad?"

Karl glared beyond the cans. "I don't know, but I sure as hell am going to find out."

His conviction made Jo pause.

"If this is someone's sick idea of a joke, I'm going to ki—"

Jo cut Drew off with a hand to his shoulder. "You'd have to find them first, and you have school to concentrate on."

Scared came out as angry in Drew's gaze. Jo attempted to smile. "C'mon." She encouraged him to walk around to the backyard so she could speak with him alone. "How was your run this morning?"

He ducked his head and walked with her.

"I don't want to talk about my workout."

"Okay."

"This is sick. First the dog, then . . ." He waved his hand toward the garbage cans. "Whatever the hell that was. I feel like every time I turn around I find something dead. When will it end?"

*When I'm dead in a trash can.* Jo winced with her thought. "Figuring out who is doing this is my number one priority, Drew. I will put a stop to it."

"I watch CSI. Psychos do this kind of shit. And they don't stop with animals."

Smart kid. "You sure you don't want to be a cop instead of a marine?"

He made a face that looked like he bit into an apple and found half a worm. "No thanks."

Jo offered a small smile and placed an arm around his shoulders. "Do you trust me?"

"Yeah."

"Good. I'll find this guy. You just pass your finals and run fast on Saturday."

"Jo?" Gill called.

They both looked up.

Gill paused, looked at Caroline and Karl, then back.

"What?"

Gill shook his head and waved her over.

"You okay?" she asked Drew.

"Yeah."

She patted him on the back before joining the others to investigate.

# Chapter Thirty

Much as Jo didn't like the thought of being there, Gill convinced her to take a trip to the cabin. The last five miles were slow, bumpy, and nerve-racking.

"When was the last time you were up here?"

She clenched her fists. "Once after my dad's death, and another time once I was elected."

"Twice?"

She nodded once.

Gill placed a hand on her knee.

"You see things I don't," he told her, "or I wouldn't have suggested you come."

Jo closed her eyes and mentally kicked herself. "I should be over this by now."

"You haven't had the opportunity to move on."

Jo covered his hand with hers. "Thank you."

"For what?"

"Getting me."

The cabin came into view as they rounded the bend. Outside of the pictures shown to her from the ladies who volunteered to clean the place every season, she hadn't experienced the vacation home for years.

Spring did wonderful things to the backdrop of the cabin. Wildflowers bloomed along the west side with new, bright green growth on the shrubs on the east. It sat on a knoll with less than a hundred yards that separated it from a hillside slope of dense pine trees that spilled into the forest. Her father had always said that a wildfire would take the place in a breath. He was right, but boy, the view was breathtaking.

The log construction was something her father had talked to her about every time they drove in. "Think of those Lincoln Logs you play with. Only these logs are filled in with a special mortar between them to keep us warm. Did you know that Abraham Lincoln was born in a log cabin?" She smiled into the memory. Her father was a patriot from the moment he was born. The fact that she'd been given Lincoln Logs to play with as a child instead of dolls said everything about how she was raised.

"My dad loved this place."

"I can see why. It has everything a man needs."

"Oh?"

Gill pulled up to the cabin and killed the engine. "A bed, a potbelly stove . . . quiet."

"I happen to like indoor plumbing."

"Men like to pee outside. Brings us back to our roots."

Jo had to smile. "Men!" Looking through the windshield, Jo gathered her courage and opened her door.

Memories trickled in as she stepped toward the cabin. If she reached back far enough, she sensed the feeling of her mother there. But that had been so early in her life she'd all but forgotten the details of the woman.

"What are you thinking about?" Gill asked as they stood staring up at the cabin.

"I'm trying to remember my mother."

Gill reached for her hand, laced his fingers through hers.

"It's hard to see her anymore. Unlike my dad. I hear him in my head just about everywhere."

"And what do you hear in this place?"

She lowered her voice in an attempt to mimic him. "'Get the groceries, JoAnne. No need to traipse dirt inside if you don't need to.' He was a little anal about cleanliness."

"Even out here?"

"A little less out here, but he'd always remind me to wipe my feet, take my shoes off."

"Those things don't seem to bother you."

She shook her head. "No. Life is too short to worry about dirt."

"Yet you keep your house nearly immaculate."

"No, I don't."

Gill tilted his head to the side.

"Okay, maybe a little. It's still his house, I guess."

Happy Gill didn't point out that it had been hers for ten years, she took the first step onto the porch and opened the door.

It smelled the same. Wood and musk from sitting unused masked the slight scent of campfire the potbelly stove would give off on cool nights. All the furniture was made of thick wood and dark-colored fabric. If dirt was brought in, Joseph couldn't see it.

This wasn't a place to watch TV or think of the world. It was a place to visit with family, eat whole foods that didn't require a microwave to cook, read a book, or play a game of cards. Considering she'd grown up with a cell phone in her back pocket, there had been trips up there she'd hated simply because she couldn't connect with Mel or Zoe. And then there were the memories of Mel and Zoe joining her. They left their phones in the truck when they arrived and didn't pick them back up until they reached the cell service back in town.

Her father would read on the porch, when he'd tell his friends he'd hunted all day. Truth was, he'd only really attempt to find venison on the day before leaving . . . or even the day of. Bleeding a deer in the woods often attracted predators that had no problem stealing her father's find. When he did manage to bring something home from his hunt, they'd freeze what they could and give the rest to various neighbors who appreciated the meat.

The taste of her father's venison stew made her mouth water.

Jo crossed to the bookshelf that sat beside the two-person sofa. Her fingers lingered over the thrillers her father had read, some he'd never gotten to.

"Your dad's?" Gill asked.

"Yeah. He was up here a lot more than I was in my last years of high school."

"Who came up here with him?"

Jo started listing names. "Karl would come up if Stan was in town, and Stan would come when Karl wasn't here. Mr. Miller, Sam. There wasn't anyone excluded from a man's trip. It came down to who could convince their wives to deal with their kids solo. He came up here alone, too."

"Or maybe he was meeting someone here," Gill suggested.

Jo lifted a novel from the shelf. "Probably. I would have at some point if I'd dated someone from town I didn't want anyone to know about."

"Is the gossip that bad?"

"Not as much as it could be, I guess. But as a public servant, there is a certain amount of scrutiny the good people of River Bend placed upon him, and now me."

Gill turned around, took in the room. "What do you see when you walk in here?"

"I see his life. I see that he's not here, and everything else is."

"Is that all?"

She allowed her eyes to settle on the new table. "No. That's not all I see."

The images snapped in the police file of her father's death showed her exactly what had happened to her dad.

His death had been instant. One bullet, point-blank. He had a closed-casket funeral as a result.

Jo shivered.

"You okay?"

"Yes."

"Liar."

She pushed the image of a dead father from her head and focused on the living soul that still lingered in the space.

"Miss Gina coordinated a cleanup . . . after."

"I noticed this table is different than those in the photos," Gill said as he tapped the kitchen-style table.

"I don't remember exactly who brought it up here. That first year was a blur."

"I assume the other one was tossed after the investigation was closed."

"Probably."

"Karl found him, right?"

"Yeah. When he didn't return for his shift, Karl drove up. Makes it difficult to point a finger at him in foul play when he had a legitimate need to be here." Jo set the book in her hand on an end table and crossed to the kitchen side of the room. There was an old icebox they'd put big bricks of dry ice in to keep their perishables cool without having to dig through an ice chest of water. Beside it was a counter for prepping food, a sink that drained to the outside. They'd use water from a nearby creek to wash pots and pans. Paper and plastic plates were a staple to cut down on the need for cleaning. They'd pack out the trash with every trip.

"Did anything else change in here? Damage to other furniture from the gun?"

She looked around. "I don't think so."

"What about on the wall behind?" Gill moved to the side of the room that needed the most cleaning.

"There might have been a picture. I don't remember."

"Do you have any photographs of an average day inside the cabin?"

She crossed to the wall of books and found a photo album her dad had kept.

Jo sat on the sofa, placed the album in her lap, and opened it. The album was one born in the days of film cameras. The images had yellowed edges from the musty conditions and sheer number of years they'd been sitting there. The thin plastic cover that was supposed to help the photos stick to the page had lost its integrity and lifted from the photographs. "I should probably take these in and have them copied digitally."

Gill sat beside her, his arm circling her back.

She walked down memory lane as she flipped through pages.

"Is that you?"

"Pigtails were all the rage when I was five."

He kissed the side of her hair. "Very cute."

Jo pointed at the image of her and her mother. "My mom."

"You look like her."

"I guess. I always thought I looked more like my dad."

The next page was of her dad on that same trip.

"I see the resemblance."

She flipped again. "Who do you take after? Mom or dad?"

"I'm the spitting image of my dad. It's scary knowing what you're going to look like when you're sixty."

"I'm sure he's handsome."

"Beer gut."

Jo laughed. "That's easily fixed."

"That's why I drink whiskey."

They both laughed as she drew a timeline of her childhood.

"Your dad and Karl?"

Jo nodded. They were so much younger. "Yep."

More pages, and fast-forwarding through the years, she found a photograph of her, Mel, and Zoe sitting at the table her father was sitting at when he died. "I'm guessing my junior year."

"Sexy."

"Jailbait," she reminded him.

"Worth the risk."

She glanced at the photograph and then to the wall across the room. "Looks like there was a picture. Probably didn't survive the blast."

Jo dug deeper into the album. The plastic pulled away from the album and a photograph slid out.

She went to put it back in and peered closer.

"That doesn't look like it was taken here," Gill said.

"No. This is in town."

"That's your dad, right?"

"Yeah, my dad, Karl, and Caroline. That must be Drew." The same mischievous smile sat on Drew's young face. He couldn't have been more than seven when this was taken.

She lifted the image closer, noticed a crease, and folded the picture where it appeared someone had done so before. When she folded the photo, Karl was taken away from the others. Only her father, Drew, and Caroline were left.

Jo's heart started to speed in her chest.

She removed her phone from her back pocket and pulled up a picture taken at the last track meet of her and Drew. Then she found a close-up of her dad and set her phone beside his picture. "Holy shit." The mouths were the same, the color of their eyes, even the goofy smiles.

She found the depths of Gill's eyes. Eyes that were drawing the same conclusion as she was.

"I think we found the mystery woman," Gill said.

"And the reason my dad didn't let anyone in town know what he had going." She couldn't stop staring.

"Karl had a motive."

Her mind wasn't moving fast enough. "My father was having an affair with a married woman."

Gill pointed to Drew on her phone. "More than just an affair. I think we need to talk to Mrs. Emery."

Jo's heart kicked hard. "I have a brother."

~

Shauna met them in Eugene at the state championships. With Jo flanking the athletes on the perimeter of the track, Gill and Shauna had the opportunity to sit in the stands with Caroline and Karl. Under the guise of new friends and a mutual association with the team, their plan was to divide and conquer.

"What does Drew run?" Shauna asked.

"The three thousand meter."

"Ouch."

"He's good, or he wouldn't be here," Karl said, pride in his voice. "But these meets last all damn day." Karl mustered up some excitement, but only for half a second.

Gill watched the man without looking straight at him. No hand holding with Caroline, no love pats or any real affection. But that didn't always say anything after twenty years of marriage.

"Is this Drew's first championship?"

"Oh, no. Last year he made it here but didn't make the podium," Caroline told them.

"Do these meets get old?" Shauna asked.

Caroline said no, Karl said yes at the same time.

Caroline shoved her husband's arm.

"What? They do. I'm here for one race and it seems like it's never going to happen, and then when it does it's not like it's over fast."

"I take it you're not a runner," Shauna kept the conversation going.

"No. I leave that to Jo."

It was Gill's turn to chime in. "I couldn't keep up with her if I tried."

"It helps that she's twenty years younger than you, Karl." Caroline leaned against the back bleachers on her elbows.

Karl started to fidget.

Gill nodded to Shauna.

"How much longer before Drew's race?" she asked.

"Couple of hours," Caroline informed them like it was old news.

Karl groaned.

"I could use a beer." Shauna stood.

"Good luck with that. This is the high school championships, not a college football game," Karl said.

"I'm starting to see what you're saying, Karl. How about we find soda and a liquor store?"

He jumped to his feet. "I like how your partner thinks, Gill."

"That's why she's my partner." Gill followed them with his eyes as they zigzagged through people and made their way out of the densely populated stands. Once out of earshot, he said, "He really doesn't like these things."

"He doesn't. Please don't say that to Drew."

"My guess is Drew knows."

Caroline scanned the field. Drew wasn't on it, they were warming up on a far end of the campus, away from spectators and the athletes who were next up to compete.

"Probably."

Gill waited a minute, sipped from his water bottle. "My question is, does Karl know?"

Caroline's look of confusion was followed by, "Does Karl know he doesn't like these things?"

Gill shook his head. "Does Karl know how much Jo and Drew look alike?"

The smile on her face slowly fell.

"Does Karl see the same smirk on his son's face that sits on Jo's . . . and from the pictures I've seen, on her late father's?"

Caroline slowly pushed off her elbows and looked behind them. Her voice was low. "What are you getting at?"

"You know what I'm getting at, Caroline."

She started to breathe faster and she rubbed her palms on her pants.

"We knew Joseph had a lover, but it wasn't until recently that we discovered who she was. It makes sense now."

"It wasn't like that."

Her confirmation of the truth in one sentence.

"What was it like?"

Her butt did a great job of cleaning the bench as she moved around. "I'm not . . . this isn't . . ."

Gill stopped her with a hand. "Does Karl know?"

"Of course not."

Which meant she didn't *think* Karl knew.

"You can't tell him." She placed her hand on Gill's shoulder. "Please. It's not fair to Drew. He's been through enough this year."

A mama bear with her hackles up.

"It's not my place to tell." Some of the color returned to her cheeks. "Who else knew?"

"No one."

"Your girlfriends?"

Caroline glared. "I am a married woman," she whispered under her breath. "We don't do that kind of thing, and if we do, we don't brag about it."

No, he was sure she didn't brag. But chances were someone knew something.

He sat forward, lowered his voice to her level. "Karl doesn't look like a stupid man to me."

"Why are we talking about this?" There was anger in her voice.

He wasn't ready to play all his cards, not in the stands at a high school track meet.

"Was there anyone else?"

Her hesitation was just long enough to say yes. "Of course not."

*Too late, sweetheart.*

# Chapter Thirty-One

"I'm not convinced it's Karl," Gill said to Shauna when she met him beside the pole vaulters.

"Me either. He's a bit of a douche, but I'm not sure he's Mr. Sociopath."

"Why a douche?"

Shauna hid behind her sunglasses, her eyes following the kid pushing off the pole and hitting the bar as he went up.

"Anyone who can't muster up some excitement for his kid at a state meet is an ass."

"It's not *his* kid."

"Yeah, well . . . he *may* know that, his wife certainly knows it, but the kid doesn't. If you're going to pretend, do it all the way. Don't screw up a kid because of your wife's sins. If Karl knows or doesn't know, he's still a douche."

Shauna was going to be a great mom someday, Gill decided. "Your take on Karl?"

"Hard to put my finger on. He's jealous of Jo's relationship with Drew . . . or he's mad they're close. Which actually should make him a suspect. But every time my head goes there, I think it's too damn convenient. Too neat."

"I hate when you think the way I do."

She clapped when the kid on the pole boomeranged over thirteen and a half feet without knocking off the bar. "What about the wife? What's your take?"

"She's a serial cheater."

Shauna glanced over the rim of her sunglasses. "Really?"

"Yep."

"Who's the other dude?"

"Don't know."

"Hmm . . . another player. Do you think she's capable of murder?"

"I think everyone is capable."

The starting gun went off on the field to announce another race.

Gill's back shot straight up.

Where was Jo?

~

The coaches from the individual schools were not allowed on the field during championships. Official refs were dressed in traditional red jackets, red hats, and holstered starting guns while they lumbered around the field qualifying and disqualifying athletes.

Jo liked this part. The excitement before the race when the athletes were stretched out, warmed up, and a medal was within their reach.

Kids were running around everywhere from dozens of different schools. But her eyes were on the colors of River Bend High. As she watched Drew warming up that morning, it was hard not to stare.

She had a brother.

Considering all of her immediate family was gone, the revelation of a new member in her life was sobering. No wonder the kid reminded her of when she was younger. They were cut from the same patriarchal cloth. Like her, Drew didn't like the label of being the kid of the town cop. Like her, Drew didn't want to follow the traditional school path. Like her, he managed to get into enough trouble to show his rebellion but not enough to end up in any serious trouble. Of course, she'd come much closer than he had. Maybe that was the influence of growing up with a mother, someone to temper and guide him when he started to waver off the straight path. Jo didn't have that luxury.

Drew and Tim were ushered onto the field along with the other three-thousand-meter runners.

"You have this, River Bend!" she shouted from across the track. The noise from the field and stands made it impossible to hear anything. Across the field Wyatt was positioned to yell out times and instructions, not that the boys didn't know what they had to do.

Jo held her stopwatch with her right hand and listened for the gun.

With eyes glued to the starting line, she studied the body language of the ref, who stood on a stepladder on the inside of the field. "C'mon, boys. Make me proud."

She heard her name from behind and ignored it. The race was about to start, and she wasn't about to take her eyes off the track.

The ref removed the .38 from his holster . . . a gun filled with blanks, but just as loud as the real thing . . . and lifted it in the air.

"Jo!"

She kept staring . . . waiting.

The sound of the gun went off and Jo flew back.

~

Gill channeled his inner linebacker as he rushed through the slow-moving crowd.

Jo stood by the fence separating the athletes from the bystanders. Her frame exposed to the world. She ignored his calls of her name.

When the gun went off, he was standing two feet behind her as she flew back from the fence.

He caught her before she hit the ground. His heart screamed.

"Jo?"

She was moaning.

The people around them stared, confused. Some by the fence glanced at them, then back to the race.

Gill shielded her with his frame in case the shooter had another round. But the crowd moved in enough to keep them hidden.

He ran his hand down her zippered sweatshirt, opened it to see her torso.

"Damn it, that hurt," Jo cussed.

"Where are you hit?" Gill yelled.

"Just damn."

"Stop talking. Point."

Someone near his side knelt down. "Hey, are you okay?"

"No. She's not. Call 911."

Jo shook her head, her eyes closed. "I'm okay."

"Jesus, Jo. You've been shot."

With his words, more heads swiveled toward them.

"I'm okay," was her breathy reply.

Gill moved to her side and lifted her bloodless T-shirt.

Jo tapped her vest with her right hand. "Still hurts like a bitch."

Gill buried his head in her good shoulder and let himself breathe. "You're killing me, JoAnne."

A frame pushed through the crowd, Gill hovered over Jo until he saw his partner. "Shauna."

"I saw her go down."

Jo tried to sit up.

Gill didn't let her. "She's wearing a vest."

"Thank God."

"We need to get you out of here."

The crowd in the stands started to cheer, announcing the end of the race. He used the noise and commotion around them to hook Jo's good arm over his shoulders and bring her to her feet.

"When they said it hurts when you're hit, they weren't kidding."

Shauna flanked them, her eyes alert. They limped through the crowd until they rounded the corner of the gym and found an open door. Only once he had Jo's shirt off and removed her vest was he convinced she wasn't full of holes.

"Our killer just changed the rules," Gill said.

∼

Drew's fifth place finish followed Tim's third. The two of them nearly knocked each other to the ground as they hugged.

They shook the hands of the winners and those of the kids that came in behind them.

"We made the podium!" Drew pumped his fist in the air.

"What a year, man. What a year." Tim patted him on the back.

Drew looked up in the stands and found his mom. She stood with a hand in the air, waving with a thumbs-up. He searched for his dad and didn't see him.

On the other side of the field, he scanned the crowd for Coach Ward. When he came up short, he assumed she'd be at the gate as they exited the field.

She wasn't.

Tina, however, was. She ran to his arms, congratulating him on his finish. "That was amazing."

"Not bad."

"What about me?" Tim asked as if Tina was going to kiss and hug him.

"Dude, I thought you had second. That Portland kid was fast."

Tim rested his hands on his knees in an attempt to capture his breath. "Goals for next year."

"In college they're going to be that much faster," Tina said.

"Good thing I'm not going to college," Drew exclaimed.

"Really, dude?"

"It's not for me."

Tim shook Drew's hand. "Then thanks for letting me beat you one last time."

Tim won fair and square. "I want a rematch."

"Name the place."

"River Bend High on our ten-year class reunion."

Tim pointed at him. "You're on."

Tina laughed. "That's one way to make sure you don't get fat before you're thirty."

Drew scanned the crowd again. "Anyone see Coach Ward?"

Tim and Tina looked around. "No."

# Chapter Thirty-Two

"The X-rays show healing ribs and clavicle."

Jo relented to a trip to the ER, so long as it wasn't in the back of an ambulance. The shot to the chest hit dead center. Good thing the shooter wasn't aiming for her head.

"Great, then I can go." Jo swung her feet over the edge of the gurney to do just that.

"Not so fast, Sheriff. You took a big punch. In light of the fact you're still recovering from a collapsed lung—"

"Recovered."

The ER doctor stood with his hands on his hips, determination in his eyes. "Your sweatshirt says track and field. Do you run, Sheriff?"

Jo looked down at herself. "Don't I look like I run?"

"How many miles did you run today?"

His point hit home. "I'm okay, Doc. Sitting here pretending to be sick is just going to piss everyone off." Besides, she had a cop killer to catch.

"Can you give us a few minutes?" Gill said to the doctor.

He closed the door behind him.

"You don't want to stay in the hospital—"

"I'm *not* staying in the hospital."

"Right now the only people that know you're here are me, you, Shauna, and the shooter."

Jo paused. "I'm listening."

"The shooter wants you dead."

"He's mucking that up."

Gill faked a smile. "We have an opportunity here to flush him out."

"How?"

"We put Shauna in your bed, say it's you . . . see if we can't get our killer to reveal himself to finish you off."

"A decoy."

"Could work."

"Why Shauna? Why not me?" Jo knew the answer before she asked.

"She's trained."

"So am I. And I'm a much better body double."

"It's too dangerous."

Jo stared. "If you're about to tell me I can't handle it, I'll remind you that I've survived two attempts on my life already." She swallowed a little bile on that statement but kept her gaze steady.

"I can't let you do it."

"Let me? I'm sorry . . ." She glanced around the room. "Did I miss the part about you having a say in what I will and won't do in my life?"

Gill's jaw tightened, his nose flared. "Let Shauna—"

"Not gonna happen. It's me, or I walk out of here." And Jo knew Gill wasn't going to let her walk out. "I finally get to figure out who has been watching me for over a year, and I'm not gonna let anyone else do that for me!"

Both hands reached for hair Gill didn't have before he cussed under his breath.

~

Gill made calls. The bureau swept in and Jo was "transferred" to an isolated ICU bed. With her status listed as critical but stable, if the shooter wanted to make sure she didn't make it out of the hospital alive, he'd come in and take her out.

Once everything was mobilized, Gill brought in the players. Luke answered the phone on the second ring.

"Hey, Miller."

"Gill, how's the track meet? Is someone putting River Bend on the map?"

"I have no idea. I'm at the hospital with Jo."

"What?" Music in the background turned off, Luke's voice sharpened. "What happened?"

"Are you alone?" The last thing Gill needed was anyone overhearing what he was about to say.

"Yes, I'm alone. Is she okay?"

"She is. This is what I need you to do."

~

The rumor mill in River Bend spread the news like a fire consumed a dead forest after ten years of drought. Luke called Maxine, the woman's whose car he was working on, and told her there'd be a delay. "Jo's been shot. I'm on my way to Eugene now."

"No, God, no."

"Yeah. Apparently she said something in the hospital about knowing who killed her dad before they had to sedate her."

Maxine ran the hair salon in town. Gossip central.

"Joseph was killed?"

"Oh, yeah. Jo's been working on the case for years. I have to run. I wanna be there when she wakes up in the morning."

"That's awful, Luke, just awful."

"I don't have time to make the calls, be sure and let people know so they can pray for her."

Maxine was a once a month Christian. Well, that and holidays.

Before he drove home to pick up Zoe, she was running from the front door. "Oh, God, no . . . Luke."

"Shh, it's okay. She's gonna be okay. C'mon inside."

He hated the stress on Zoe's face and quickly put her at ease. Although the ease was temporary. "Someone shot her?"

"She was wearing her vest. She's fine. Gill and the FBI think they can flush this person out."

"They're using her as bait?"

"My guess is Jo asked to be put on the hook."

"This has got to stop."

Luke agreed. "C'mon, babe. Let's get in the car and drive to Eugene like we normally would."

"I need to call Miss Gina, tell her she's okay."

"No. No one else. I didn't even tell my parents."

"But Miss Gina—"

"Gill said no one. Now let's go."

All the way to Eugene, Zoe's phone lit up. Every conversation, every text was the same. Someone tried to kill Jo. The doctors were waiting for the morning to take her out of sedation to let her lungs heal. And the last bit of gossip let everyone in River Bend know that Jo knew the name of the person who killed her father.

~

Considering Drew almost never used his phone to talk, the fact that it rang caught him by surprise.

"Dude!"

It was Gustavo.

"Hey."

"What the hell happened? Is Coach Ward okay?"

Drew was sitting in a group of athletes with his right hand plugging an ear and his left pressing the phone to the other. "What are you talking about?"

"She was shot."

"What the fu—"

"I heard she was in the ICU again. Didn't you see anything?"

"No. I haven't heard a thing." Drew jumped to his feet and scanned the field, hoping Gustavo was wrong and Coach Ward was standing close.

"What's wrong?" Tina asked.

"Coach Ward is in the hospital."

Gustavo yelled into the phone. "Call me back when you find out what's going on. There are all kinds of rumors spinning around here."

"I will." Drew hung up. Coach Gibson and his wife were standing among a handful of parents from River Bend. One was his dad. He ran to the group and knew they were talking about Coach Ward.

"I just heard," he said. "Is she okay?"

His dad placed an arm on his shoulder. "She's going to be okay."

"I knew something was wrong." She'd missed the picture opportunity on the podium. The disappointment he'd felt seemed trivial now.

"I heard something about Jo knowing who killed her father," Principal Mason, who stood next to Coach Gibson, said.

Drew looked to his father.

"I never liked the fact Joseph's death was deemed accidental. The man was too smart to leave a bullet in a gun he was cleaning."

"Why are we standing here talking?" Drew asked. "We should be at the hospital."

"Does anyone know where she was shot?" Principal Mason asked.

"I heard it was here," Tim's mother said.

"We would have heard something if that was the case," Karl said.

"That doesn't make sense," Coach Gibson added.

When the starting gun went off, all heads turned.

Drew's dad stepped closer to his side. "We're outta here."

"I need to get my stuff."

"Screw your stuff. We're leaving."

"Gather your athletes, Wyatt. This meet is over for River Bend."

~

All Jo had to do was lie there and wait.

Not an easy task regardless of how many FBI personnel were surrounding her. One of the nurses in the station worked with Gill, a man posing as an orderly carried a gun.

The vital signs pinging on the monitor were not her own, the blankets and dressings masked the dripping IV that wasn't connected to her arm.

And now she waited.

Even when her friends walked into the room, she didn't open her eyes. Zoe didn't stay long, and Mel left even quicker. Good thing, too, because as Mel was walking out of the room, Karl and Drew stepped in.

The room held one camera that could be viewed from the nurse's station, and audio recording hid within the wires of medical equipment.

Jo counted her breaths to keep them even.

"Oh, man." Drew's voice was a whisper.

"They said she's going to be okay," Karl said.

"This looks bad."

"She's a very strong woman, Drew. One of the strongest I've ever met. She's going to be fine."

Jo heard footsteps cross and had to keep her hand limp when one of them reached for it. Drew's voice cracked. "I made fifth place. Tim came in third."

She bit her tongue and kept her smile away.

"She'll be proud," Karl assured his son.

"Oh, man . . . I can't do this."

"You're fine. Go on. I'll be just a minute," Karl said.

The sound from outside her door amplified and then dissipated as someone exited the room.

She heard a chair scrape along the floor and the sound of Karl's breath. "Damn it, JoAnne. It's so hard to stay mad at you when you keep ending up in the hospital."

*Breathe in . . . one, two, three.*

*Breathe out . . . four, five, six.*

"I've been told that people hear things and remember things said when they were unconscious in hospital rooms. So I'm promising this to you now, not because I don't want you to remember it, but because I do. I always believed your father was murdered. But I was too afraid to look for his killer. You see, I learned he was Drew's real dad just months before Joseph's death. I know how it would have looked then, and I know how it looks now."

Karl rested a hand on her arm.

Jo didn't flinch.

"I didn't kill him. And I would never harm you. The fact some in River Bend think I'm capable grabs my balls and twists them in knots. I guess I should learn to be a little more diplomatic. A little more laid-back like you. My guess is you know about Drew, which is why you've taken him under your wing."

She heard Karl sniffle and had to force herself not to join his emotions.

"I didn't want him gaining a sister to be the same thing that removes me as his dad. I know it's selfish of me, but I would have liked to keep who his real father was from him. I see now that isn't possible. It's only fair that someday he knows he has a sister." Karl patted her arm, and the sound of a chair scooting back reached her ears. "Anyway. It looks like they have you well protected here. I'm going to get back to town and make sure everything is ready for your return."

A few footsteps, the sound of the ICU . . . the door closed.

And Jo released a long-suffering sigh.

~

Gill had a remote mic in his ear from Jo's room. There was no way of knowing if Karl's bedside confessions were made because he'd spotted the recording devices or if they were as heartfelt as they sounded. Living by the standard of *believe none of what you hear and half of what you see* forced Gill to hold his opinions of the man until he could prove him right.

As he sat in the ICU waiting room, Drew spoke with Wyatt and Mel and allowed his mother to hug him. Eighteen was such a hard year for boys, technically a man but still too young to process his emotions without tears.

All eyes went to the door when Karl walked in.

Drew walked right up to his dad, stuck his chin in the air. "We need to find out who did this to her."

Gill liked the word *we*.

Karl placed a hand on Drew's shoulder. "We will." He looked at his wife. "Why don't you take Drew home."

"I wanna stay."

"We'll come back tomorrow. There is a reason visitors aren't allowed in the ICU all day. Jo needs her rest."

It looked like Drew was going to argue, then reconsidered.

"Go on, Caroline. Take him home."

Once they'd left the room, Karl turned to Gill. "A moment of your time?"

They stepped outside hearing range of the others, and Gill crossed his arms over his chest.

"I'm being set up."

Gill lifted his eyebrows, didn't deny the claim.

"You know about Drew." It wasn't a question.

"I do."

"I didn't kill Joseph."

"Who did?"

The expression on his face said he had a name. "I started thinking, after finding the dog . . . then the rabbit. This happened before. Right before Joseph. After, it all stopped, and I didn't revisit those cases since they were only pets."

"Where are those files?" Gill had skimmed through a lot of Joseph Ward's cases but didn't remember seeing anything that resembled the hanging dog.

"I don't know. I searched the paper trail and came up cold. Glynis may have scanned them already, and I just haven't found them."

"Or . . ."

"Or someone removed them and there isn't a paper trail. Which means whoever removed them was worried something will link them to Joseph's murder, or Jo's attempted . . ." Karl didn't say *murder*, which suited Gill just fine. "To Jo. Or whoever removed them knows it would look bad for me."

"Because you have access to remove files and destroy them," Gill concluded.

Karl nodded.

"Who is your suspect?" Gill asked.

Karl blinked. "My wife isn't capable of murder."

Gill sighed. "Everyone is capable of murder under the right circumstances."

"She wouldn't."

Gill wasn't so sure. "Where were you when Jo was shot today?"

"When did she go down?"

"With the starting gun of your son's race."

"I was by the long jump pits on the other side of the fence. I wanted Drew to see me, but all he saw was the finish line."

"Did anyone see you there?" His off-the-record questions would be asked again if needed.

"Probably. No one I knew."

Karl knew he was being interrogated and took it in stride.

"What about Caroline? Where was she?"

It took Karl a few seconds to answer. "I don't know. She was upset."

"Why was she upset?"

"You tell me. She was close to tears after sitting with you in the stands."

Right . . . that would be after Gill let her know he'd unearthed her secret.

Gill wondered just how much Karl knew about his wife. "Do you know why repeat offenders repeat their crimes?" he asked.

"Because they're not caught," Karl responded. "Or because their punishment wasn't enough to make them stop."

"When you found out about your wife and Joseph, did you confront her?"

Karl glanced behind Gill's shoulder, his jaw tightened.

"Did Caroline's life change in any way?"

"She's not capable, Gill. I'm telling you."

"Of murder? Maybe not . . . but of finding another lover . . ."

Karl's Adam's apple bobbed in his neck.

# Chapter Thirty-Three

Drew pulled the car around from the hospital parking lot and waited for his mother.

While sitting in the pickup line, his head was buried in his phone, texting. The group text included Tina, Tim, and the rest of the cross-country team.

This is wrong. Someone shot our coach! Drew sent out.

No one wants to kill a coach, someone shot our Sheriff. Tim texted.

Yeah, Drew figured that out.

"Hey, honey."

Drew looked out the passenger window to see his mom standing there. "Want me to drive?" he asked.

She opened the door, dropped her purse in the seat. "Sure, that's fine—" she stopped with one foot inside. "I forgot something. I'll be right back."

His mom closed the car door and Drew went back to his phone. The group was going back and forth with their idea of a round-the-clock babysitting service for Coach Ward once she recovered.

His mother's phone buzzed from the passenger seat.

Ignoring it, he went back to his own conversation.

The buzz a second and third time surprised him. Without thought, he moved his mother's purse to find that her cell phone had slid out. He picked it up and caught a glimpse of the green text message. The name on the sender was Stella.

Drew didn't know a Stella.

We are not over. Don't ever say that! The message coming in flashed on the home screen.

Drew attempted to open his mother's messages and found it locked.

Why would his mother lock her phone?

Baby, I've done everything for you. Don't do this!

Drew's hands started to sweat. He looked over the hood of the car, watching for his mother. His own phone pinged, and he glanced at the screen on his phone.

He realized almost all the names he had in his phone were nicknames. Most of which were things like Slowpoke and Yard Time.

Answer my text, baby. I know you're reading them.

Drew saw his mother's orange shirt walking from the sliding doors of the hospital. He dropped her phone on the seat, knocked her purse over, and stared at his screen without reading a word.

"Forgot my purse," his mom said as she reached through the window and grabbed it, and the phone. "I'm getting a soda from the gift shop before we head back. Want something?"

Drew shook his head. "I'm good."

As soon as she turned away, Drew followed her. He saw her feet hesitate as she neared the doors of the hospital. She wasn't inside a minute before she walked back out. This time she came to his side of the car and leaned in. "You know what, I'm going to drive back with your father. I'm worried about him."

"You sure?"

Her tight smile scared him.

"Positive. Drive careful."

"Let me know if something changes," he told her.

"I will. Love you."

"Yeah, okay. See you at home."

She stepped away from the car and headed inside.

Drew pulled out of the turnaround, his eyes on the rearview mirror. For good measure, he pulled out of the lot and rounded the corner, doubling back. He cut the engine and waited.

It didn't take long for his mom to walk back outside, look around, and then disappear into a three-story parking structure on the west side of the hospital.

"Holy shit."

Drew sat in his mother's car refusing to leave the parking lot. His mother didn't reappear from the parking structure, and since there were two ways a car could exit the three-story garage, he had no way of knowing if she left with someone else. It would have to be someone else, since Drew noticed his father's squad car pulling out of one of the emergency spaces designated for the police.

His phone buzzed with texts that went unanswered from his friends.

Drew couldn't stop thinking about what he'd read on his mother's phone. No one called another person *baby* unless . . .

His parents had been fighting a lot in the past year, but he never thought one of them could cheat.

He waited an hour before calling his dad.

"Hi, Dad."

"You're not talking on the phone while you're driving, are you?"

"You mean like you are."

"That's different." Yeah, cops seemed to think those rules didn't apply to them.

"Ha." Drew tried to laugh, and it came out strained. "Uhm, is Mom with you?"

"I thought she was with you."

"She ran back into the hospital, said she was going to ride back with you."

His dad was silent on the other end.

"Dad?"

"Yeah, I'm here. I'll head back and pick her up."

"I can do it. I didn't get far. I wanted a burger."

"No, no . . . you go on home. I'll find your mother." His dad sounded angry.

"You sure?"

"Positive. You've had a long day. I'd hate you driving tired."

"Okay."

"Hey, Drew?"

"Yeah?"

"Proud of you today. I know I don't say that enough."

His praise formed a knot in Drew's throat. "Thanks, Dad."

Drew was about to give up on spying on his parents when he saw his mother running from the parking garage. She appeared to be chasing down his dad . . . only it wasn't his dad. He wore the same uniform, was similar in size . . . but it wasn't his dad.

She caught the man by his arm, and he pulled away and shoved himself right up against her chest.

Drew reached for the car door to jump out.

He was halfway across the parking lot when he recognized the man in the uniform.

Stopping, Drew took in what he was seeing.

A man he'd known since birth pulled his mother into his arms, kissed her roughly, then stormed into the hospital.

Sensing his stare, his mother twisted her head and met his accusing gaze. Both her hands flew to her face as if she could hide the truth.

~

Jo's butt hurt from lying in bed for hours. The sun outside the window was starting to set and she was beginning to think their playing possum was a bust. Well, outside of Karl's confession, which, if she was honest with herself, was worth the whole ruse.

The adrenaline that had brought her to the hospital was finally waning and mixed with the boredom of waiting. Jo realized she had fallen asleep when noise from outside her room woke her.

"It's okay. Take a break, get some coffee."

It sounded like Stan, her temporary deputy and longtime family friend, telling the uniformed officer outside her door to grab some coffee.

*Breathe in . . . one, two, three.*

*Breathe out . . . one, two, three.*

"Jo?"

"Jo?" he said a little louder.

She felt a finger poking her shoulder through the covers. "Jo?"

He sighed. "You are one tough broad."

~

"What are you doing, Mom?"

She sobbed, her body shaking with every breath.

"I'm sorry."

Her apology doubled as a confession.

"Deputy Fitzpatrick? Really?"

"It isn't what you think."

Drew had a hard time looking at her. "I'm young, not stupid."

She bit her lips as if trying to stop her tears. "I'm not having this conversation with you."

"What about Dad? Are you going to have this conversation with Dad?" How could she do this to them? Why?

The woman who raised him wore her nerves in her shaking hands. "I need to talk to Jo's boyfriend."

"Gill?"

"Stan isn't right. He's been acting strange."

"Men act that way when their *girlfriends* are breaking up with them," Drew said.

His mother stiffened her shoulders, stared at him.

"I read your texts."

"You need to respect my privacy."

"You need to respect our family."

His mother didn't get angry often, but he saw irritation in her eyes before she walked past him and into the hospital.

~

Jo kept her breathing even, kept her eyes closed with only a slit casting shadows behind her lids.

Stan said next to nothing as he moved around the room.

His silence disarmed her.

Stan moved back to her bedside. The tubes of the IV line pulled against the tape on her arm.

His breath became quick, short pants.

Another tug on her arm.

The scent of his breath came close, his lips next to her ear. "JoAnne?"

*Slow breaths. Slow breaths!*

His chest pressed against her left arm and she felt his fingers grip her shoulder. "Sorry, Jo. It's better this way. Would have been better if you'd just left River Bend after Daddy died."

Jo felt a scrape on her arm and she jumped.

Her free hand reached out to grasp Stan's, and the door to the room burst open.

Stan was in motion, a syringe in his right hand, Jo's shoulder in his left.

Gill stood in the doorway, Caroline and Drew running toward them.

"Drop it!" Gill pointed his weapon at Stan's chest.

The deputy didn't stop, he jerked Jo's injured arm and shielded his body with hers. She cried out in pain.

The shot was too close. Gill didn't take it.

Caroline screamed Stan's name, telling him to stop.

Drew shoved his mother behind him.

"Put the syringe down," Gill ordered.

That's when Jo noticed the grip Stan's hand had on the syringe he'd destined for her. The pain in her shoulder and chest stopped being of any concern.

"Drop it."

"What are you doing, Stan?" Jo asked.

Stan's eyes were on Caroline. "See what you made me do? This is your fault."

"Stanley, please."

The other agents filled in around them, guns pointing at Stan. If he did manage to bury that needle in her arm, it would be the last thing he did.

"I was the only one you needed. But no. You couldn't leave that weasel husband. Had to spread for this one's daddy." Stan shifted Jo side to side, his arm around her neck, the needle scraping her bare arm.

"Get them out of here," Gill yelled at no one in particular.

Agents pushed in, dragged Caroline and Drew aside.

"Don't do this, Stan." Jo kept her voice even. Calculated her next move.

"You're like a damn cat that just won't die."

"You're not going to make it out of here."

"No. Maybe not." His voice was too calm, too controlled. "Doesn't matter now."

Jo caught movement in front of her. There were five weapons pointing at them.

She sought Gill's eyes.

Without hesitation and ignoring the pain in her arm, she maneuvered her bare leg around Stan's, grasped the hand he held the needle in with both of hers, and twisted her body toward his as she'd been taught in Virginia. He wasn't expecting her move, but that didn't mean he went down easy. Jo focused on the needle as they fell to the floor.

Pain shot through her body, and air left her lungs.

The room exploded when Gill charged. All Jo saw was Gill's meaty hand grasping Stan's. If his fingers didn't break, they were made of titanium.

Stan's grip on Jo broke loose, and someone pulled her back.

Grunts and the sound of a hospital room being destroyed filled the empty sound outside the walls.

Stan went down kicking.

But he went down.

# Chapter Thirty-Four

As Gill led Stan from the hospital floor, Jo allowed the real doctor to check her arm and vital signs before pulling on her clothes and letting her best friends hug the life out of her.

"Damn it, Jo. Don't you ever, ever do this again." Zoe shook her finger at her and then hugged her a second time.

"Watch the arm, cupcake."

"Sorry." Zoe pulled back but still didn't let her go.

"I hope you have good insurance," Mel dug in. "You've been in more hospitals than me, and I'm knocked up."

In the last month Mel had started to actually show.

"I miss you guys," Jo said.

"We've been right here." Zoe pushed a lock of hair behind her shoulder.

"I know. I just haven't been able to take a breath in what feels like forever."

Mel rolled her eyes. "You might wanna stop poking holes in your lungs then."

Jo looked down at her arm that sat in a new sling. Her shoulder stung like a bitch.

"So Stan—" Mel looked over at the agents who had pulled Caroline aside. Karl stood by Drew as questions were asked.

"All for a stupid love triangle," Jo said.

"I thought Stan was married," Mel sighed.

"I haven't seen his wife in years."

"Do you think he killed your dad?" Zoe asked.

"It makes sense. If he wanted my job, he takes care of my dad, discredits Karl, takes the position."

"Only you step up," Mel reminded her.

"Yeah. So why did he wait until now to make another move?"

Gill led Caroline out of the room and nodded to Jo for her to follow. "I don't know, but I'm gonna find out." She caught Drew watching. "Do me a favor, distract Drew."

Mel and Zoe exchanged glances. "On it," Zoe said.

The room Gill used to question Caroline was one the ICU staff reserved for talking to distressed families.

Gill no sooner closed the door behind them than Caroline burst into tears. "I'm sorry, JoAnne."

Jo's back teeth ground to the point of pain. "Prove it, Caroline. Don't make me wait for answers."

Gill lifted a hand. "You do have a right to an attorney."

Jo caught his gaze. "Have you read her her rights?"

Gill turned to Caroline, recited her Miranda rights, and waited.

"I'm not proud of my behavior," Caroline started.

"Did you kill my dad?"

"No! God, no. I'm guilty of adultery, not murder. Stan and I . . . we've both . . . We knew it wasn't right. Karl and I were having a hard time trying to have a baby. I was tested. I was fine. The doctor never flat-out said Karl couldn't have a child, so we kept trying."

"So you started your affair to have a child?"

"No . . . yes, I don't know." Her tears increased, and large black smudges of mascara blotted the top of her cheeks.

"Which is it?"

"I wanted a baby. Only it didn't happen."

"So you went looking for another man?" Jo fisted her hands, thinking her father had been played.

"After your mother passed, Joseph would come around once in a while, asking what a woman would do in regards to raising you." Caroline rubbed her palms against her pants. "Your father was a good man."

"I get it. So you had an affair."

Caroline stared at the ground.

"How long did it last?"

"About a year."

Jo's heart slammed hard in her chest. The thought of her father sleeping with a married woman for a year made her sick.

"You got pregnant?"

She agreed with a single nod.

"Did my dad know?"

"He figured it out . . . later. I didn't tell Karl."

"So who broke it off, you or my dad?"

Caroline wove her fingers together, nerves at the surface of her movements. "When Karl told him he was going to be a father, your dad said we were over."

Well, at least Jo had to give him that. "Where did Stan come back in?"

Caroline was silent.

"We'll get the answers from him," Gill said.

"Stan has always been around. He wanted more than I was willing to give him. When he divorced Helen, he assumed I would leave Karl."

"But you didn't," Gill stated.

"Stan started acting strange right after his divorce was filed. Kept saying he had given up everything for me, and I still wasn't happy. I assumed he meant his divorce, but then he said a few things that made me wonder if there was more to his statement."

Jo and Gill silently stared at each other.

Gill took that moment to sit down. Jo kept her back to the door, her good arm cradling the one in the sling.

"Like what things?"

"He said Karl was behind the dog killing."

"A lot of people thought that."

Caroline tilted her head to the side. "He isn't. And Stan was over the day Drew found the . . ." She swallowed hard.

"So you figured Stan was behind the animals."

"Yes."

"Did that scare you?"

The tears in her eyes started to spill harder. "Yes. He told me Karl wanted your job and was willing to do anything to get it."

"Is that true?"

"No. Would Karl like to be the sheriff? Yes, but not at your expense."

"Caroline." Jo caught the woman's attention. "What do you remember about the night my father died?"

Fear replaced Caroline's tears. "I was at home, Karl was on duty since your dad was up at the cabin. Stan wanted to come to see me, but I didn't want to take the risk. We argued."

"What did you argue about?"

"The usual. We should both file for a divorce, I could move in with him in Waterville."

"But you didn't want that."

"No. I didn't want to live in Waterville, I like River Bend. I didn't want to move Drew away from his friends. I know it's hard to believe, but I love Karl. I never wanted any of this to happen."

Jo kept her disgust toward the woman to herself.

"So you and Stan argued. What then?"

"He said he would arrange it so that he would move to River Bend."

Jo narrowed her eyes at Caroline. "And isn't that exactly what he did once my father was murdered?"

Caroline winced. "Stan commuted, would stay at the hotel outside of town once in a while."

"And since he and Karl were working opposite shifts, Stan was able to spend more time with you."

Silence.

It took everything in Jo to keep from saying what she truly wanted to say. "Someone shot me today. Was it you?"

"No." Caroline shot her eyes toward Jo.

"Was it Karl?"

"No, he wouldn't."

"Was it Stan?" Jo asked.

"I don't know."

She did know, she just couldn't admit it, even to herself.

"One more question, Caroline." Jo leaned forward.

Caroline bit her bottom lip.

"Did Stan kill my father?"

The woman JoAnne had known most of her life, the mother of her half-brother, brought her hand to her mouth and cried.

"Why now? Why, after all these years, has Stan made me his target?"

"I don't know! He'd tell me that if all the obstacles were gone, we'd be happy together. Karl has come home every night stressed, angry . . . everyone was turning against him. The last time that had happened was right after your dad died. When you came back in town and the election made you sheriff, Stan all but disappeared. Then after a year he was back, flirting, asking me to meet him. It wasn't often, just once in a while."

Like Jo cared.

"Next thing I know he was getting divorced and making me choose."

"Why go after me? Why not go after Karl?"

Caroline's back straightened, her lips pushed together. "Karl's a good, honorable man."

"A man you've cheated on for years."

Caroline swallowed hard.

Gill moved between them, blocking Jo's eye contact.

"It looks to me as if Stan has been framing Karl from the start . . . JoAnne's father's death, the attempts on Jo's life. Even all the animals."

Caroline nodded.

"If Stan discredits Karl, maybe Karl doesn't hold the same 'honorable' mention in your head."

Caroline stared, mouth open.

"Maybe Karl is deemed the bad guy in all of his, the man responsible for killing the father of his illegitimate son, and maybe then taking the life of the woman who took the job he should have had."

Horror reached Caroline's eyes.

"And maybe then all those obstacles are gone, and you'd have nowhere else to go but into his arms."

Gill stopped watching Caroline and stared at Jo.

While her heart tore open, some of it healed.

At least now she knew.

~

Jo stumbled outside the room, leaving Gill and Caroline. Jo met Drew's gaze.

She attempted a grin. If there was a silver lining to any of this, it was the fact she had a brother.

Karl stood at Drew's side. The sight of the two of them together twisted her gut.

Drew said something to his dad, and Karl offered a half smile to Jo before nodding in her direction.

"Hey." Jo sat on a waiting room couch, patted the seat beside her.

Drew, still wearing the uniform for the day's track meet and the scent of a kid who had been running most of the day, sat beside her. "How are you feeling?" he asked.

"I'm fine, Drew. Pissed off about Stan, but . . ."

Drew huffed. "We're all ticked off at him."

"There are some things you need to know," she said.

"My mom's been messing with him." Drew's words cut her off.

"I know."

"Is my mom in trouble?"

"We have a lot of questions for her."

Drew bit his bottom lip. "Is what he said about your dad true?"

Jo covered her hand with his. "Yes."

Drew sucked in three rapid breaths. "Does that mean . . . ?" His question hung in the air.

Jo found Karl watching them, humility on his face.

She squeezed his hand. "You still have a father, Drew. But . . ."

He turned and looked at her.

"You've gained a sister."

Moisture filled his eyes.

Damn hers for doing the same thing.

"I like that," he said.

She needed a bigger smile on Drew's face. The adrenaline of the day was starting to dump out of her system, and she guessed it was doing the same in his. "Just means I get more than chocolate at Christmas."

He found his grin. The sneaky-ass one she saw many times in her own mirror. "Means I get to call you JoAnne."

Her smile dropped. "No one calls me JoAnne."

Drew did one of those faces kids do to pretend he was contemplating her suggestion. "Well, as I see it, you can't fail me in track . . . you can't take away my diploma . . . and Christmas is months away, *JoAnne*."

She swallowed hard. "I see how this is going to be."

"No, you don't. You might be many things before I was . . . but we became family at the exact same time." He squeezed her hand back. "We're going to learn this together."

Damn kid was going to make her cry.

"Dork."

Drew pulled her into a quick hug before moving back to his father.

# Epilogue

Caroline stayed through Drew's graduation before packing her belongings and leaving River Bend. The investigation didn't find her guilty of anything other than infidelity. The town gossip spread like a case of the flu, especially when it came to light that Joseph Ward . . . trusted sheriff of River Bend . . . was just as guilty as Caroline for their transgressions.

Standing beside Drew and her deputy, Karl, Gill held Jo's hand during the graduation ceremonies of River Bend High.

They were a strange family, one born of lies and deceit. But Jo was happy for it.

Jo had a brother. While she never thought she was missing something in her life, she realized when he became more than just another kid on the field, another attitude-filled teen, she missed a whole lot.

Gill insisted on staying with her the week that followed.

Mel and Zoe moved into the role of reunion alumni committee without having any connection with the class that had graduated three years after them.

The six of them stood around the bar, listening to Principal Mason score free drinks off the graduating class of ten years before. With little to entertain the small town, many showed up regardless of the fact that several of them had graduated more than twenty years before.

"Can you believe this? Thirteen years since we left this school," Zoe said as she leaned on Luke's arm.

"I don't feel like I've ever left, and this isn't where I grew up," Wyatt said, laughing.

"So, Zoe," Jo said. "What are you going to do with the family home?" Zoe's siblings had been paid for their portion, her mother was still serving time, and her father was dead. But the house that had haunted Jo's BFF still stood.

"Felix had a great idea," she told them. Felix was her longtime director and friend.

"Oh?"

"Yeah . . . we're gonna blow it up."

Jo paused. Gill squeezed her hand.

"Blow it up?" Gill asked.

"Kitchen disasters. You know. The typical 'I blew up my kitchen cooking a turkey' episode."

Mel frowned. "No one blows up a kitchen cooking a turkey."

Wyatt nudged her.

"I didn't blow up anything. That stove was defective!"

They all laughed.

The music slowed, and Luke pulled Zoe onto the dance floor.

Mel and Wyatt followed.

"Wanna dance?" Gill asked.

Jo put the drink in her hand down and shook her head. "No. Dancing isn't what I want to do."

Gill raised an eyebrow and grinned.

Two hours later, as they rolled over on the bed long after they'd exercised every possible muscle either of them owned, Jo snuggled into the crook of Gill's arm.

"I've been thinking," Gill said.

"Sounds like trouble."

He laughed. "There's a promotion available for me with the bureau."

"That's a good thing, right?"

"It is. I wouldn't have to leave Eugene."

She didn't even realize she'd been holding her breath. "Are you taking it?"

"I'm thinking about it. Which means that Shauna will need a new partner."

Jo shifted her weight, damn shoulder still ached, even though the sling had been off for less than a week. "Sucks for her."

He paused. "Unless it's you."

Jo lay perfectly still. "Me?"

"Well, I mean . . . you'd have to apply, pass the agility, which you'd ace. You might be eligible with your years of experience as a sheriff, and if not, a few classes to get your degree can work."

Jo leaned up on an elbow. "You think I need to go back to school?"

"If the agent thing interests you."

Her heartbeat pulsed in her head. "I don't think I ever thought about it."

"You have some time. I wouldn't take the promotion until after the first of the year."

"You think they'd hire me?"

Gill tucked a strand of hair behind her ear. "They'd be fools not to."

Could she? Was she capable? "The FBI," she whispered.

"Something to think about."

Jo looked around the room. Her father's room, albeit a different color with different furniture.

"You've made things right here in River Bend, JoAnne. Maybe it's time for you to make things right for you."

She was smiling as she slipped back into the crook of his arm. "I'd have to live in Eugene."

"Yeah. But I have that part covered," he told her.

"How's that?"

"You'd live with me."

They already bunked up whenever they were in the same town.

"Live with you?"

"Of course. Where else would you live?" The foregone conclusion laced the tone in his voice.

"My own place . . . an apartment?"

It was Gill's turn to pull away and make sure she saw his eyes. "Why?"

"I don't know—"

"No. You live with me. You've burned through three lives since we met. I don't trust you on your own."

"Don't trust me?"

"Nope. Sorry. So you move in with me. We can visit here on the weekends—"

"Whoa, back up. I have a life here."

"No. You've been living here. Your life is with me."

"My life has been in River Bend."

He hesitated. "I'd make a really bad deputy sheriff."

The thought of him in her uniform made her laugh.

"See."

"You would suck."

"But you." He kissed her nose. "You'd make a stellar agent."

Jo placed a fist on his chest, rested her chin on it. "Stellar, huh?"

"You kicked ass at Quantico."

"All my friends are here, Miss Gina . . ."

"And you'll only be two hours away and you'd visit often."

She sighed, already halfway making up her mind. She'd never had the option before. "I'll consider it."

His smile was a slow, easy grin. "So . . . shack up, get married?"

Jo narrowed her eyes. "Was that a proposal?"

He rolled his eyes. Which Jo wasn't sure she'd ever seen him do before. "It's a conversation before a proposal. It isn't like we've been outside of a hospital long enough to know that's what we want."

"True."

His hand lingered on the skin of her naked back as they spoke. "I like the idea of getting married," he told her as if he had just figured that out. "My parents did it the other way, but I don't know . . . maybe—"

"Wait, wait . . . your parents aren't married?"

Gill shook his head. "God, no. Hippies to the core. Miss Gina would love them."

"And that worked?"

"Worked for . . ." Gill looked at the ceiling for the answer. "Going on thirty-six years now."

Jo blew out a breath.

"As far as I see it, when two people love each other, a piece of paper is just that. But if you want it, I get it."

"I don't think that was a proposal either." She was teasing him, and his words of love hadn't escaped her.

"So you're a proposal girl . . ." He winked. "Got it."

"Well, I want a ring at least."

"Duh. I can't have men hitting on you," he said.

"Oh, they're gonna hit on me."

He frowned. "Good thing I'm a big man." His hand moved over the curve of her ass and squeezed.

"You know I love you," she told him for the first time.

"I know. And I, my sexy sheriff, love you. But you know that, too."

She crawled up his chest, intending to make sure he knew just how deep her affection was, when the sound of something soft hit the side of the house.

They both stiffened.

Jo relaxed first.

"I'll get my gun." Gill tried to move her off of him.

"Don't you dare," she told him, pinning him back to the bed.

"Someone is outside."

She nodded. "Yep."

He tried moving her again.

"You can't shoot my brother."

"Drew?"

"Yeah . . . it's reunion night."

"What does that mean?"

"You'll see . . ." Jo pressed her lips to Gill's and made him forget all about the noise outside the walls of her father's home.

The next morning, when she and Gill stood outside in a sea of toilet paper–laden trees, he turned to her and said, "We are moving to Eugene."

"Fine. But I'm keeping the house."

"And I'm using the cabin."

"It will be a great place to take kids."

Gill squeezed her close. "I really hope you're talking about our kids."

She sighed. "I think I'm gonna need that proposal before we talk about children."

He kissed the side of her head as moist, sodden toilet paper dripped from the roof.

Rocco, her rottweiler pup, barked at their heels.

# Acknowledgments

So many people to thank . . . where to begin? Let me start with Kari and Brandy, my inspirations for this series. Our friendship grounded me as a kid growing up and inspires me as an adult today. Thank you, Kari, for the information on Quantico that you could share. I hope the places I strayed from reality weren't completely off the mark. And if they are, well, this *is* a work of fiction.

To Dawna, my second mom . . . while you were nothing like my Miss Gina, you were the one I ran to for advice and safety when I needed an adult. You will always hold a special place in my heart.

To Suzie, the cop's daughter in the neighborhood . . . when I think back on the things you used to do to tick off your dad . . . and how much restraint he displayed by not throttling you. Those guys next door, however, were worth the risk!

To all the track and field coaches who have dedicated their knowledge and skills to my boys over the years, thank you!

To Jane, my forever agent and friend.

To Kelli and everyone at Montlake for your understanding my fire delays this year. I'm happy to have changed my original ending of . . . "And then a fire swept through River Bend and everyone died. THE END." I think this one was better.

Now back to Andrea:

To my Andi. When I wrote the dedications to Brandy and Kari in the first two books of this series, I realized that I perhaps needed to dedicate a book to myself. Mainly because Zoe's book so closely resembles my life. But things happen for a reason. So as I sat down to write this dedication and acknowledgment, I saw Jo standing over her father's final resting place and pictured me standing over yours. I spent half of my working life saving lives as a nurse, partly because I wanted to save yours. But life doesn't work that way. And when you live your life to please someone else, you aren't living, you're simply alive.

I miss you, my dear baby sister, and promise to live my life fully, for the both of us.

*Catherine*

# About the Author

Photo © 2015 Julianne Gentry

Catherine Bybee is a *New York Times*, *Wall Street Journal*, and *USA Today* bestselling author of twenty-five books that have collectively sold more than three million copies and have been translated into twelve languages. Raised in Washington State, Bybee moved to Southern California in hopes of becoming a movie star. After growing bored with waiting tables, she returned to school and became a registered nurse, spending most of her career in urban emergency rooms. She now writes full-time and has penned the Not Quite series, the Weekday Brides series, and the Most Likely To series.